# The Abinger Edition
## of E. M. Forster

*Edited by*
OLIVER STALLYBRASS

Volume 1

# Where Angels Fear to Tread

## E. M. Forster

© text ... Introduction ... Oliver Stallybrass

First published 1905
First published in the Abinger Edition ...
Edward Arnold (Publishers) Ltd
25 Hill Street, London W1X 8LL

ISBN 0 7131 5813 8

All rights reserved. No part of this publication
may be reproduced, stored in a retrieval system, or
transmitted in any form or by any means, electronic,
mechanical, photo-copying, recording ...
without the prior permission of
Edward Arnold (Publishers) Ltd.

Printed in Great Britain by
The Camelot Press Ltd, Southampton

Edward Arnold

First published 1905
First published in the Abinger Edition 1975 by
Edward Arnold (Publishers) Ltd
25 Hill Street, London W1X 8LL

ISBN 0 7131 5815 8

Printed in Great Britain by
The Camelot Press Ltd, Southampton

# Contents

# Contents

v

# Editor's Introduction

On 3 October 1901 E. M. Forster, then twenty-two, set out with his mother on a prolonged visit to Italy. "Start as bad as can well be imagined," his diary records: by Dover his mother had a headache, and at 12.20 a.m. they arrived at Calais to find that the through train to Basle had been cancelled, so that they had to go via Paris instead. Paris was fogbound and apparently cableless, there was a row with the station people over tickets, no buffet was open at the Gare de l'Est, they had to walk back to the Gare du Nord ("M.'s head now awful"); and when they finally escaped from Paris the country was frightful, the tea on the train disgusting as well as expensive. At the German frontier there was more trouble with officials, and when they reached Basle their heavy luggage had vanished. Next day it caught up with them, but "M. had a splitting sick head-ache, & couldn't eat or drink", and the departure for Lucerne moved Forster to record: "The porters always grumble at what I give, so shall try less." Lucerne provided a breathing-space, but in the St Gotthard tunnel "everyone smoked and the carriage was boiling hot", so that at Como, two days later, "still we have not recovered from the St Gotthard tunnel", not to mention the appalling custom house examination at Chiasso. It was an irritable couple who took tickets to Milan.

If that last sentence sounds vaguely familiar, the explanation will be found on p. 76, where an almost identical sentence rounds off another paragraph-long travellers' tale of woe. Even before Como, however, Forster had managed to forget his mother for long enough to note that "at Lugano the sun was setting, and the whole lake filled with light. Everything began to look like Italy." And despite the horrors of those first six days—and even these could be put to artistic use—Forster had embarked on the most fruitful journey of his life: out of it sprang his earliest stories and two of his first three novels. He himself has expressed, more than once, his sense of debt to Italy. In 1962, for example, addressing an Italian audience, he described how a valley near Ravello inspired "The Story of a Panic", how "Italy pushed it into my mind, almost with physical force, and set me going as a novelist". After that

I wrote ahead. The creative element had been freed, and two of my novels—*Where Angels Fear to Tread* and *A Room with a View*—are mainly Italian. Your country had taught me much. Unfortunately she did not teach me everything. She did not teach me the Italian language as Italians have chosen to speak it. . . . And she did not introduce me into any section of Italian society, which has been a disadvantage to me as a novelist. The tourist may be intelligent, warm-hearted and alert, and I think I was that much, but he has to go back every evening to his hotel or pension, and he can know very little of the class-structure of the country he is visiting, or of its economic problems. My limitations were grave. Fortunately I was unaware of them, and plunged ahead. *Where Angels Fear to Tread* rests on a piece of effrontery. In a hotel lounge one day—at Siena or that sort of place—I overheard an English lady talking to another English lady about a third English lady who had married an Italian far beneath her socially and also much younger, and how most unfortunate it was. This sorry bit of twaddle stuck in my mind. I worked at it until it became alive and grew into a novel of contrasts. On the one hand was the English suburbs with the gray inhibited life that I knew only too well, and on the other hand was Monteriano, a romantic hill town which I established in Tuscany on the basis of San Gimignano. The English ladies go there to look at the frescoes, and one of them falls in love with Gino, a charming local youth, and they marry. The consequences of the *mésalliance* were tragic but do not here concern us. What's so remarkable is my own temerity. For I placed Gino firmly in his society although I knew nothing about it. I guessed at his relatives, his daily life, his habits, his house, and his sketchy conception of housekeeping. I gave him not only a personal outfit but a social surround. Italian friends who have read the book say that I have not done so badly. If that is true I am indeed proud. One of them, a charming girl, added that I must not think Gino is a typical Italian. There is not much danger of my doing this, since I do not think anyone is a typical anything. I am a novelist and my business lies with individuals, not with classifications.[1]

If "Siena or that sort of place" was indeed Siena, the "sorry bit of twaddle" could well have been overheard in July 1901, when Forster spent four days in the city; San Gimignano he had visited the previous month. In that case, however, the first seeds of *Where Angels Fear to Tread* were sown some three years before they began to bear fruit; meanwhile Forster had busied himself with more short stories, essays, and two successive attempts at another novel with an Italian setting, and a heroine called Lucy—the novel that eventually turned into *A Room with a View*. For a time he appears to have been working simultaneously on both novels, but by 2 December 1904 the newcomer has taken the lead: "Lucy novel laid aside for a bit, at ch. IX. Gino one needs two chapters to finish it." And by the end of the year the Gino novel—now tentatively called "Rescue"—"only needs revising". At the end of his twenty-sixth year, Forster had completed his first novel.

Three further pieces of the raw material for it deserve mention: a place, a person and an operatic performance. Just as Monteriano is based on San Gimignano, so Sawston has its real-life counterpart, both here and in *The Longest Journey*: Tonbridge, Kent, where Forster had lived while attending the school as a dayboy.[2] The person is the musicologist E. J. Dent, Forster's slightly older contemporary at King's College, Cambridge, and at this date one of his closest friends. Dent's contribution is multiple, as a letter to him from Forster written on 22 March 1950 suggests:

[1] From "Three Countries" (typescript at King's College, Cambridge).
[2] It has been suggested by John Purkis in an excellent booklet on *Where Angels Fear to Tread* (Milton Keynes, Open University Press, 1973) that in this novel Sawston may stand for Tunbridge Wells. Forster, however, has confirmed the Sawston = Tonbridge equation in an inscribed copy belonging to the American artist Paul Cadmus.

Dear Dent,

I am going through old letters and have come across a number of yours—mostly from about 1902, when you were helping me, in all sorts of ways, to get into touch with Italy. They have reminded me of how much I owe you. I was grateful then, I hope, and I certainly am now.

More specifically, Dent contributed (as we shall see) the novel's title—and two-thirds of the character of Philip Herriton. In Forster's words:

If Forster has been to Italy, signs will appear in his Italian novels of course. Similarly with people whom he has met. A useful trick is to look back upon such a person with half-closed eyes, wilfully obscuring certain characteristics. I am then left with about ⅔ of a human being and can get to work. This is what I did with E. J. Dent, who became Philip in *Where Angels*. . . .[3]

Finally, Dent was present with Forster at a performance, on 12 May 1903, of *Lucia di Lammermoor*. In a letter to Dent written eighteen months earlier, Forster had declared: "I do not think I shall ever enjoy the Italian opera. All the conventions are so irritating"—and Dent may have needed to use persuasion before Forster agreed to give the genre another try. If so, we owe to Dent the magnificent opera scene in chapter 6:

I based this account on a performance I had heard at Florence at the beginning of the century where Lucia was sung by a little-known soprano. Her name was Tetrazzini. She had come along in a travelling company from Faenza. We all thought her splendid, but had no conception of her great future and international fame. It is amusing that I should have popped her into my little book without the least idea of her approaching celebrity. As the years passed and she was singing over the world, I sometimes thought I would write to her, for I believe that she was an amiable lady as well as a great artist. I decided not to write and I think you will agree I was wise. No artist, however great, no lady, however amiable, likes to be called ugly and stout.[4]

[3] From a manuscript memoir at King's College, Cambridge.
[4] See note 1 (p. ix).

Because of its modest length—possibly under the 50,000 words which in *Aspects of the Novel* he was to suggest as the minimum length for a novel—Forster offered "Monteriano", as he now called it, to *Blackwood's Magazine*. Instead, the Edinburgh firm of William Blackwood offered publication in volume form.

> The great news . . . is that Blackwood has written offering to publish my novel. It was for the Magazine that I sent it them, and the terms they offer are not at all good. I have written trying to do better, and meantime am trying to find out whether Blackwoods as *publishers* are a good firm, as though I don't mind much about money it's important to be in the hands of people who will advertise you well. Methuen or Heinemann are the firms I should have naturally tried first. The title has to be changed, which is very sad, but I see their point of view. (Letter to his mother, 9 April 1905.)

Four days later he spells out his complaints about the terms:

> Blackwood's terms are really no money at all: in other words nothing on the first 300 copies sold, 10% on the next 1,000, 15% up to 2,500, and 1/- a copy on all copies after 2,500. They haven't yet said, either, what price the book is to be sold at.

Both letters were written from Nassenheide, the baronial residence in Pomerania where Forster was currently installed as tutor to the children of the Gräfin von Arnim, alias "Elizabeth" of the German garden. In July ("at last"—i.e. a mere three months after acceptance) proofs began to arrive,

> and I sat correcting them in my room while she sat typing her novel *The Princess Priscilla's Fortnight* in the summer house. She read my proofs and she hated the book because it spoke of underdone meat and spittle. "Pfui, Mr Forster! Disgusting."

That was what Forster recalled, or chose to recall, in a memoir on Nassenheide written many years later.[5] At the time, in another letter to his mother (8 July 1905), he recorded a more mixed reaction:

> E. is very funny over it. She read ch. 1-3, and said it was very clever, but most unattractive, and she felt as if she wanted a

[5] Typescript at King's College, Cambridge.

bath. Then she read ch. 4 and said it was really beautiful, and she wanted to retract. Now she has read ch. 5 & ch. 6—you wouldn't remember, but it was the one that you rather liked—and has gone back to her original opinion.

Blackwood's having jibbed at "Monteriano", Forster asked Dent to suggest alternative titles. Dent offered "Where Angels Fear to Tread" and "From a Sense of Duty"; Forster passed both suggestions on, and Blackwood's chose the former. Somewhat nervously, Forster announced the decision to his mother, whose characteristic reaction can be inferred from his next letter (18 August 1905):

> I fear it is too late about the title, and am sorry you dislike it so much: I quite agree it isn't "me", and it was perhaps unwise to accept it: Elizabeth urged me to it so strongly (and though Blackwood's finally permitted "Monteriano" I did not dare, because they said it would be so detrimental to the sale). With all its faults—and it has many—it has the merit of describing the contents.

The Gräfin von Arnim's "Pfui, Mr Forster!" is not quite the earliest surviving comment on a Forster novel. That distinction belongs to Forster's friend H. O. Meredith, who in February had written to say that, after reading Turgenev "all last week", and then "Monteriano",

> I feel that you and Geo. M. [i.e. George Meredith] are the only living Eng. writers who can stand beside him. Of course you have an immense amount to learn yet especially in the management of your subordinate scenes and your treatment of the characters which you dislike. But it will be worth going through with it even if no one will publish or buy your books (which I don't for a moment believe) because you really understand tragedy. The death of the baby and the last conversation between Miss Abbott and Herriton are magnificent. I don't believe anyone else would have dared to write "baby" instead of "child". . . . The scene in the theatre in a different way is of course immensely good.

Forster himself, commenting on this letter in a diary entry of 26 February 1905, expressed the view that *Where Angels*

*Fear to Tread* was "not more than careful and praiseworthy".
All the same, he kept Meredith's letter; a less flattering
one from R. C. Trevelyan ("Bob Trevy", himself to make a
modest literary career) has vanished. Forster's reply, however, has survived, together with a further letter from
Trevelyan, whose further criticisms are kindly, solemn, and
almost entirely misguided. He finds Forster's style "often far
too conversational and even slangy, e.g. p. [76], where
'beastly Italy' is merely beastly indeed", and is particularly
severe on the delightful first new paragraph on p. 75, with its
well-judged chiasmus in the first sentence and the vivid
freshness of "waltzing". The incomplete exchange is something of a curiosity, and is included as Appendix A; from
it we learn that Desmond MacCarthy, Goldsworthy Lowes
Dickinson, Maynard Keynes and Edward Dent all thought
better of the novel than Trevelyan did.

One last private reaction deserves to be mentioned, before
we turn to the novel's more public reception. Snow
Wedgwood

> told him my fundamental objection to the story was that he did
> not make up his mind at the start whether it was to be tragedy
> or comedy. It seemed quite a new idea to him . . . that one
> ought to have any conception of one's intentions in this respect.
> I feel that in a tragedy everything ought to convey some
> intimation of seriousness and *Ahnung* [foreboding]. The
> lighting of the stage should be different. He writes in a jeering
> Retla-ish [?] spirit and interpolates a claim on one's tears.
> I am not certain whether I got him to agree in this as an
> aim so *a fortiori* I don't know whether I made him feel he had
> failed in it. . . . I even managed to say what was difficult, how
> much I felt the want of more elaboration of Gino's infidelity.
> Impropriety should be worth while.
> I begged him to fall in love before writing another novel. . . .[6]

(An elderly maiden lady in 1906, even one capable of
believing that "impropriety should be worth while", was
unlikely to guess what Forster later acknowledged: that the

[6] Letter to Laura Forster, 27 April 1906. For Snow Wedgwood see *Two
Cheers for Democracy*.

scene where Gino tortures Philip had "stirred" him, though at the time he "neither knew nor wondered why".)[7]

*Where Angels Fear to Tread* was published at the beginning of October 1905, in the same year as *Kipps*. (*Jude the Obscure* was nine years old, *Anna of the Five Towns* three, *The Way of All Flesh* two, *Nostromo* and *The Golden Bowl* one; *The Forsyte Saga* would be inaugurated in the following year; James Joyce had started writing the stories collected in *Dubliners*, but D. H. Lawrence's first novel was six years away, Virginia Woolf's a decade, as was *The Good Soldier*.) The number of copies printed was no more than 1,050, from which, if the terms were as quoted by Forster, he should have earned £22 10s.; from a second impression of 526 copies in January 1906, a further £19 18s. 1d. Hardly a fortune. More to the point, this first novel earned him golden opinions of a fair number of people. If his earliest reviewer (*Times Literary Supplement*, 29 September 1905) found "some of the incidents . . . so original as to be almost farcical", at least he recognized the originality, "an odd kind of individuality . . . which is worth exploring". The *Bookman*, similarly, found the book "unusual and convincing, with its uniqueness and its persuasion accomplished in an unexpectedly fresh manner". "Fresh and convincing" were two adjectives used also by the *Glasgow Herald*, while "original" occurs in several other reviews: in the *Manchester Guardian* ("almost startlingly original"), the *Speaker* ("brilliantly original") and the *Spectator*—which, however, hoped "that so original and searching a talent may yet give us a story in which the fallibility of goodness and the callousness of respectability are less uncompromisingly insisted upon". This disturbing quality, again, was felt by others: the *Manchester Guardian* reviewer wondered whether Forster "could be a little more charitable", his colleague on the *Manchester Courier* whether "the writer handles his creations a little too savagely". These reservations must be the reason why Blackwood's advertised the book, somewhat perversely, as "a story which puzzles the critics".[8] Most of

[7] See note 3 (p. x).
[8] *Saturday Review of Literature*, 18 November 1905.

the critics had, on the contrary, shown themselves to be perceptive as well as appreciative. The *Bookman*, for example, had gone right to the heart of Forster in noting that "the main issues of life are confronting us where we looked for trivialities". Most perceptive of all was C. F. G. Masterman, then literary editor of the *Daily News* (later a Liberal M.P. and junior Minister), and a consistent admirer of Forster's work—he also reviewed *The Longest Journey* and *A Room with a View*. His review of *Where Angels Fear to Tread* opens:

> *Where Angels Fear to Tread* is a remarkable book. Not often has the reviewer to welcome a new writer and a new novel so directly conveying the impression of power and an easy mastery of material. Here there are qualities of style and thought which awaken a sense of satisfaction and delight; a taste in the selection of words; a keen insight into the humour (and not merely the humours) of life; and a challenge to its accepted courses.

and ends:

> It is told with a deftness, a lightness, a grace of touch, and a radiant atmosphere of humour, which mark a strength and capacity giving large promise for the future.

The whole review well repays reading.[9]

By general consensus, Forster's first and shortest novel is a remarkable achievement in which all his characteristic gifts are displayed. "It would not be excessive," writes Virginia Woolf in 1927, "if we discovered in this slight first novel evidence of powers which only needed, one might hazard, a more generous diet to ripen into wealth and beauty."[10] And Elizabeth Bowen: "*Where Angels Fear to Tread* . . . contained in embryo all the other books."[11] F. R. Leavis goes further, rating it "the most successful of the pre-war novels".[12] After repeated re-readings, I would agree: unlike the more

[9] It is included, as are all the other reviews quoted above, in Philip Gardner's invaluable *E. M. Forster: the Critical Heritage* (London, Routledge & Kegan Paul, 1973), where full publication details are given.

[10] *The Death of the Moth, and Other Essays* (London, Hogarth Press, 1942), p. 105.

[11] *The Spectator*, 20 March 1936, p. 521.

[12] *The Common Pursuit* (London, Chatto & Windus, 1952), p. 262.

ambitious *Howards End*, I find it flawless—in the perfection oᴵ its structure, its subtle use of leitmotifs, its sureness of touch and tone, the deftness of its comedy, and the skill with which (*pace* Snow Wedgwood) the comedy modulates via scenes of nightmare into a poignancy and pathos unsurpassed in Forster's work.

I am grateful, once again, to Mr P. N. Furbank for help in answering countless questions. At King's College many people, and particularly Mrs Penelope Bulloch, have, once again, been unstinting in their kindness. For help at various stages in collating editions and reading proofs I am indebted to Professor George H. Thomson, Miss Laurie Cherbonnier, Miss Jennifer Fellows, Mrs Susan Burton, and (as always) Mr T. S. Matthews. Finally I owe thanks to Mr Julian Trevelyan for permission to quote the late R. C. Trevelyan's letter which forms part of Appendix A.

OLIVER STALLYBRASS

# Chapter 1

They were all at Charing Cross to see Lilia off—Philip, Harriet, Irma, Mrs Herriton herself. Even Mrs Theobald, squired by Mr Kingcroft, had braved the journey from Yorkshire to bid her only daughter goodbye. Miss Abbott was likewise attended by numerous relatives, and the sight of so many people talking at once and saying such different things caused Lilia to break into ungovernable peals of laughter.

"Quite an ovation," she cried, sprawling out of her first-class carriage. "They'll take us for royalty. Oh, Mr Kingcroft, get us foot-warmers."

The good-natured young man hurried away, and Philip, taking his place, flooded her with a final stream of advice and injunctions—where to stop, how to learn Italian, when to use mosquito-nets, what pictures to look at. "Remember," he concluded, "that it is only by going off the track that you get to know the country. See the little towns—Gubbio, Pienza, Cortona, San Gimignano, Monteriano. And don't, let me beg you, go with that awful tourist idea that Italy's only a museum of antiquities and art. Love and understand the Italians, for the people are more marvellous than the land."

"How I wish you were coming, Philip," she said, flattered at the unwonted notice her brother-in-law was giving her.

"I wish I were." He could have managed it without great difficulty, for his career at the Bar was not so intense as to prevent occasional holidays. But his family disliked his continual visits to the Continent, and he himself often found pleasure in the idea that he was too busy to leave town.

"Goodbye, dear everyone. What a whirl!" She caught sight of her little daughter Irma, and felt that a touch of maternal solemnity was required. "Goodbye, darling. Mind you're always good, and do what Granny tells you."

She referred not to her own mother, but to her mother-in-law, Mrs Herriton, who hated the title of Granny.

Irma lifted a serious face to be kissed, and said cautiously, "I'll do my best."

"She is sure to be good," said Mrs Herriton, who was standing pensively a little out of the hubbub. But Lilia was already calling to Miss Abbott, a tall, grave, rather nice-looking young lady who was conducting her adieus in a more decorous manner on the platform.

"Caroline, my Caroline! Jump in, or your chaperon will go off without you."

And Philip, whom the idea of Italy always intoxicated, had started again, telling her of the supreme moments of her coming journey—the Campanile of Airolo, which would burst on her when she emerged from the St Gotthard tunnel, presaging the future; the view of the Ticino and Lago Maggiore as the train climbed the slopes of Monte Ceneri; the view of Lugano, the view of Como—Italy gathering thick around her now—the arrival at her first resting-place, when, after long driving through dark and dirty streets, she should at last behold, amid the roar of trams and the glare of arc lamps, the buttresses of the cathedral of Milan.

"Handkerchiefs and collars," screamed Harriet, "in my inlaid box! I've lent you my inlaid box."

"Good old Harry!" She kissed everyone again, and there was a moment's silence. They all smiled steadily, excepting Philip, who was choking in the fog, and old Mrs Theobald, who had begun to cry. Miss Abbott got into the carriage. The guard himself shut the door, and told Lilia that she would be all right. Then the train moved, and they all moved with it a couple of steps, and waved their handkerchiefs, and uttered cheerful little cries. At that moment Mr Kingcroft reappeared, carrying a foot-warmer by both ends, as if it was a tea-tray. He was sorry that he was too late, and called out in a quavering voice: "Goodbye, Mrs Charles. May you enjoy yourself, and may God bless you."

Lilia smiled and nodded, and then the absurd position of the foot-warmer overcame her, and she began to laugh again.

"Oh, I am so sorry," she cried back, "but you do look so funny. Oh, you all look so funny waving! Oh, pray!" And laughing helplessly she was carried out into the fog.

"High spirits to begin so long a journey," said Mrs Theobald, dabbing her eyes.

Mr Kingcroft solemnly moved his head in token of agreement. "I wish," said he, "that Mrs Charles had gotten the foot-warmer. These London porters won't take heed to a country chap."

"But you did your best," said Mrs Herriton. "And I think it simply noble of you to have brought Mrs Theobald all the way here on such a day as this." Then, rather hastily, she shook hands, and left him to take Mrs Theobald all the way back.

Sawston, her own home, was within easy reach of London, and they were not late for tea. Tea was in the dining-room, with an egg for Irma, to keep up the child's spirits. The house seemed strangely quiet after a fortnight's bustle, and their conversation was spasmodic and subdued. They wondered whether the travellers had got to Folkestone, whether it would be at all rough, and if so what would happen to poor Miss Abbott.

"And, Granny, when will the old ship get to Italy?" asked Irma.

" 'Grandmother', dear; not 'Granny'," said Mrs Herriton, giving her a kiss. "And we say 'a boat' or 'a steamer', not 'a ship'. Ships have sails. And mother won't go all the way by sea. You look at the map of Europe, and you'll see why. Harriet, take her. Go with Aunt Harriet, and she'll show you the map."

"Right-o!" said the little girl, and dragged the reluctant Harriet into the library. Mrs Herriton and her son were left alone. There was immediately confidence between them.

"Here beginneth the New Life," said Philip.

3

"Poor child, how vulgar!" murmured Mrs Herriton. "It's surprising that she isn't worse. But she has got a look of poor Charles about her."

"And—alas, alas!—a look of old Mrs Theobald. What appalling apparition was that? I did think the lady was bedridden as well as imbecile. Why ever did she come?"

"Mr Kingcroft made her. I am certain of it. He wanted to see Lilia again, and this was the only way."

"I hope he is satisfied. I did not think my sister-in-law distinguished herself in her farewells."

Mrs Herriton shuddered. "I mind nothing, so long as she has gone—and gone with Miss Abbott. It is mortifying to think that a widow of thirty-three requires a girl ten years younger to look after her."

"I pity Miss Abbott. Fortunately one admirer is chained to England. Mr Kingcroft cannot leave the crops or the climate or something. I don't think, either, he improved his chances today. He, as well as Lilia, has the knack of being absurd in public."

Mrs Herriton replied, "When a man is neither well-bred, nor well-connected, nor handsome, nor clever, nor rich, even Lilia may discard him in time."

"No. I believe she would take anyone. Right up to the last, when her boxes were packed, she was 'playing' the chinless curate. Both the curates are chinless, but hers had the dampest hands. I came on them in the Park. They were speaking of the Pentateuch."

"My dear boy! If possible, she has got worse and worse. It was your idea of Italian travel that saved us!"

Philip brightened at the little compliment. "The odd part is that she was quite eager—always asking me for information; and of course I was very glad to give it. I admit she is a philistine, appallingly ignorant, and her taste in art is false. Still, to have any taste at all is something. And I do believe that Italy really purifies and ennobles all who visit her. She is the school as well as the playground of the world. It is really to Lilia's credit that she wants to go there."

4

"She would go anywhere," said his mother, who had heard enough of the praises of Italy. "I and Caroline Abbott had the greatest difficulty in dissuading her from the Riviera."

"No, mother; no. She was really keen on Italy. This travel is quite a crisis for her." He found the situation full of whimsical romance: there was something half attractive, half repellent in the thought of this vulgar woman journeying to places he loved and revered. Why should she not be transfigured? The same had happened to the Goths.

Mrs Herriton did not believe in romance, nor in transfiguration, nor in parallels from history, nor in anything else that may disturb domestic life. She adroitly changed the subject before Philip got excited. Soon Harriet returned, having given her lesson in geography. Irma went to bed early, and was tucked up by her grandmother. Then the two ladies worked and played cards. Philip read a book. And so they all settled down to their quiet profitable existence, and continued it without interruption through the winter.

It was now nearly ten years since Charles had fallen in love with Lilia Theobald because she was pretty, and during that time Mrs Herriton had hardly known a moment's rest. For six months she schemed to prevent the match, and when it had taken place she turned to another task—the supervision of her daughter-in-law. Lilia must be pushed through life without bringing discredit on the family into which she had married. She was aided by Charles, by her daughter Harriet, and, as soon as he was old enough, by the clever one of the family, Philip. The birth of Irma made things still more difficult. But fortunately old Mrs Theobald, who had attempted interference, began to break up. It was an effort to her to leave Whitby, and Mrs Herriton discouraged the effort as far as possible. That curious duel which is fought over every baby was fought and decided early. Irma belonged to her father's family, not to her mother's.

Charles died, and the struggle recommenced. Lilia tried to assert herself, and said that she should go to take care of

Mrs Theobald. It required all Mrs Herriton's kindness to prevent her. A house was finally taken for her at Sawston, and there for three years she lived with Irma, continually subject to the refining influences of her late husband's family.

During one of her rare Yorkshire visits trouble began again. Lilia confided to a friend that she liked a Mr Kingcroft extremely, but that she was not exactly engaged to him. The news came round to Mrs Herriton, who at once wrote, begging for information, and pointing out that Lilia must either be engaged or not, since no intermediate state existed. It was a good letter, and flurried Lilia extremely. She left Mr Kingcroft without even the pressure of a rescue-party. She cried a great deal on her return to Sawston, and said she was very sorry. Mrs Herriton took the opportunity of speaking more seriously about the duties of widowhood and motherhood than she had ever done before. But somehow things never went easily after. Lilia would not settle down in her place among Sawston matrons. She was a bad house-keeper, always in the throes of some domestic crisis, which Mrs Herriton, who kept her servants for years, had to step across and adjust. She let Irma stop away from school for insufficient reasons, and she allowed her to wear rings. She learned to bicycle, for the purpose of waking the place up, and coasted down the High Street one Sunday evening, falling off at the turn by the church. If she had not been a relative, it would have been entertaining. But even Philip, who in theory loved outraging English conventions, rose to the occasion, and gave her a talking which she remembered to her dying day. It was just then, too, that they discovered that she still allowed Mr Kingcroft to write to her "as a gentleman friend", and to send presents to Irma.

Philip thought of Italy, and the situation was saved. Caroline, charming sober Caroline Abbott, who lived two turnings away, was seeking a companion for a year's travel. Lilia gave up her house, sold half her furniture, left the other half and Irma with Mrs Herriton, and had now departed, amid universal approval, for a change of scene.

She wrote to them frequently during the winter—more frequently than she wrote to her mother. Her letters were always prosperous. Florence she found perfectly sweet, Naples a dream, but very whiffy. In Rome one had simply to sit still and feel. Philip, however, declared that she was improving. He was particularly gratified when in the early spring she began to visit the smaller towns that he had recommended. "In a place like this," she wrote, "one really does feel in the heart of things, and off the beaten track. Looking out of a Gothic window every morning, it seems impossible that the Middle Ages have passed away." The letter was from Monteriano, and concluded with a not unsuccessful description of the wonderful little town.

"It is something that she is contented," said Mrs Herriton. "But no one could live three months with Caroline Abbott and not be the better for it."

Just then Irma came in from school, and she read her mother's letter to her, carefully correcting any grammatical errors, for she was a loyal supporter of parental authority. Irma listened politely, but soon changed the subject to hockey, in which her whole being was absorbed. They were to vote for colours that afternoon—yellow and white or yellow and green. What did her grandmother think?

Of course Mrs Herriton had an opinion, which she sedately expounded, in spite of Harriet, who said that colours were unnecessary for children, and of Philip, who said that they were ugly. She was getting proud of Irma, who had certainly greatly improved, and could no longer be called that most appalling of things—a vulgar child. She was anxious to form her before her mother returned. So she had no objection to the leisurely movements of the travellers, and even suggested that they should overstay their year if it suited them.

Lilia's next letter was also from Monteriano, and Philip grew quite enthusiastic.

"They've stopped there over a week!" he cried. "Why! I shouldn't have done as much myself. They must be really keen, for the hotel's none too comfortable."

7

"I cannot understand people," said Harriet. "What can they be doing all day? And there is no church there, I suppose."

"There is Santa Deodata, one of the most beautiful churches in Italy."

"Of course I mean an English church," said Harriet stiffly. "Lilia promised me that she would always be in a large town on Sundays."

"If she goes to a service at Santa Deodata's, she will find more beauty and sincerity than there is in all the Back Kitchens of Europe."

The Back Kitchen was his nickname for St James's, a small and depressing edifice much patronized by his sister. She always resented any slight on it, and Mrs Herriton had to intervene.

"Now, dears, don't. Listen to Lilia's letter. 'We love this place, and I do not know how I shall ever thank Philip for telling me it. It is not only so quaint, but one sees the Italians unspoiled in all their simplicity and charm here. The frescoes are wonderful. Caroline, who grows sweeter every day, is very busy sketching.' "

"Everyone to his taste!" said Harriet, who always delivered a platitude as if it was an epigram. She was curiously virulent about Italy, which she had never visited, her only experience of the Continent being an occasional six weeks in the Protestant parts of Switzerland.

"Oh, Harriet is a bad lot!" said Philip as soon as she left the room. His mother laughed, and told him not to be naughty; and the appearance of Irma, just off to school, prevented further discussion. Not only in tracts is a child a peacemaker.

"One moment, Irma," said her uncle. "I'm going to the station. I'll give you the pleasure of my company."

They started together. Irma was gratified; but conversation flagged, for Philip had not the art of talking to the young. Mrs Herriton sat a little longer at the breakfast-table, rereading Lilia's letter. Then she helped the cook to clear, ordered dinner, and started the housemaid turning

8

out the drawing-room, Tuesday being its day. The weather was lovely, and she thought she would do a little gardening, as it was quite early. She called Harriet, who had recovered from the insult to St James's, and together they went to the kitchen-garden and began to sow some early vegetables.

"We will save the peas to the last; they are the greatest fun," said Mrs Herriton, who had the gift of making work a treat. She and her elderly daughter always got on very well, though they had not a great deal in common. Harriet's education had been almost too successful. As Philip once said, she had bolted all the cardinal virtues and couldn't digest them. Though pious and patriotic, and a great moral asset for the house, she lacked that pliancy and tact which her mother so much valued, and had expected her to pick up for herself. Harriet, if she had been allowed, would have driven Lilia to an open rupture, and, what was worse, she would have done the same to Philip two years before, when he returned full of passion for Italy, and ridiculing Sawston and its ways.

"It's a shame, mother!" she had cried. "Philip laughs at everything—the Book Club, the Debating Society, the Progressive Whist, the bazaars. People won't like it. We have our reputation. A house divided against itself cannot stand."

Mrs Herriton replied in the memorable words, "Let Philip say what he likes, and he will let us do what we like." And Harriet had acquiesced.

They sowed the duller vegetables first, and a pleasant feeling of righteous fatigue stole over them as they addressed themselves to the peas. Harriet stretched a string to guide the row straight, and Mrs Herriton scratched a furrow with a pointed stick. At the end of it she looked at her watch.

"It's twelve! The second post's in. Run and see if there are any letters."

Harriet did not want to go. "Let's finish the peas. There won't be any letters."

"No, dear; please go. I'll sow the peas, but you shall cover them up—and mind the birds don't see 'em!"

9

Mrs Herriton was very careful to let those peas trickle evenly from her hand, and at the end of the row she was conscious that she had never sown better. They were expensive too.

"Actually old Mrs Theobald!" said Harriet, returning. "Read me the letter. My hands are dirty. How intolerable the crested paper is!"

Harriet opened the envelope.

"I don't understand," she said; "it doesn't make sense."

"Her letters never did."

"But it must be sillier than usual," said Harriet, and her voice began to quaver. "Look here, read it, mother; I can't make head or tail."

Mrs Herriton took the letter indulgently. "What is the difficulty?" she said after a long pause. "What is it that puzzles you in this letter?"

"The meaning—" faltered Harriet. The sparrows hopped nearer and began to eye the peas.

"The meaning is quite clear—Lilia is engaged to be married. Don't cry, dear; please me by not crying—don't talk at all. It's more than I could bear. She is going to marry someone she has met in a hotel. Take the letter and read for yourself." Suddenly she broke down over what might seem a small point. "How dare she not tell me direct! How dare she write first to Yorkshire! Pray, am I to hear through Mrs Theobald—a patronizing, insolent letter like this? Have I no claim at all? Bear witness, dear"—she choked with passion—"bear witness that for this I'll never forgive her!"

"Oh, what is to be done?" moaned Harriet. "What is to be done?"

"This first!" She tore the letter into little pieces and scattered it over the mould. "Next, a telegram for Lilia! No: a telegram for Miss Caroline Abbott. She, too, has something to explain."

"Oh, what is to be done?" repeated Harriet, as she followed her mother to the house. She was helpless before such effrontery. What awful thing—what awful person had come to Lilia? "Someone in the hotel." The letter only said that. What kind of person? A gentleman? An Englishman? The letter did not say.

"Wire reason of stay at Monteriano. Strange rumours," read Mrs Herriton, and addressed the telegram to Abbott, Stella d'Italia, Monteriano, Italy. "If there is an office there," she added, "we might get an answer this evening. Since Philip is back at seven, and the eight-fifteen catches the midnight boat at Dover—Harriet, when you go with this, get a hundred pounds in five-pound notes at the bank."

"But why—what—"

"Go, dear, at once; do not talk. I see Irma coming back; go quickly. . . . Well, Irma dear, and whose team are you in this afternoon—Miss Edith's or Miss May's?"

But as soon as she had behaved as usual to her grand-daughter she went to the library and took out the large atlas, for she wanted to know about Monteriano. The name was in the smallest print, in the midst of a woolly-brown tangle of hills which were called the "Sub-Apennines". It was not so very far from Siena, which she had learned at school. Past it there wandered a thin black line, notched at intervals like a saw, and she knew that this was a railway. But the map left a good deal to imagination, and she had not got any. She looked up the place in *Childe Harold*, but Byron had not been there. Nor did Mark Twain visit it in the *Tramp Abroad*. The resources of literature were ex-hausted; she must wait till Philip came home. And the thought of Philip made her try Philip's room, and there she found *Central Italy*, by Baedeker, and opened it for the first time in her life and read in it as follows:

**Monteriano** (pop. 4,800). *Hotels*: Stella d'Italia, moderate only; Globo, dirty. *Caffè Garibaldi. Post and Telegraph office in Corso Vittorio Emmanuele, next to Theatre. Photographs at Seghena's (cheaper in Florence). Diligence (1 lira) meets principal trains.

*Chief attractions* (*2–3 hours*): Santa Deodata, Palazzo Pubblico, Sant' Agostino, Santa Caterina, Sant' Ambrogio, Palazzo

11

Capocchi. Guide (2 lire) unnecessary. A walk round the Walls should on no account be omitted. The view from the Rocca (small gratuity) is finest at sunset.

*History*: Monteriano, the Mons Rianus of Antiquity, whose Ghibelline tendencies are noted by Dante (Purg. xx), definitely emancipated itself from Poggibonsi in 1261. Hence the distich, '*Poggibonizzi, fatti in là, che Monteriano si fa città!*' till recently inscribed over the Siena gate. It remained independent till 1530, when it was sacked by the Papal troops and became part of the Grand Duchy of Tuscany. It is now of small importance, and seat of the district prison. The inhabitants are still noted for their agreeable manners.

The traveller will proceed direct from the Siena gate to the COLLEGIATE CHURCH OF SANTA DEODATA, and inspect (5th chapel on right) the charming *Frescoes. . . .

Mrs Herriton did not proceed. She was not one to detect the hidden charms of Baedeker. Some of the information seemed to her unnecessary, all of it was dull. Whereas Philip could never read "The view from the Rocca (small gratuity) is finest at sunset" without a catching at the heart. Restoring the book to its place, she went downstairs and looked up and down the asphalt paths for her daughter. She saw her at last, two turnings away, vainly trying to shake off Mr Abbott, Miss Caroline Abbott's father. Harriet was always unfortunate. At last she returned, hot, agitated, crackling with bank-notes, and Irma bounced to greet her, and trod heavily on her corn.

"Your feet grow larger every day," said the agonized Harriet, and gave her niece a violent push. Then Irma cried, and Mrs Herriton was annoyed with Harriet for betraying irritation. Lunch was nasty; and during pudding news arrived that the cook, by sheer dexterity, had broken a very vital knob off the kitchen-range. "It is too bad," said Mrs Herriton. Irma said it was three bad, and was told not to be rude. After lunch Harriet would get out Baedeker, and read in injured tones about Monteriano, the Mons Rianus of Antiquity, till her mother stopped her.

"It's ridiculous to read, dear. She's not trying to marry

anyone in the place. Some tourist, obviously, who's stopping in the hotel. The place has nothing to do with it at all."

"But what a place to go to! What nice person, too, do you meet in a hotel?"

"Nice or nasty, as I have told you several times before, is not the point. Lilia has insulted our family, and she shall suffer for it. And when you speak against hotels I think you forget that I met your father at Chamonix. You can contribute nothing, dear, at present, and I think you had better hold your tongue. I am going to the kitchen, to speak about the range."

She spoke just too much, and the cook said that if she could not give satisfaction she had better leave. A small thing at hand is greater than a great thing remote, and Lilia, misconducting herself upon a mountain in Central Italy, was immediately hidden. Mrs Herriton flew to a registry office, failed; flew to another, failed again; came home, was told by the housemaid that things seemed so unsettled that she had better leave as well; had tea, wrote six letters, was interrupted by cook and housemaid, both weeping, asking her pardon, and imploring to be taken back. In the flush of victory the doorbell rang, and there was the telegram: "Lilia engaged to Italian nobility. Writing. Abbott."

"No answer," said Mrs Herriton. "Get down Mr Philip's gladstone from the attic."

She would not allow herself to be frightened by the unknown. Indeed, she knew a little now. The man was not an Italian noble, otherwise the telegram would have said so. It must have been written by Lilia. None but she would have been guilty of the fatuous vulgarity of "Italian nobility". She recalled phrases of this morning's letter: "We love this place—Caroline is sweeter than ever, and busy sketching—Italians full of simplicity and charm." And the remark of Baedeker, "the inhabitants are still noted for their agreeable manners", had a baleful meaning now. If Mrs Herriton had no imagination, she had intuition, a more useful quality, and the picture she made to herself of Lilia's fiancé did not prove altogether wrong.

So Philip was received with the news that he must start in half an hour for Monteriano. He was in a painful position. For three years he had sung the praises of the Italians, but he had never contemplated having one as a relative. He tried to soften the thing down to his mother, but in his heart of hearts he agreed with her when she said: "The man may be a duke or he may be an organ-grinder. That is not the point. If Lilia marries him she insults the memory of Charles, she insults Irma, she insults us. Therefore I forbid her, and if she disobeys we have done with her for ever."

"I will do all I can," said Philip in a low voice. It was the first time he had had anything to do. He kissed his mother and sister and puzzled Irma. The hall was warm and attractive as he looked back into it from the cold March night, and he departed for Italy reluctantly, as for something commonplace and dull.

Before Mrs Herriton went to bed she wrote to Mrs Theobald, using plain language about Lilia's conduct, and hinting that it was a question on which everyone must definitely choose sides. She added, as if it was an afterthought, that Mrs Theobald's letter had arrived that morning.

Just as she was going upstairs she remembered that she never covered up those peas. It upset her more than anything, and again and again she struck the banisters with vexation. Late as it was, she got a lantern from the toolshed and went down the garden to rake the earth over them. The sparrows had taken every one. But countless fragments of the letter remained, disfiguring the tidy ground.

# Chapter 2

When the bewildered tourist alights at the station o Monteriano, he finds himself in the middle of the country. There are a few houses round the railway, and many more dotted over the plain and the slopes of the hills, but of a town, medieval or otherwise, not the slightest sign. He must take what is suitably termed a *legno*—a piece of wood—and drive up eight miles of excellent road into the Middle Ages. For it is impossible, as well as sacrilegious, to be as quick as Baedeker.

It was three in the afternoon when Philip left the realms of common sense. He was so weary with travelling that he had fallen asleep in the train. His fellow passengers had the usual Italian gift of divination, and when Monteriano came they knew he wanted to go there, and dropped him out. His feet sank into the hot asphalt of the platform, and in a dream he watched the train depart, while the porter who ought to have been carrying his bag ran up the line playing touch-you-last with the guard. Alas! he was in no humour for Italy. Bargaining for a *legno* bored him unutterably. The man asked six lire; and, though Philip knew that for eight miles it should scarcely be more than four, yet he was about to give what he was asked, and so make the man discontented and unhappy for the rest of the day. He was saved from this social blunder by loud shouts, and looking up the road saw one cracking his whip and waving his reins and driving two horses furiously, and behind him there appeared the swaying figure of a woman, holding starfish fashion onto anything she could touch. It was Miss Abbott, who had just received his letter from Milan announcing the time of his arrival, and had hurried down to meet him.

He had known Miss Abbott for years, and had never had

15

much opinion about her one way or the other. She was good, quiet, dull and amiable, and young only because she was twenty-three: there was nothing in her appearance or manner to suggest the fire of youth. All her life had been spent at Sawston with a dull and amiable father, and her pleasant, pallid face, bent on some respectable charity, was a familiar object of the Sawston streets. Why she had ever wished to leave them was surprising; but, as she truly said, "I am John Bull to the backbone, yet I do want to see Italy, just once. Everybody says it is marvellous, and that one gets no idea of it from books at all." The curate suggested that a year was a long time; and Miss Abbott, with decorous playfulness, answered him: "Oh, but you must let me have my fling! I promise to have it once, and once only. It will give me things to think about and talk about for the rest of my life." The curate had consented; so had Mr Abbott. And here she was in a *legno*, solitary, dusty, frightened, with as much to answer and to answer for as the most dashing adventuress could desire.

They shook hands without speaking. She made room for Philip and his luggage amidst the loud indignation of the unsuccessful driver, whom it required the combined eloquence of the station-master and the station beggar to confute. The silence was prolonged until they started. For three days he had been considering what he should do, and still more what he should say. He had invented a dozen imaginary conversations, in all of which his logic and eloquence procured him certain victory. But how to begin? He was in the enemy's country, and everything—the hot sun, the cold air behind the heat, the endless rows of olives, regular yet mysterious—seemed hostile to the placid atmosphere of Sawston in which his thoughts took birth. At the outset he made one great concession. If the match was really suitable, and Lilia were bent on it, he would give in, and trust to his influence with his mother to set things right. He would not have made the concession in England; but here in Italy Lilia, however wilful and silly, was at all events growing to be a human being.

"Are we to talk it over now?" he asked.

"Certainly, please," said Miss Abbott, in great agitation. "If you will be so very kind."

"Then how long has she been engaged?"

Her face was that of a perfect fool—a fool in terror.

"A short time—quite a short time," she stammered, as if the shortness of the time would reassure him.

"I should like to know how long, if you can remember."

She entered into elaborate calculations on her fingers. "Exactly eleven days," she said at last.

"How long have you been here?"

More calculations, while he tapped irritably with his foot. "Close on three weeks."

"Did you know him before you came?"

"No."

"Oh! Who is he?"

"A native of the place."

The second silence took place. They had left the plain now and were climbing up the outposts of the hills, the olive-trees still accompanying. The driver, a jolly, fat man, had got out to ease the horses, and was walking by the side of the carriage.

"I understood they met at the hotel."

"It was a mistake of Mrs Theobald's."

"I also understand that he is a member of the Italian nobility."

She did not reply.

"May I be told his name?"

Miss Abbott whispered "Carella". But the driver heard her, and a grin split over his face. The engagement must be known already.

"Carella? Conte or Marchese, or what?"

"Signor," said Miss Abbott, and looked helplessly aside.

"Perhaps I bore you with these questions. If so, I will stop."

"Oh no, please; not at all. I am here—my own idea—to give all information which you very naturally—and to see if somehow—please ask anything you like."

"Then how old is he?"

"Oh, quite young. Twenty-one, I believe."

There burst from Philip the exclamation, "Good Lord!"

"One would never believe it," said Miss Abbott, flushing. "He looks much older."

"And is he good-looking?" he asked, with gathering sarcasm.

She became decisive. "Very good-looking. All his features are good, and he is well built—though I dare say English standards would find him too short."

Philip, whose one physical advantage was his height, felt annoyed at her implied indifference to it.

"May I conclude that you like him?"

She replied decisively again, "As far as I have seen him, I do."

At that moment the carriage entered a little wood, which lay brown and sombre across the cultivated hill. The trees of the wood were small and leafless, but noticeable for this —that their stems stood in violets as rocks stand in the summer sea. There are such violets in England, but not so many. Nor are there so many in art, for no painter has the courage. The cart-ruts were channels, the hollows lagoons; even the dry white margin of the road was splashed, like a causeway soon to be submerged under the advancing tide of spring. Philip paid no attention at the time; he was thinking what to say next. But his eyes had registered the beauty, and next March he did not forget that the road to Monteriano must traverse innumerable flowers.

"As far as I have seen him, I do like him," repeated Miss Abbott, after a pause.

He thought she sounded a little defiant, and crushed her at once.

"What is he, please? You haven't told me that. What's his position?"

She opened her mouth to speak, and no sound came from it. Philip waited patiently. She tried to be audacious, and failed pitiably.

"No position at all. He is kicking his heels, as my father

18

would say. You see, he has only just finished his military service."

"As a private?"

"I suppose so. There is general conscription. He was in the Bersaglieri, I think. Isn't that the crack regiment?"

"The men in it must be short and broad. They must also be able to walk six miles an hour."

She looked at him wildly, not understanding all that he said, but feeling that he was very clever. Then she continued her defence of Signor Carella.

"And now, like most young men, he is looking out for something to do."

"Meanwhile?"

"Meanwhile, like most young men, he lives with his people—father, mother, two sisters, and a tiny tot of a brother."

There was a grating sprightliness about her that drove him nearly mad. He determined to silence her at last.

"One more question, and only one more. What is his father?"

"His father," said Miss Abbott. "Well, I don't suppose you'll think it a good match. But that's not the point. I mean the point is not—I mean that social differences—love, after all—not but what—"

Philip ground his teeth together and said nothing.

"Gentlemen sometimes judge hardly. But I feel that you, and at all events your mother—so really good in every sense, so really unworldly—after all, love—marriages are made in heaven."

"Yes, Miss Abbott, I know. But I am anxious to hear heaven's choice. You arouse my curiosity. Is my sister-in-law to marry an angel?"

"Mr Herriton, don't—please, Mr Herriton—a dentist. His father's a dentist."

Philip gave a cry of personal disgust and pain. He shuddered all over, and edged away from his companion. A dentist! A dentist at Monteriano! A dentist in fairyland! False teeth and laughing-gas and the tilting chair at a place which knew the Etruscan League, and the Pax Romana, and Alaric himself, and the Countess Matilda, and the Middle Ages, all fighting and holiness, and the Renaissance, all fighting and beauty! He thought of Lilia no longer. He was anxious for himself: he feared that Romance might die.

Romance only dies with life. No pair of pincers will ever pull it out of us. But there is a spurious sentiment which cannot resist the unexpected and the incongruous and the grotesque. A touch will loosen it, and the sooner it goes from us the better. It was going from Philip now, and therefore he gave the cry of pain.

"I cannot think what is in the air," he began. "If Lilia was determined to disgrace us, she might have found a less repulsive way. A boy of medium height with a pretty face, the son of a dentist at Monteriano. Have I put it correctly? May I surmise that he has not got one penny? May I also surmise that his social position is nil? Furthermore—"

"Stop! I'll tell you no more."

"Really, Miss Abbott, it is a little late for reticence. You have equipped me admirably!"

"I'll tell you not another word!" she cried, with a spasm of terror. Then she got out her handkerchief, and seemed as if she would shed tears. After a silence, which he intended to symbolize to her the dropping of a curtain on the scene, he began to talk of other subjects.

They were among olives again, and the wood with its beauty and wildness had passed away. But as they climbed higher the country opened out, and there appeared, high on a hill to the right, Monteriano. The hazy green of the olives rose up to its walls, and it seemed to float in isolation between trees and sky, like some fantastic ship city of a dream. Its colour was brown, and it revealed not a single house—nothing but the narrow circle of the walls, and behind them seventeen towers—all that was left of the fifty-two that had filled the city in her prime. Some were only stumps, some were inclining stiffly to their fall, some were still erect, piercing like masts into the blue. It was impossible to praise it as beautiful, but it was also impossible to damn it as quaint.

Meanwhile Philip talked continually, thinking this to be great evidence of resource and tact. It showed Miss Abbott that he had probed her to the bottom, but was able to conquer his disgust, and by sheer force of intellect continue to be as agreeable and amusing as ever. He did not know that he talked a good deal of nonsense, and that the sheer force of his intellect was weakened by the sight of Monteriano, and by the thought of dentistry within those walls.

The town above them swung to the left, to the right, to the left again, as the road wound upward through the trees, and the towers began to glow in the descending sun. As they drew near, Philip saw the heads of people gathering black upon the walls, and he knew well what was happening—how the news was spreading that a stranger was in sight, and the beggars were aroused from their content and bid to adjust their deformities; how the alabaster man was running for his wares, and the Authorized Guide running for his peaked cap and his two cards of recommendation—one from Miss M'Gee, Maida Vale, the other, less valuable, from an Equerry to the Queen of Peru; how someone else was running to tell the landlady of the Stella d'Italia to put on her pearl necklace and brown boots and empty the slops from the spare bedroom; and how the landlady was running to tell Lilia and her boy that their fate was at hand.

Perhaps it was a pity Philip had talked so profusely. He had driven Miss Abbott half demented, but he had given himself no time to concert a plan. The end came so suddenly. They emerged from the trees onto the terrace before the walls, with the vision of half Tuscany radiant in the sun behind them, and then they turned in through the Siena gate, and their journey was over. The *dogana* men admitted them with an air of gracious welcome, and they clattered up the narrow dark street, greeted by that mixture of curiosity and kindness which makes each Italian arrival so wonderful.

He was stunned and knew not what to do. At the hotel he received no ordinary reception. The landlady wrung him by the hand; one person snatched his umbrella, another his bag; people pushed each other out of his way. The entrance seemed blocked with a crowd. Dogs were barking, bladder whistles being blown, women waving their handkerchiefs, excited children screaming on the stairs, and at the top of the stairs was Lilia herself, very radiant, with her best blouse on.

"Welcome!" she cried. "Welcome to Monteriano!" He greeted her, for he did not know what else to do, and a sympathetic murmur rose from the crowd below.

"You told me to come here," she continued, "and I don't forget it. Let me introduce Signor Carella!"

Philip discerned in the corner behind her a young man who might eventually prove handsome and well-made, but certainly did not seem so then. He was half enveloped in the drapery of a cold dirty curtain, and nervously stuck out a hand, which Philip took and found thick and damp. There were more murmurs of approval from the stairs.

"Well, din-din's nearly ready," said Lilia. "Your room's down the passage, Philip. You needn't go changing."

He stumbled away to wash his hands, utterly crushed by her effrontery.

"Dear Caroline!" whispered Lilia as soon as he had gone. "What an angel you've been to tell him! He takes it so well. But you must have had a *mauvais quart d'heure*."

Miss Abbot's long terror suddenly turned into acidity. "I've told nothing," she snapped. "It's all for you—and if it only takes a quarter of an hour you'll be lucky!"

Dinner was a nightmare. They had the smelly dining-room to themselves. Lilia, very smart and vociferous, was at the head of the table; Miss Abbott, also in her best, sat by Philip, looking, to his irritated nerves, more like the tragedy confidante every moment. That scion of the Italian nobility, Signor Carella, sat opposite. Behind him loomed a bowl of goldfish, who swam round and round, gaping at the guests.

The face of Signor Carella was twitching too much for Philip to study it. But he could see the hands, which were not particularly clean, and did not get cleaner by fidgeting amongst the shining slabs of hair. His starched cuffs were no clean either, and as for his suit, it had obviously been bought for the occasion as something really English—a gigantic check, which did not even fit. His handkerchief he had forgotten, but never missed it. Altogether, he was quite unpresentable, and very lucky to have a father who was a dentist in Monteriano. And why even Lilia—but as soon as the meal began it furnished Philip with an explanation.

For the youth was hungry, and his lady filled his plate with spaghetti, and when those delicious slippery worms were flying down his throat his face relaxed and became for a moment unconscious and calm. And Philip had seen that face before in Italy a hundred times—seen it and loved it, for it was not merely beautiful, but had the charm which is the rightful heritage of all who are born on that soil. But he did not want to see it opposite him at dinner. It was not the face of a gentleman.

Conversation, to give it that name, was carried on in a mixture of English and Italian. Lilia had picked up hardly any of the latter language, and Signor Carella had not yet learned any of the former. Occasionally Miss Abbott had to act as interpreter between the lovers, and the situation became uncouth and revolting in the extreme. Yet Philip was too cowardly to break forth and denounce the engagement. He thought he should be more effective with Lilia if he had her alone, and pretended to himself that he must hear her defence before giving judgement.

Signor Carella, heartened by the spaghetti and the throat-rasping wine, attempted to talk, and, looking politely towards Philip, said: "England is a great country. The Italians love England and the English."

Philip, in no mood for international amenities, merely bowed.

"Italy too," the other continued a little resentfully, "is a great country. She has produced many famous men—for example, Garibaldi and Dante. The latter wrote the *Inferno*, the *Purgatorio*, the *Paradiso*. The *Inferno* is the most beautiful." And, with the complacent tone of one who has received a solid education, he quoted the opening lines—

Nel mezzo del cammin di nostra vita
Mi ritrovai per una selva oscura,
Che la diritta via era smarrita—

a quotation which was more apt than he supposed.

Lilia glanced at Philip to see whether he noticed that she was marrying no ignoramus. Anxious to exhibit all the good qualities of her betrothed, she abruptly introduced the subject of *pallone*, in which, it appeared, he was a proficient player. He suddenly became shy, and developed a conceited grin—the grin of the village yokel whose cricket score is mentioned before a stranger. Philip himself had loved to watch *pallone*, that entrancing combination of lawn-tennis and fives. But he did not expect to love it quite so much again.

"Oh, look!" exclaimed Lilia, "the poor wee fish!"

A starved cat had been worrying them all for pieces of the purple quivering beef they were trying to swallow. Signor Carella, with the brutality so common in Italians, had caught her by the paw and flung her away from him. Now she had climbed up to the bowl and was trying to hook out the fish. He got up, drove her off, and, finding a large glass stopper by the bowl, entirely plugged up the aperture with it.

"But may not the fish die?" said Miss Abbott. "They have no air."

"Fish live on water, not on air," he replied in a knowing voice, and sat down. Apparently he was at his ease again, for he took to spitting on the floor. Philip glanced at Lilia, but did not detect her wincing. She talked bravely till the end of the disgusting meal, and then got up saying: "Well, Philip, I am sure you are ready for bye-bye. We shall meet at twelve o'clock lunch tomorrow, if we don't meet before. They give us *caffè-latte* in our rooms."

It was a little too impudent. Philip replied, "I should like to see you now, please, in my room, as I have come all the way on business." He heard Miss Abbott gasp. Signor Carella, who was lighting a rank cigar, had not understood.

It was as he expected. When he was alone with Lilia he lost all nervousness. The remembrance of his long intellectual supremacy strengthened him, and he began volubly—

"My dear Lilia, don't let's have a scene. Before I arrived I thought I might have to question you. It is unnecessary. I know everything. Miss Abbott has told me a certain amount, and the rest I see for myself."

"See for yourself?" she exclaimed, and he remembered afterwards that she had flushed crimson.

"That he is probably a ruffian and certainly a cad."

"There are no cads in Italy," she said quickly.

He was taken aback. It was one of his own remarks. And she further upset him by adding: "He is the son of a dentist. Why not?"

"Thank you for the information. I know everything, as I told you before. I am also aware of the social position of an Italian who pulls out teeth in a minute provincial town."

He was not aware of it, but he ventured to conclude that it was pretty low. Nor did Lilia contradict him. But she was sharp enough to say: "Indeed, Philip, you surprise me. I understood you went in for equality and so on."

"And I understood that Signor Carella was a member of the Italian nobility."

"Well, we put it like that in the telegram so as not to shock dear Mrs Herriton. But it is true. He is a younger branch. Of course families ramify—just as in yours there is your cousin Joseph." She adroitly picked out the only undesirable member of the Herriton clan. "Gino's father is courtesy itself, and rising rapidly in his profession. This very month he leaves Monteriano, and sets up at Poggibonsi. And for my own poor part, I think what people *are* is what matters, but I don't suppose you'll agree. And I should like you to know that Gino's uncle is a priest—the same as a clergyman at home."

Philip was aware of the social position of an Italian priest, and said so much about it that Lilia interrupted him with, "Well, his cousin's a lawyer at Rome."

"What kind of 'lawyer'?"

25

"Why, a lawyer just like you are—except that he has lots to do and can never get away."

The remark hurt more than he cared to show. He changed his method, and in a gentle, conciliatory tone delivered the following speech:

"The whole thing is like a bad dream—so bad that it cannot go on. If there was one redeeming feature about the man I might be uneasy. As it is I can trust to time. For the moment, Lilia, he has taken you in, but you will find him out soon. It is not possible that you, a lady, accustomed to ladies and gentlemen, will tolerate a man whose position is—well, not equal to the son of the servants' dentist in Coronation Place. I am not blaming you now. But I blame the glamour of Italy—I have felt it myself, you know—and I greatly blame Miss Abbott."

"Caroline! Why blame her? What's all this to do with Caroline?"

"Because we expected her to—" He saw that the answer would involve him in difficulties, and, waving his hand, continued: "So I am confident, and you in your heart agree, that this engagement will not last. Think of your life at home—think of Irma! And I'll also say, think of us; for you know, Lilia, that we count you more than a relation. I should feel I was losing my own sister if you did this, and my mother would lose a daughter."

She seemed touched at last, for she turned away her face and said, "I can't break it off now!"

"Poor Lilia," said he, genuinely moved. "I know it may be painful. But I have come to rescue you, and, book-worm though I may be, I am not frightened to stand up to a bully. He's merely an insolent boy. He thinks he can keep you to your word by threats. He will be different when he sees he has a man to deal with."

What follows should be prefaced with some simile—the simile of a powder-mine, a thunderbolt, an earthquake—for it blew Philip up in the air and flattened him on the ground and swallowed him up in the depths. Lilia turned on her gallant defender and said:

"For once in my life I'll thank you to leave me alone. I'll thank your mother too. For twelve years you've trained me and tortured me, and I'll stand it no more. Do you think I'm a fool? Do you think I never felt? Ah! when I came to your house a poor young bride, how you all looked me over —never a kind word—and discussed me, and thought I might just do; and your mother corrected me, and your sister snubbed me, and you said funny things about me to show how clever you were! And when Charles died I was still to run in strings for the honour of your beastly family, and I was to be cooped up at Sawston and learn to keep house, and all my chances spoilt of marrying again. No, thank you! No, thank you! 'Bully'? 'Insolent boy'? Who's that, pray, but you? But, thank goodness, I can stand up against the world now, for I've found Gino, and this time I marry for love!"

The coarseness and truth of her attack alike overwhelmed him. But her supreme insolence found him words, and he too burst forth.

"Yes! And I forbid you to do it! You despise me, perhaps, and think I'm feeble. But you're mistaken. You are ungrateful and impertinent and contemptible, but I will save you in order to save Irma and our name. There is going to be such a row in this town that you and he'll be sorry you came to it. I shall shrink from nothing, for my blood is up. It is unwise of you to laugh. I forbid you to marry Carella, and I shall tell him so now."

"Do," she cried. "Tell him so now. Have it out with him. Gino! Gino! Come in! Avanti! Fra Filippo forbids the banns!"

Gino appeared so quickly that he must have been listening outside the door.

"Fra Filippo's blood's up. He shrinks from nothing. Oh, take care he doesn't hurt you!" She swayed about in vulgar imitation of Philip's walk, and then, with a proud glance at the square shoulders of her betrothed, flounced out of the room.

Did she intend them to fight? Philip had no intention of

doing so; and no more, it seemed, had Gino, who stood nervously in the middle of the room with twitching lips and eyes.

"Please sit down, Signor Carella," said Philip in Italian. "Mrs Herriton is rather agitated, but there is no reason we should not be calm. Might I offer you a cigarette? Please sit down."

He refused the cigarette and the chair, and remained standing in the full glare of the lamp. Philip, not averse to such assistance, got his own face into shadow.

For a long time he was silent. It might impress Gino, and it also gave him time to collect himself. He would not this time fall into the error of blustering, which he had caught so unaccountably from Lilia. He would make his power felt by restraint.

Why, when he looked up to begin, was Gino convulsed with silent laughter? It vanished immediately; but he became nervous, and was even more pompous than he intended.

"Signor Carella, I will be frank with you. I have come to prevent you marrying Mrs Herriton, because I see you will both be unhappy together. She is English, you are Italian; she is accustomed to one thing, you to another. And—pardon me if I say it—she is rich and you are poor."

"I am not marrying her because she is rich," was the sulky reply.

"I never suggested that for a moment," said Philip courteously. "You are honourable, I am sure; but are you wise? And let me remind you that we want her with us at home. Her little daughter will be motherless, our home will be broken up. If you grant my request you will earn our thanks—and you will not be without a reward for your disappointment."

"Reward—what reward?" He bent over the back of a chair and looked earnestly at Philip. They were coming to terms pretty quickly. Poor Lilia!

Philip said slowly, "What about a thousand lire?"

His soul went forth into one exclamation, and then he

was silent, with gaping lips. Philip would have given double; he had expected a bargain.

"You can have them tonight."

He found words, and said, "It is too late."

"But why?"

"Because—" His voice broke. Philip watched his face—a face without refinement, perhaps, but not without expression—watched it quiver and re-form and dissolve from emotion into emotion. There was avarice at one moment, and insolence, and politeness, and stupidity, and cunning —and let us hope that sometimes there was love. But gradually one emotion dominated, the most unexpected of all; for his chest began to heave and his eyes to wink and his mouth to twitch, and suddenly he stood erect and roared forth his whole being in one tremendous laugh.

Philip sprang up, and Gino, who had flung wide his arms to let the glorious creature go, took him by the shoulders and shook him, and said: "Because we are married—married —married as soon as I knew you were coming. There was no time to tell you. Oh, oh! You have come all the way for nothing. Oh! And oh, your generosity!" Suddenly he became grave, and said: "Please pardon me; I am rude. I am no better than a peasant, and I—" Here he saw Philip's face, and it was too much for him. He gasped and exploded and crammed his hands into his mouth and spat them out in another explosion, and gave Philip an aimless push, which toppled him onto the bed. He uttered a horrified "Oh!" and then gave up, and bolted away down the passage, shrieking like a child, to tell the joke to his wife.

For a time Philip lay on the bed, pretending to himself that he was hurt grievously. He could scarcely see for temper, and in the passage he ran against Miss Abbott, who promptly burst into tears.

"I sleep at the Globo," he told her, "and start for Sawston tomorrow morning early. He has assaulted me. I could prosecute him. But shall not."

"I can't stop here," she sobbed. "I daren't stop here. You will have to take me with you!"

29

# Chapter 3

Opposite the Volterra gate of Monteriano, outside the city, is a very respectable whitewashed mud wall, with a coping of red crinkled tiles to keep it from dissolution. It would suggest a gentleman's garden if there was not in its middle a large hole, which grows larger with every rainstorm. Through the hole is visible, firstly, the iron gate that is intended to close it; secondly, a square piece of ground which, though not quite mud, is at the same time not exactly grass; and, finally, another wall, stone this time, which has a wooden door in the middle and two wooden-shuttered windows each side, and apparently forms the façade of a one-storey house.

This house is bigger than it looks, for it slides for two storeys down the hill behind, and the wooden door, which is always locked, really leads into the attic. The knowing person prefers to follow the precipitous mule-track round the turn of the mud wall till he can take the edifice in the rear. Then—being now on a level with the cellars—he lifts up his head and shouts. If his voice sounds like something light —a letter, for example, or some vegetables, or a bunch of flowers—a basket is let out of the first-floor windows by a string, into which he puts his burden and departs. But if he sounds like something heavy, such as a log of wood, or a piece of meat, or a visitor, he is interrogated, and then bidden or forbidden to ascend. The ground floor and the upper floor of that battered house are alike deserted, and the inmates keep to the central portion, just as in a dying body all life retires to the heart. There is a door at the top of the first flight of stairs, and if the visitor is admitted he will find a welcome which is not necessarily cold. There are several rooms, some dark and mostly stuffy—a reception-

room adorned with horsehair chairs, woolwork stools, and a
stove that is never lit—German bad taste without German
domesticity broods over that room; also a living-room, which
insensibly glides into a bedroom when the refining influence
of hospitality is absent, and real bedrooms; and last, but not
least, the loggia, where you can live day and night if you
feel inclined, drinking vermouth and smoking cigarettes,
with leagues of olive-trees and vineyards and blue-green
hills to watch you.

It was in this house that the brief and inevitable tragedy
of Lilia's married life took place. She made Gino buy it for
her, because it was there she had first seen him, sitting on the
mud wall that faced the Volterra gate. She remembered
how the evening sun had struck his hair, and how he had
smiled down at her, and, being both sentimental and un-
refined, was determined to have the man and the place
together. Things in Italy are cheap for an Italian, and,
though he would have preferred a house in the piazza, or
better still a house at Siena, or, bliss above bliss, a house
at Leghorn, he did as she asked, thinking that perhaps
she showed her good taste in preferring so retired an
abode.

The house was far too big for them, and there was a
general concourse of his relatives to fill it up. His father
wished to make it a patriarchal concern, where all the
family should have their rooms and meet together for meals,
and was perfectly willing to give up the new practice at
Poggibonsi and preside. Gino was quite willing too, for he
was an affectionate youth who liked a large home-circle, and
he told it as a pleasant bit of news to Lilia, who did not
attempt to conceal her horror.

At once he was horrified too; saw that the idea was
monstrous; abused himself to her for having suggested it;
rushed off to tell his father that it was impossible. His father
complained that prosperity was already corrupting him and
making him unsympathetic and hard; his mother cried; his
sisters accused him of blocking their social advance. He was
apologetic, and even cringing, until they turned on Lilia.

31

Then he turned on them, saying that they could not understand, much less associate with, the English lady who was his wife; that there should be one master in that house —himself.

Lilia praised and petted him on his return, calling him brave and a hero and other endearing epithets. But he was rather blue when his clan left Monteriano in much dignity —a dignity which was not at all impaired by the acceptance of a cheque. They took the cheque not to Poggibonsi, after all, but to Empoli—a lively, dusty town some twenty miles off. There they settled down in comfort; and the sisters said they had been driven to it by Gino.

The cheque was, of course, Lilia's, who was extremely generous, and was quite willing to know anybody so long as she had not to live with them, relations-in-law being on her nerves. She liked nothing better than finding out some obscure and distant connection—there were several of them—and acting the lady bountiful, leaving behind her bewilderment, and too often discontent. Gino wondered how it was that all his people, who had formerly seemed so pleasant, had suddenly become plaintive and disagreeable. He put it down to his lady-wife's magnificence, in comparison with which all seemed common. Her money flew apace, in spite of the cheap living. She was even richer than he expected; and he remembered with shame how he had once regretted his inability to accept the thousand lire that Philip Herriton offered him in exchange for her. It would have been a short-sighted bargain.

Lilia enjoyed settling into the house, with nothing to do except give orders to smiling workpeople, and a devoted husband as interpreter. She wrote a jaunty account of her happiness to Mrs Herriton, and Harriet answered the letter saying (1) that all future communications should be addressed to the solicitors; (2) would Lilia return an inlaid box which Harriet had lent her—lent, not given—to keep handkerchiefs and collars in?

"Look what I am giving up to live with you!" she said to Gino, never unwilling to lay stress on her condescension.

He took her to mean the inlaid box, and said that she need not give it up at all.

"Silly fellow, no! I mean the life. Those Herritons are very well connected. They lead Sawston society. But what do I care so long as I have my silly fellow!" She always treated him as a boy, which he was, and as a fool, which he was not, thinking herself so immeasurably superior to him that she neglected opportunity after opportunity of establishing her rule. He was good-looking and indolent; therefore he must be stupid. He was poor; therefore he would never dare to criticize his benefactress. He was passionately in love with her; therefore she could do exactly as she liked.

"It mayn't be heaven below," she thought, "but it's better than Charles."

And all the time the boy was watching her, and growing up.

She was reminded of Charles by a disagreeable letter from the solicitors, bidding her disgorge a large sum of money for Irma, in accordance with her late husband's will. It was just like Charles's suspicious nature to have provided against a second marriage. Gino was equally indignant, and between them they composed a stinging reply, which had no effect. He then said that Irma had better come out and live with them. "The air is good, so is the food; she will be happy here, and we shall not have to part with the money." But Lilia had not the courage even to suggest this to the Herritons, and an unexpected terror seized her at the thought of Irma or any English child being educated at Monteriano.

Gino became terribly depressed over the solicitors' letter, more depressed than she thought necessary. There was no more to do in the house, and he spent whole days in the loggia leaning over the parapet or sitting astride it disconsolately.

"Oh, you idle boy!" she cried, pinching his muscles. "Go and play *pallone*."

"I am a married man," he answered, without raising his head. "I do not play games any more."

"Go and see your friends then."

33

"I have no friends now."

"Silly, silly, silly! You can't stop indoors all day!"

"I want to see no one but you." He spat onto an olive-tree.

"Now, Gino, don't be silly. Go and see your friends, and bring them to see me. We both of us like society."

He looked puzzled, but allowed himself to be persuaded, went out, found that he was not as friendless as he supposed, and returned after several hours in altered spirits. Lilia congratulated herself on her good management.

"I'm ready, too, for people now," she said. "I mean to wake you all up, just as I woke up Sawston. Let's have plenty of men—and make them bring their womenkind. I mean to have real English tea-parties."

"There is my aunt and her husband; but I thought you did not want to receive my relatives."

"I never said such a—"

"But you would be right," he said earnestly. "They are not for you. Many of them are in trade, and even we are little more; you should have gentlefolk and nobility for your friends."

"Poor fellow," thought Lilia. "It is sad for him to discover that his people are vulgar." She began to tell him that she loved him just for his silly self, and he flushed and began tugging at his moustache.

"But besides your relatives I must have other people here. Your friends have wives and sisters, haven't they?"

"Oh yes; but of course I scarcely know them."

"Not know your friends' people?"

"Why, no. If they are poor and have to work for their living I may see them—but not otherwise. Except—" He stopped. The chief exception was a young lady, to whom he had once been introduced for matrimonial purposes. But the dowry had proved inadequate, and the acquaintance terminated.

"How funny! But I mean to change all that. Bring your friends to see me, and I will make them bring their people."

He looked at her rather hopelessly.

34

"Well, who are the principal people here? Who leads society?"

The governor of the prison, he supposed, and the officers who assisted him.

"Well, are they married?"

"Yes."

"There we are. Do you know them?"

"Yes—in a way."

"I see," she exclaimed angrily. "They look down on you, do they, poor boy? Wait!" He assented. "Wait! I'll soon stop that. Now, who else is there?"

"The Marchese, sometimes, and the canons of the Collegiate Church."

"Married?"

"The canons—" he began with twinkling eyes.

"Oh, I forgot your horrid celibacy. In England they would be the centre of everything. But why shouldn't I know them? Would it make it easier if I called all round? Isn't that your foreign way?"

He did not think it would make it easier.

"But I must know someone! Who were the men you were talking to this afternoon?"

Low-class men. He could scarcely recollect their names.

"But, Gino dear, if they're low-class, why did you talk to them? Don't you care about your position?"

All Gino cared about at present was idleness and pocket-money, and his way of expressing it was to exclaim: "Ouf —pouf! How hot it is in here. No air; I sweat all over. I expire. I must cool myself, or I shall never get to sleep." In his funny abrupt way he ran out onto the loggia, where he lay full length on the parapet, and began to smoke and spit under the silence of the stars.

Lilia gathered somehow from this conversation that continental society was not the go-as-you-please thing she had expected. Indeed, she could not see where continental society was. Italy is such a delightful place to live in if you happen to be a man. There one may enjoy that exquisite luxury of socialism—that true socialism which is based not on equality of income or character, but on the equality of manners. In the democracy of the *caffè* or the street the great question of our life has been solved, and the brotherhood of man is a reality. But it is accomplished at the expense of the sisterhood of women. Why should you not make friends with your neighbour at the theatre or in the train, when you know and he knows that feminine criticism and feminine insight and feminine prejudice will never come between you! Though you become as David and Jonathan, you need never enter his home, nor he yours. All your lives you will meet under the open air, the only roof-tree of the South, under which he will spit and swear, and you will drop your h's, and nobody will think the worse of either.

Meanwhile the women—they have, of course, their house and their church, with its admirable and frequent services, to which they are escorted by the maid. Otherwise they do not go out much, for it is not genteel to walk, and you are too poor to keep a carriage. Occasionally you will take them to the *caffè* or theatre, and immediately all your wonted acquaintance there desert you, except those few who are expecting and expected to marry into your family. It is all very sad. But one consolation emerges—life is very pleasant in Italy if you are a man.

Hitherto Gino had not interfered with Lilia. She was so much older than he was, and so much richer, that he regarded her as a superior being who answered to other laws. He was not wholly surprised, for strange rumours were always blowing over the Alps of lands where men and women had the same amusements and interests, and he had often met that privileged maniac, the lady tourist, on her solitary walks. Lilia took solitary walks, too, and only that week a tramp had grabbed at her watch—an episode which is supposed to be indigenous in Italy, though really less frequent there than in Bond Street. Now that he knew her better, he was inevitably losing his awe; no one could live with her and keep it, especially when she had been so silly as to lose a gold watch and chain. As he lay thoughtful along the parapet, he realized for the first time the responsibilities of married life. He must save her from dangers, physical and social, for after all she was a woman. "And I," he reflected, "though I am young, am at all events a man, and know what is right."

He found her still in the living-room, combing her hair, for she had something of the slattern in her nature, and there was no need to keep up appearances.

"You must not go out alone," he said gently. "It is not safe. If you want to walk, Perfetta shall accompany you." Perfetta was a widowed cousin, too humble for social aspirations, who was living with them as factotum.

"Very well," smiled Lilia, "very well"—as if she were addressing a solicitous kitten. But for all that she never took a solitary walk again, with one exception, till the day of her death.

Days passed, and no one called except poor relatives. She began to feel dull. Didn't he know the *Sindaco* or the bank-manager? Even the landlady of the Stella d'Italia would be better than no one. She, when she went into the town, was pleasantly received; but people naturally found a difficulty in getting on with a lady who could not learn their language. And the tea-party, under Gino's adroit management, receded ever and ever before her.

He had a good deal of anxiety over her welfare, for she did not settle down in the house at all. But he was comforted by a welcome and unexpected visitor. As he was going one afternoon for the letters—they were delivered at the door, but it took longer to get them at the office—someone humorously threw a cloak over his head, and when he disengaged himself he saw his very dear friend Spiridione Tesi of the custom-house at Chiasso, whom he had not met for two years. What joy! What salutations! So that all the passers-by smiled with approval on the amiable scene. Spiridione's brother was now station-master at Bologna, and thus he himself could spend his holiday travelling over Italy at the public expense. Hearing of Gino's marriage, he had come to see him on his way to Siena, where lived his own uncle, lately married too.

"They all do it," he exclaimed, "myself excepted." He was not quite twenty-three. "But tell me more. She is English. That is good, very good. An English wife is very good indeed. And she is rich?"

"Immensely rich."

"Blonde or dark?"

"Blonde."

"Is it possible!"

"It pleases me very much," said Gino simply. "If you remember, I always desired a blonde." Three or four men had collected, and were listening.

"We all desire one," said Spiridione. "But you, Gino, deserve your good fortune, for you are a good son, a brave man and a true friend, and from the very first moment I saw you I wished you well."

"No compliments, I beg," said Gino, standing with his hands crossed on his chest and a smile of pleasure on his face.

Spiridione addressed the other men, none of whom he had ever seen before. "Is it not true? Does not he deserve this wealthy blonde?"

"He does deserve her," said all the men.

It is a marvellous land, whether you love it or hate it.

There were no letters, and of course they sat down at the Caffè Garibaldi, by the Collegiate Church—quite a good *caffè*, that, for so small a city. There were marble-topped tables, and pillars terracotta below and gold above, and on the ceiling was a fresco of the battle of Solferino. One could not have desired a prettier room. They had vermouth and little cakes with sugar on the top, which they chose gravely at the counter, pinching them first to be sure they were fresh. And, though vermouth is barely alcoholic, Spiridione drenched his with soda-water to be sure that it should not get into his head.

They were in high spirits, and elaborate compliments alternated curiously with gentle horse-play. But soon they put up their legs on a pair of chairs and began to smoke.

"Tell me," said Spiridione—"I forgot to ask—is she young?"

38

"Thirty-three."

"Ah, well, we cannot have everything."

"But you would be surprised. Had she told me twenty-eight, I should not have disbelieved her."

"Is she *simpatica*?" (Nothing will translate that word.)

Gino dabbed at the sugar and said after a silence, "Sufficiently so."

"It is a most important thing."

"She is rich, she is generous, she is affable, she addresses her inferiors without haughtiness."

There was another silence. "It is not sufficient," said the other. "One does not define it thus." He lowered his voice to a whisper. "Last month a German was smuggling cigars. The custom-house was dark. Yet I refused because I did not like him. The gifts of such men do not bring happiness. Non era simpatico. He paid for every one, and the fine for deception besides."

"Do you gain much beyond your pay?" asked Gino, diverted for an instant.

"I do not accept small sums now. It is not worth the risk. But the German was another matter. But listen, my Gino, for I am older than you and more full of experience. The person who understands us at first sight, who never irritates us, who never bores, to whom we can pour forth every thought and wish, not only in speech but in silence—that is what I mean by *simpatico*."

"There are such men, I know," said Gino. "And I have heard it said of children. But where will you find such a woman?"

"That is true. Here you are wiser than I. Sono poco simpatiche le donne. And the time we waste over them is much." He sighed dolefully, as if he found the nobility of his sex a burden.

"One I have seen who may be so. She spoke very little, but she was a young lady—different to most. She, too, was English, the companion of my wife here. But Fra Filippo, the brother-in-law, took her back with him. I saw them start. He was very angry."

39

Then he spoke of his exciting and secret marriage, and they made fun of the unfortunate Philip, who had travelled over Europe to stop it.

"I regret, though," said Gino, when they had finished laughing, "that I toppled him onto the bed. A great tall man! And when I am really amused I am often impolite."

"You will never see him again," said Spiridione, who carried plenty of philosophy about with him. "And by now the scene will have passed from his mind."

"It sometimes happens that such things are recollected longest. I shall never see him again, of course; but it is no benefit to me that he should wish me ill. And even if he has forgotten, I am still sorry that I toppled him onto the bed."

So their talk continued, at one moment full of childishness and tender wisdom, the next moment scandalously gross. The shadows of the terracotta pillars lengthened, and tourists, flying through the Palazzo Pubblico opposite, could observe how the Italians wasted time.

The sight of tourists reminded Gino of something he might say. "I want to consult you since you are so kind as to take an interest in my affairs. My wife wishes to take solitary walks."

Spiridione was shocked.

"But I have forbidden her."

"Naturally."

"She does not yet understand. She asked me to accompany her sometimes—to walk without object! You know, she would like me to be with her all day."

"I see, I see." He knitted his brows and tried to think how he could help his friend. "She needs employment. Is she a Catholic?"

"No."

"That is a pity. She must be persuaded. It will be a great solace to her when she is alone."

"I am a Catholic, but of course I never go to church."

"Of course not. Still, you might take her at first. That is what my brother has done with his wife at Bologna, and he has joined the Freethinkers. He took her once or twice himself, and now she has acquired the habit and continues to go without him."

"Most excellent advice, and I thank you for it. But she wishes to give tea-parties—men and women together whom she has never seen."

"Oh, the English! They are always thinking of tea. They carry it by the kilogram in their trunks, and they are so clumsy that they always pack it at the top. But it is absurd!"

"What am I to do about it?"

"Do nothing. Or ask me!"

"Come!" cried Gino, springing up. "She will be quite pleased."

The dashing young fellow coloured crimson. "Of course I was only joking."

"I know. But she wants me to take my friends. Come now! Waiter!"

"If I do come," cried the other, "and take tea with you, this bill must be my affair."

"Certainly not; you are in my country!"

A long argument ensued, in which the waiter took part, suggesting various solutions. At last Gino triumphed. The bill came to eightpence-halfpenny, and a halfpenny for the waiter brought it up to ninepence. Then there was a shower of gratitude on one side and of deprecation on the other, and when courtesies were at their height they suddenly linked arms and swung down the street, tickling each other with lemonade-straws as they went.

Lilia was delighted to see them, and became more animated than Gino had known her for a long time. The tea tasted of chopped hay, and they asked to be allowed to drink it out of a wineglass, and refused milk; but, as she repeatedly observed, this was something like. Spiridione's manners were very agreeable. He kissed her hand on introduction, and, as his profession had taught him a little English, conversation did not flag.

"Do you like music?" she asked.

"Passionately," he replied. "I have not studied scientific music, but the music of the heart, yes."

So she played on the humming piano, very badly, and he sang, not so badly. Gino got out a guitar and sang too, sitting out on the loggia. It was a most agreeable visit.

Gino said he would just walk his friend back to his lodgings. As they went he said, without the least trace of malice or satire in his voice: "I think you are quite right. I shall not bring people to the house any more. I do not see why an English wife should be treated differently. This is Italy."

"You are very wise," exclaimed the other; "very wise indeed. The more precious a possession the more carefully it should be guarded."

They had reached the lodging, but went on as far as the Caffè Garibaldi, where they spent a long and most delightful evening.

# Chapter 4

The advance of regret can be so gradual that it is impossible to say, "Yesterday I was happy, today I am not." At no one moment did Lilia realize that her marriage was a failure; yet during the summer and autumn she became as unhappy as it was possible for her nature to be. She had no unkind treatment, and few unkind words, from her husband. He simply left her alone. In the morning he went out to do "business", which, as far as she could discover, meant sitting in the *farmacia*. He usually returned to lunch, after which he retired to another room and slept. In the evening he grew vigorous again, and took the air on the ramparts, often having his dinner out, and seldom returning till midnight or later. There were, of course, the times when he was away altogether—at Empoli, Siena, Florence, Bologna—for he delighted in travel, and seemed to pick up friends all over the country. Lilia often heard what a favourite he was.

She began to see that she must assert herself, but she could not see how. Her self-confidence, which had overthrown Philip, had gradually oozed away. If she left the strange house there was the strange little town. If she were to disobey her husband and walk in the country, that would be stranger still—vast slopes of olives and vineyards, with chalk-white farms, and in the distance other slopes, with more olives and more farms, and more little towns outlined against the cloudless sky. "I don't call this country," she would say. "Why, it's not as wild as Sawston Park!" And, indeed, there was scarcely a touch of wildness in it—some of those slopes had been under cultivation for two thousand years. But it was terrible and mysterious all the same, and its continued presence made Lilia so uncomfortable that she forgot her nature and began to reflect.

She reflected chiefly about her marriage. The ceremony had been hasty and expensive, and the rites, whatever they were, were not those of the Church of England. Lilia had no religion in her; but for hours at a time she would be seized with a vulgar fear that she was not "married properly", and that her social position in the next world might be as obscure as it was in this. It might be safer to do the thing thoroughly, and one day she took the advice of Spiridione and joined the Roman Catholic Church, or, as she called it, "Santa Deodata's". Gino approved; he, too, thought it safer. And it was fun confessing, though the priest was a stupid old man; and the whole thing was a good slap in the face for the people at home.

The people at home took the slap very soberly; indeed, there were few left for her to give it to. The Herritons were out of the question; they would not even let her write to Irma, though Irma was occasionally allowed to write to her. Mrs Theobald was rapidly subsiding into dotage, and, as far as she could be definite about anything, had definitely sided with the Herritons. And Miss Abbott did likewise. Night after night did Lilia curse this false friend, who had agreed with her that the marriage would "do", and that the Herritons would come round to it, and then, at the first hint of opposition, had fled back to England, shrieking and distraught. Miss Abbott headed the long list of those who should never be written to, and who should never be forgiven. Almost the only person who was not on that list was Mr Kingcroft, who had unexpectedly sent an affectionate and inquiring letter. He was quite sure never to cross the Channel, and Lilia drew freely on her fancy in the reply.

At first she had seen a few English people, for Monteriano was not the end of the earth. One or two inquisitive ladies, who had heard at home of her quarrel with the Herritons, came to call. She was very sprightly, and they thought her quite unconventional, and Gino a charming boy, so all that was to the good. But by May the season, such as it was, had finished, and there would be no one till next spring. As Mrs Herriton had often observed, Lilia had no resources.

She did not like music, or reading, or work. Her one qualification for life was rather blowsy high spirits, which turned
querulous or boisterous according to circumstances. She was
not obedient, but she was cowardly; and in the most gentle
way, which Mrs Herriton might have envied, Gino made her
do what he wanted. At first it had been rather fun to let
him get the upper hand. But it was galling to discover that
he could not do otherwise. He had a good strong will when
he chose to use it, and would not have had the least scruple
in using bolts and locks to put it into effect. There was
plenty of brutality deep down in him, and one day Lilia
nearly touched it.

It was the old question of going out alone.

"I always do it in England."

"This is Italy."

"Yes, but I'm older than you, and I'll settle."

"I am your husband," he said smiling. They had finished
their midday meal, and he wanted to go and sleep. Nothing
would rouse him up, until at last Lilia, getting more and
more angry, said, "And I've got the money."

He looked horrified.

Now was the moment to assert herself. She made the
statement again. He got up from his chair.

"And you'd better mend your manners," she continued,
"for you'd find it awkward if I stopped drawing cheques."

She was no reader of character, but she quickly became
alarmed. As she said to Perfetta afterwards, "None of his
clothes seemed to fit—too big in one place, too small in
another." His figure rather than his face altered, the
shoulders falling forward till his coat wrinkled across the
back and pulled away from the wrists. He seemed all arms.
He edged round the table to where she was sitting, and she
sprang away and held the chair between them, too frightened
to speak or to move. He looked at her with round expression-
less eyes, and slowly stretched out his left hand.

Perfetta was heard coming up from the kitchen. It
seemed to wake him up, and he turned away and went to
his room without a word.

"What has happened?" cried Lilia, nearly fainting. "He is ill—ill."

Perfetta looked suspicious when she heard the account. "What did you say to him?" She crossed herself.

"Hardly anything," said Lilia, and crossed herself also. Thus did the two women pay homage to their outraged male.

It was clear to Lilia at last that Gino had married her for money. But he had frightened her too much to leave any place for contempt. His return was terrifying, for he was frightened too, imploring her pardon, lying at her feet, embracing her, murmuring "It was not I", striving to define things which he did not understand. He stopped in the house for three days, positively ill with physical collapse. But for all his suffering he had tamed her, and she never threatened to cut off supplies again.

Perhaps he kept her even closer than convention demanded. But he was very young, and he could not bear it to be said of him that he did not know how to treat a lady —or to manage a wife. And his own social position was uncertain. Even in England a dentist is a troublesome creature, whom careful people find difficult to class. He hovers between the professions and the trades; he may be only a little lower than the doctors, or he may be down among the chemists, or even beneath them. The son of the Italian dentist felt this too. For himself nothing mattered; he made friends with the people he liked, for he was that glorious invariable creature, a man. But his wife should visit nowhere rather than visit wrongly; seclusion was both decent and safe. The social ideals of North and South had had their brief contention, and this time the South had won.

It would have been well if he had been as strict over his own behaviour as he was over hers. But the incongruity never occurred to him for a moment. His morality was that of the average Latin, and as he was suddenly placed in the position of a gentleman he did not see why he should not behave as such. Of course, had Lilia been different, had she asserted herself and got a grip on his character, he might possibly—though not probably—have been made a better husband as well as a better man, and at all events he could have adopted the attitude of the Englishman, whose standard is higher even when his practice is the same. But had Lilia been different she might not have married him.

The discovery of his infidelity—which she made by accident—destroyed such remnants of self-satisfaction as her life might yet possess. She broke down utterly, and sobbed and cried in Perfetta's arms. Perfetta was kind and even sympathetic, but cautioned her on no account to speak to Gino, who would be furious if he was suspected. And Lilia agreed, partly because she was afraid of him, partly because it was, after all, the best and most dignified thing to do. She had given up everything for him—her daughter, her relatives, her friends, all the little comforts and luxuries of a civilized life—and even if she had the courage to break away there was no one who would receive her now. The Herritons had been almost malignant in their efforts against her, and all her friends had one by one fallen off. So it was better to live on humbly, trying not to feel, endeavouring by a cheerful demeanour to put things right. "Perhaps," she thought, "if I have a child he will be different. I know he wants a son."

Lilia had achieved pathos despite herself, for there are some situations in which vulgarity counts no longer. Not Cordelia nor Imogen more deserve our tears.

She herself cried frequently, making herself look plain and old, which distressed her husband. He was particularly kind to her when he hardly ever saw her, and she accepted his kindness without resentment, even with gratitude, so docile had she become. She did not hate him, even as she had never loved him; with her it was only when she was excited that the semblance of either passion arose. People said she was headstrong, but really her weak brain left her cold.

Suffering, however, is more independent of temperament, and the wisest of women could hardly have suffered more.

As for Gino, he was quite as boyish as ever, and carried

his iniquities like a feather. A favourite speech of his was: "Ah, one ought to marry! Spiridione is wrong; I must persuade him. Not till marriage does one realize the pleasures and the possibilities of life." So saying, he would take down his felt hat, strike it in the right place as infallibly as a German strikes his in the wrong place, and leave her.

One evening, when he had gone out thus, Lilia could stand it no longer. It was September. Sawston would be just filling up after the summer holidays. People would be running in and out of each other's houses all along the road. There were bicycle gymkhanas, and on the 30th Mrs Herriton would be holding the annual bazaar in her garden for the C.M.S. It seemed impossible that such a free, happy life could exist. She walked out onto the loggia. Moonlight and stars in a soft purple sky. The walls of Monteriano should be glorious on such a night as this. But the house faced away from them.

Perfetta was banging in the kitchen, and the stairs down led past the kitchen door. But the stairs up to the attic— —the stairs no one ever used—opened out of the living-room, and by unlocking the door at the top one might slip out onto the square terrace above the house, and thus for ten minutes walk in freedom and peace.

The key was in the pocket of Gino's best suit—the English check—which he never wore. The stairs creaked and the keyhole screamed; but Perfetta was growing deaf. The walls were beautiful, but as they faced west they were in shadow. To see the light upon them she must walk round the town a little, till they were caught by the beams of the rising moon. She looked anxiously at the house, and started.

It was easy walking, for a little path ran all outside the ramparts. The few people she met wished her a civil good-night, taking her, in her hatless condition, for a peasant. The walls trended round towards the moon; and presently she came into its light, and saw all the rough towers turn into pillars of silver and black, and the ramparts into cliffs of pearl. She had no great sense of beauty, but she was sentimental, and she began to cry; for here, where a great

cypress interrupted the monotony of the girdle of olives, she
had sat with Gino one afternoon in March, her head upon
his shoulder, while Caroline was looking at the view and
sketching. Round the corner was the Siena gate, from which
the road to England started, and she could hear the rumble
of the diligence which was going down to catch the night
train to Empoli. The next moment it was upon her, for the
highroad came towards her a little before it began its long
zigzag down the hill.

The driver slackened, and called to her to get in. He did
not know who she was. He hoped she might be coming to
the station.

"Non vengo!" she cried.

He wished her goodnight, and turned his horses down the
corner. As the diligence came round she saw that it was
empty.

"Vengo . . ."

Her voice was tremulous, and did not carry. The horses
swung off.

"Vengo! Vengo!"

He had begun to sing, and heard nothing. She ran down
the road screaming to him to stop—that she was coming;
while the distance grew greater and the noise of the diligence
increased. The man's back was black and square against the
moon, and if he would but turn for an instant she would be
saved. She tried to cut off the corner of the zigzag, stumbling
over the great clods of earth, large and hard as rocks, which
lay between the eternal olives. She was too late; for, just
before she regained the road, the thing swept past her,
thunderous, ploughing up choking clouds of moonlit dust.

She did not call any more, for she felt very ill, and fainted;
and when she revived she was lying in the road, with dust
in her eyes, and dust in her mouth, and dust down her ears.
There is something very terrible in dust at night-time.

"What shall I do?" she moaned. "He will be so angry."

And without further effort she slowly climbed back to
captivity, shaking her garments as she went.

Ill-luck pursued her to the end. It was one of the nights

when Gino happened to come in. He was in the kitchen, swearing and smashing plates, while Perfetta, her apron over her head, was weeping violently. At the sight of Lilia he turned upon her and poured forth a flood of miscellaneous abuse. He was far more angry but much less alarming than he had been that day when he edged after her round the table. And Lilia gained more courage from her bad conscience than she ever had from her good one, for as he spoke she was seized with indignation and feared him no longer, and saw him for a cruel, worthless, hypocritical, dissolute upstart, and spoke in return.

Perfetta screamed, for she told him everything—all she knew and all she thought. He stood with open mouth, all the anger gone out of him, feeling ashamed, and an utter fool. He was fairly and rightfully cornered. When had husband so given himself away before? She finished; and he was dumb, for she had spoken truly. Then, alas! the absurdity of his own position grew upon him, and he laughed—as he would have laughed at the same situation on the stage.

"You laugh?" stammered Lilia.

"Ah," he cried, "who could help it? I, who thought you knew and saw nothing—I am tricked—I am conquered. I give in. Let us talk of it no more."

He touched her on the shoulder like a good comrade, half amused and half penitent, and then, murmuring and smiling to himself, ran quietly out of the room.

Perfetta burst into congratulations. "What courage you have!" she cried; "and what good fortune! He is angry no longer! He has forgiven you!"

Neither Perfetta nor Gino nor Lilia herself knew the true reason of all the misery that followed. To the end he thought that kindness and a little attention would be enough to set things straight. His wife was a very ordinary woman, and why should her ideas differ from his own? No one realized that more than personalities were engaged; that the struggle was national; that generations of ancestors, good, bad or indifferent, forbade the Latin man to be chivalrous to the northern woman, the northern woman to forgive the Latin

man. All this might have been foreseen; Mrs Herriton
foresaw it from the first.

Meanwhile Lilia prided herself on her high personal
standard, and Gino simply wondered why she did not come
round. He hated discomfort, and yearned for sympathy, but
shrank from mentioning his difficulties in the town in case
they were put down to his own incompetence. Spiridione
was told, and replied in a philosophical but not very helpful
letter. His other great friend, whom he trusted more, was
still serving in Eritrea or some other desolate outpost. It
would take too long to explain everything to him. And,
besides, what was the good of letters? Friends cannot travel
through the post.

Lilia, so similar to her husband in many ways, yearned
for comfort and sympathy too. The night he laughed at her
she wildly took up paper and pen and wrote page after page,
analysing his character, enumerating his iniquities, reporting
whole conversations, tracing all the causes and the growth
of her misery. She was beside herself with passion, and
though she could hardly think or see she suddenly attained
to magnificence and pathos which a practised stylist might
have envied. It was written like a diary, and not till its
conclusion did she realize for whom it was meant.

"Irma, darling Irma, this letter is for you. I almost forget
I have a daughter. It will make you unhappy, but I want
you to know everything, and you cannot learn things too
soon. God bless you, my dearest, and save you. God bless
your miserable mother."

Fortunately Mrs Herriton was in when the letter arrived.
She seized it and opened it in her bedroom. Another
moment, and Irma's placid childhood would have been
destroyed for ever.

Lilia received a brief note from Harriet, again forbidding
direct communication between mother and daughter, and
concluding with formal condolences. It nearly drove her
mad.

"Gently! Gently!" said her husband. They were sitting
together on the loggia when the letter arrived. He often sat

51

with her now, watching her for hours, puzzled and anxious, but not contrite.

"It's nothing." She went in and tore it up, and then began to write—a very short letter, whose gist was "Come and save me".

It is not good to see your wife crying when she writes—especially if you are conscious that, on the whole, your treatment of her has been reasonable and kind. It is not good, when you accidentally look over her shoulder, to see that she is writing to a man. Nor should she shake her fist at you when she leaves the room, under the impression that you are engaged in lighting a cigar and cannot see her.

Lilia went to the post herself. But in Italy so many things can be arranged. The postman was a friend of Gino's, and Mr Kingcroft never got his letter.

So she gave up hope, became ill, and all through the autumn lay in bed. Gino was distracted. She knew why: he wanted a son. He could talk and think of nothing else. His one desire was to become the father of a man like himself, and it held him with a grip he only partially understood, for it was the first great desire, the first great passion of his life. Falling in love was a mere physical triviality, like warm sun or cool water, beside this divine hope of immortality: "I continue." He gave candles to Santa Deodata, for he was always religious at a crisis, and sometimes he went to her himself and prayed the crude uncouth demands of the simple. Impetuously he summoned all his relatives back to bear him company in his time of need, and Lilia saw strange faces flitting past her in the darkened room.

"My love!" he would say, "my dearest Lilia! Be calm. I have never loved anyone but you."

She, knowing everything, would only smile gently, too broken by suffering to make sarcastic repartees.

Before the child was born he gave her a kiss, and said, "I have prayed all night for a boy."

Some strangely tender impulse moved her, and she said faintly, "You are a boy yourself, Gino."

He answered, "Then we shall be brothers."

He lay outside the room with his head against the door like a dog. When they came to tell him the glad news they found him half unconscious, and his face was wet with tears.

As for Lilia, someone said to her, "It is a beautiful boy!" But she had died in giving birth to him.

# Chapter 5

At the time of Lilia's death Philip Herriton was just twenty-four years of age—indeed, the news reached Sawston on his birthday. He was a tall, weakly-built young man, whose clothes had to be judiciously padded on the shoulder in order to make him pass muster. His face was plain rather than not, and there was a curious mixture in it of good and bad. He had a fine forehead and a good large nose, and both observation and sympathy were in his eyes. But below the nose and eyes all was confusion, and those people who believe that destiny resides in the mouth and chin shook their heads when they looked at him.

Philip himself, as a boy, had been keenly conscious of these defects. Sometimes when he had been bullied or hustled about at school he would retire to his cubicle and examine his features in a looking-glass, and he would sigh and say: "It is a weak face. I shall never carve a place for myself in the world." But as years went on he became either less self-conscious or more self-satisfied. The world, he found, made a niche for him as it did for everyone. Decision of character might come later—or he might have it without knowing. At all events he had got a sense of beauty and a sense of humour, two most desirable gifts. The sense of beauty developed first. It caused him at the age of twenty to wear parti-coloured ties and a squashy hat, to be late for dinner on account of the sunset, and to catch art from Burne-Jones to Praxiteles. At twenty-two he went to Italy with some cousins, and there he absorbed into one aesthetic whole olive-trees, blue sky, frescoes, country inns, saints, peasants, mosaics, statues, beggars. He came back with the air of a prophet who would either remodel Sawston or reject it. All the energies and enthusiasms of a rather friendless life had passed into the championship of beauty.

In a short time it was over. Nothing had happened either in Sawston or within himself. He had shocked half a dozen people, squabbled with his sister, and bickered with his mother. He concluded that nothing could happen, not knowing that human love and love of truth sometimes conquer where love of beauty fails.

A little disenchanted, a little tired, but aesthetically intact, he resumed his placid life, relying more and more on his second gift, the gift of humour. If he could not reform the world, he could at all events laugh at it, thus attaining at least an intellectual superiority. Laughter, he read and believed, was a sign of good moral health, and he laughed on contentedly, till Lilia's marriage toppled contentment down for ever. Italy, the land of beauty, was ruined for him. She had no power to change men and things who dwelt in her. She, too, could produce avarice, brutality, stupidity—and what was worse, vulgarity. It was on her soil and through her influence that a silly woman had married a cad. He hated Gino, the betrayer of his life's ideal, and now that the sordid tragedy had come it filled him with pangs, not of sympathy, but of final disillusion.

The disillusion was convenient for Mrs Herriton, who saw a trying little period ahead of her, and was glad to have her family united.

"Are we to go into mourning, do you think?" She always asked her children's advice where possible.

Harriet thought that they should. She had been detestable to Lilia while she lived, but she always felt that the dead deserve attention and sympathy. "After all she has suffered. That letter kept me awake for nights. The whole thing is like one of those horrible modern plays where no one is in the right. But if we have mourning it will mean telling Irma."

"Of course we must tell Irma!" said Philip.

"Of course," said his mother. "But I think we can still not tell her about Lilia's marriage."

"I don't think that. And she must have suspected something by now."

"So one would have supposed. But she never cared for her mother, and little girls of nine don't reason clearly. She looks on it as a long visit. And it is important, most important, that she should not receive a shock. All a child's life depends on the ideal it has of its parents. Destroy that and everything goes—morals, behaviour, everything. Absolute trust in someone else is the essence of education. That is why I have been so careful about talking of poor Lilia before her."

"But you forget this wretched baby. Waters & Adamson write that there is a baby."

"Mrs Theobald must be told. But she doesn't count. She is breaking up very quickly. She doesn't even see Mr Kingcroft now. He, thank goodness, I hear, has at last consoled himself with someone else."

"The child must know some time," persisted Philip, who felt a little displeased, though he could not tell with what.

"The later the better. Every moment she is developing."

"I must say it seems rather hard luck, doesn't it?"

"On Irma? Why?"

"On us, perhaps. We have morals and behaviour also, and I don't think this continual secrecy improves them."

"There's no need to twist the thing round to that," said Harriet, rather disturbed.

"Of course there isn't," said her mother. "Let's keep to the main issue. This baby's quite beside the point. Mrs Theobald will do nothing, and it's no concern of ours."

"It will make a difference in the money, surely," said he.

"No, dear; very little. Poor Charles provided for every kind of contingency in his will. The money will come to you and Harriet, as Irma's guardians."

"Good. Does the Italian get anything?"

"He will get all hers. But you know what that is."

"Good. So those are our tactics—to tell no one about the baby, not even Miss Abbott."

"Most certainly this is the proper course," said Mrs

56

Herriton, preferring "course" to "tactics" for Harriet's sake. "And why ever should we tell Caroline?"

"She was so mixed up in the affair."

"Poor silly creature. The less she hears about it the better she will be pleased. I have come to be very sorry for Caroline. She, if anyone, has suffered and been penitent. She burst into tears when I told her a little, only a little, of that terrible letter. I never saw such genuine remorse. We must forgive her and forget. Let the dead bury their dead. We will not trouble her with them."

Philip saw that his mother was scarcely logical. But there was no advantage in saying so. "Here beginneth the New Life, then. Do you remember, mother, that was what we said when we saw Lilia off?"

"Yes, dear; but now it is really a New Life, because we are all at accord. Then you were still infatuated with Italy. It may be full of beautiful pictures and churches, but we cannot judge a country by anything but its men."

"That is quite true," he said sadly. And as the tactics were now settled he went out and took an aimless and solitary walk.

By the time he came back two important things had happened. Irma had been told of her mother's death, and Miss Abbott, who had called for a subscription, had been told also.

Irma had wept loudly, had asked a few sensible questions and a good many silly ones, and had been content with evasive answers. Fortunately the school prizegiving was at hand, and that, together with the prospect of new black clothes, kept her from meditating on the fact that Lilia, who had been absent so long, would now be absent for ever.

"As for Caroline," said Mrs Herriton, "I was almost frightened. She broke down utterly. She cried even when she left the house. I comforted her as best I could, and I kissed her. It is something that the breach between her and ourselves is now entirely healed."

"Did she ask no questions—as to the nature of Lilia's death, I mean?"

"She did. But she has a mind of extraordinary delicacy. She saw that I was reticent, and she did not press me. You see, Philip, I can say to you what I could not say before Harriet. Her ideas are so crude. Really we do not want it known in Sawston that there is a baby. All peace and comfort would be lost if people came inquiring after it."

His mother knew how to manage him. He agreed enthusiastically. And a few days later, when he chanced to travel up to London with Miss Abbott, he had all the time the pleasant thrill of one who is better informed. Their last journey together had been from Monteriano back across Europe. It had been a ghastly journey, and Philip, from the force of association, rather expected something ghastly now.

He was surprised. Miss Abbott, between Sawston and Charing Cross, revealed qualities which he had never guessed her to possess. Without being exactly original, she did show a commendable intelligence, and though at times she was gauche and even uncourtly he felt that here was a person whom it might be well to cultivate.

At first she annoyed him. They were talking, of course, about Lilia, when she broke the thread of vague commiseration and said abruptly: "It is all so strange as well as so tragic. And what I did was as strange as anything."

It was the first reference she had ever made to her contemptible behaviour. "Never mind," he said. "It's all over now. Let the dead bury their dead. It's fallen out of our lives."

"But that's why I can talk about it and tell you everything. I have always wanted to. You thought me stupid and sentimental and wicked and mad, but you never really knew how much I was to blame."

"Indeed, I never think about it now," said Philip gently. He knew that her nature was in the main generous and upright; it was unnecessary of her to reveal her thoughts.

"The first evening we got to Monteriano," she persisted, "Lilia went out for a walk alone, saw that Italian in a picturesque position on a wall, and fell in love. He was shabbily dressed, and she did not even know he was the son of a dentist. I must tell you I was used to this sort of thing. Once or twice before I had had to send people about their business."

"Yes; we counted on you," said Philip with sudden sharpness. After all, if she would reveal her thoughts, she must take the consequences.

"I know you did," she retorted with equal sharpness. "Lilia saw him several times again, and I knew I ought to interfere. I called her to my bedroom one night. She was very frightened, for she knew what it was about and how severe I could be. 'Do you love this man?' I asked. 'Yes or no?' She said 'Yes.' And I said, 'Why don't you marry him if you think you'll be happy?'"

"Really—really," exploded Philip, as exasperated as if the thing had happened yesterday. "You knew Lilia all your life. Apart from everything else—as if she could choose what would make her happy!"

"Had you ever let her choose?" she flashed out. "I'm afraid that's rude," she added, trying to calm herself.

"Let us rather say unhappily expressed," said Philip, who always adopted a dry satirical manner when he was puzzled.

"I want to finish. Next morning I found Signor Carella and said the same to him. He—well, he was willing. That's all."

"And the telegram?" He looked scornfully out of the window.

Hitherto her voice had been hard, possibly in self-accusation, possibly in defiance. Now it became unmistakably sad. "Ah, the telegram! That was wrong. Lilia there was more cowardly than I was. We should have told the truth. It lost me my nerve, at all events. I came to the station meaning to tell you everything then. But we had started with a lie, and I got frightened. And at the end, when you left, I got frightened again and came with you."

"Did you really mean to stop?"

"For a time, at all events."

"Would that have suited a newly married pair?"

"It would have suited them. Lilia needed me. And as for

him—I can't help feeling I might have got influence over him."

"I am ignorant of these matters," said Philip; "but I should have thought that would have increased the difficulty of the situation."

The crisp remark was wasted on her. She looked hopelessly at the raw over-built country, and said, "Well, I have explained."

"But pardon me, Miss Abbott; of most of your conduct you have given a description rather than an explanation."

He had fairly caught her, and expected that she would gape and collapse. To his surprise she answered with some spirit, "An explanation may bore you, Mr Herriton: it drags in other topics."

"Oh, never mind."

"I hated Sawston, you see."

He was delighted. "So did and do I. That's splendid. Go on."

"I hated the idleness, the stupidity, the respectability, the petty unselfishness."

"Petty selfishness," he corrected. Sawston psychology had long been his speciality.

"Petty unselfishness," she repeated. "I had got an idea that everyone here spent their lives in making little sacrifices for objects they didn't care for, to please people they didn't love; that they never learned to be sincere—and, what's as bad, never learned how to enjoy themselves. That's what I thought—what I thought at Monteriano."

"Why, Miss Abbott," he cried, "you should have told me this before! Think it still! I agree with lots of it. Magnificent!"

"Now Lilia," she went on, "though there were things about her I didn't like, had somehow kept the power of enjoying herself with sincerity. And Gino, I thought, was splendid, and young, and strong not only in body, and sincere as the day. If they wanted to marry, why shouldn't they do so? Why shouldn't she break with the deadening life where she had got into a groove, and would go on in it, getting more and more—worse than unhappy—apathetic till she died? Of course I was wrong. She only changed one groove for another—a worse groove. And as for him—well, you know more about him than I do. I can never trust myself to judge character again. But I still feel he cannot have been quite bad when we first met him. Lilia—that I should dare to say it!—must have been cowardly. He was only a boy—just going to turn into something fine, I thought —and she must have mismanaged him. So that is the one time I have gone against what is proper, and there are the results. You have an explanation now."

"And much of it has been most interesting, though I don't understand everything. Did you never think of the disparity of their social position?"

"We were mad—drunk with rebellion. We had no common sense. As soon as you came, you saw and foresaw everything."

"Oh, I don't think that." He was vaguely displeased at being credited with common sense. For a moment Miss Abbott had seemed to him more unconventional than himself.

"I hope you see," she concluded, "why I have troubled you with this long story. Women—I heard you say the other day—are never at ease till they tell their faults out loud. Lilia is dead and her husband gone to the bad—all through me. You see, Mr Herriton, it makes me specially unhappy; it's the only time I've ever gone into what my father calls 'real life'—and look what I've made of it! All that winter I seemed to be waking up to beauty and splendour and I don't know what; and when the spring came I wanted to fight against the things I hated—mediocrity and dullness and spitefulness and society. I actually hated society for a day or two at Monteriano. I didn't see that all these things are invincible, and that if we go against them they will break us to pieces. Thank you for listening to so much nonsense."

"Oh, I quite sympathize with what you say," said Philip encouragingly; "it isn't nonsense, and a year or two ago I should have been saying it too. But I feel differently now,

and I hope that you also will change. Society *is* invincible
—to a certain degree. But your real life is your own, and
nothing can touch it. There is no power on earth that can
prevent your criticizing and despising mediocrity—nothing
that can stop you retreating into splendour and beauty—
into the thoughts and beliefs that make the real life—the
real you."

"I have never had that experience yet. Surely I and my
life must be where I live."

Evidently she had the usual feminine incapacity for
grasping philosophy. But she had developed quite a per-
sonality, and he must see more of her. "There is another
great consolation against invincible mediocrity," he said—
"the meeting a fellow victim. I hope that this is only the
first of many discussions that we shall have together."

She made a suitable reply. The train reached Charing
Cross, and they parted—he to go to a matinée, she to buy
petticoats for the corpulent poor. Her thoughts wandered
as she bought them: the gulf between herself and Mr
Herriton, which she had always known to be great, now
seemed to her immeasurable.

These events and conversations took place at Christmas-
time. The New Life initiated by them lasted some seven
months. Then a little incident—a mere little vexatious
incident—brought it to its close.

Irma collected picture-postcards, and Mrs Herriton or
Harriet always glanced first at all that came, lest the child
should get hold of something vulgar. On this occasion the
subject seemed perfectly inoffensive—a lot of ruined factory
chimneys—and Harriet was about to hand it to her niece
when her eye was caught by the words on the margin. She
gave a shriek and flung the card into the grate. Of course
no fire was alight in July, and Irma only had to run and
pick it out again.

"How dare you!" screamed her aunt. "You wicked girl!
Give it here!"

Unfortunately Mrs Herriton was out of the room. Irma,
who was not in awe of Harriet, danced round the table,

reading as she did so, "View of the superb city of Monteriano—from your lital brother."

Stupid Harriet caught her, boxed her ears, and tore the postcard into fragments. Irma howled with pain, and began shouting indignantly: "Who is my little brother? Why have I never heard of him before? Grandmamma! Grandmamma! Who is my little brother? Who is my—"

Mrs Herriton swept into the room, saying: "Come with me, dear, and I will tell you. Now it is time for you to know."

Irma returned from the interview sobbing, though, as a matter of fact, she had learned very little. But that little took hold of her imagination. She had promised secrecy —she knew not why. But what harm in talking of the little brother to those who had heard of him already?

"Aunt Harriet!" she would say. "Uncle Phil! Grandmamma! What do you suppose my little brother is doing now? Has he begun to play? Do Italian babies talk sooner than us, or would he be an English baby born abroad? Oh, I do long to see him, and be the first to teach him the Ten Commandments and the Catechism."

The last remark always made Harriet look grave.

"Really," exclaimed Mrs Herriton, "Irma is getting too tiresome. She forgot poor Lilia soon enough."

"A living brother is more to her than a dead mother," said Philip dreamily. "She can knit him socks."

"I stopped that. She is bringing him in everywhere. It is most vexatious. The other night she asked if she might include him in the people she mentions specially in her prayers."

"What did you say?"

"Of course I allowed her," she replied coldly. "She has a right to mention anyone she chooses. But I was annoyed with her this morning, and I fear that I showed it."

"And what happened this morning?"

"She asked if she could pray for her 'new father'—for the Italian!"

"Did you let her?"

"I got up without saying anything."

"You must have felt just as you did when I wanted to pray for the devil."

"He is the devil," cried Harriet.

"No, Harriet; he is too vulgar."

"I will thank you not to scoff against religion!" was Harriet's retort. "Think of that poor baby. Irma is right to pray for him. What an entrance into life for an English child!"

"My dear sister, I can reassure you. Firstly, the beastly baby is Italian. Secondly, it was promptly christened at Santa Deodata's, and a powerful combination of saints watch over—"

"Don't, dear. And, Harriet, don't be so serious—I mean not so serious when you are with Irma. She will be worse than ever if she thinks we have something to hide."

Harriet's conscience could be quite as tiresome as Philip's unconventionality. Mrs Herriton soon made it easy for her daughter to go for six weeks to the Tirol. Then she and Philip began to grapple with Irma alone.

Just as they had got things a little quiet the beastly baby sent another picture-postcard—a comic one, not particularly proper. Irma received it while they were out, and all the trouble began again.

"I cannot think," said Mrs Herriton, "what his motive is in sending them."

Two years before, Philip would have said that the motive was to give pleasure. Now he, like his mother, tried to think of something sinister and subtle.

"Do you suppose that he guesses the situation—how anxious we are to hush the scandal up?"

"That is quite possible. He knows that Irma will worry us about the baby. Perhaps he hopes that we shall adopt it to quiet her."

"Hopeful indeed."

"At the same time he has the chance of corrupting the child's morals." She unlocked a drawer, took out the postcard, and regarded it gravely. "He entreats her to send the baby one," was her next remark.

"She might do it too!"

"I told her not to; but we must watch her carefully, without, of course, appearing to be suspicious."

Philip was getting to enjoy his mother's diplomacy. He did not think of his own morals and behaviour any more.

"Who's to watch her at school, though? She may bubble out any moment."

"We can but trust to our influence," said Mrs Herriton.

Irma did bubble out, that very day. She was proof against a single postcard, not against two. A new little brother is a valuable sentimental asset to a schoolgirl, and her school was then passing through an acute phase of baby-worship. Happy the girl who had her quiver full of them, who kissed them when she left home in the morning, who had the right to extricate them from mail-carts in the interval, who dangled them at tea ere they retired to rest! That one might sing the unwritten song of Miriam, blessed above all school-girls, who was allowed to hide her baby brother in a squashy place, where none but herself could find him!

How could Irma keep silent when pretentious girls spoke of baby cousins and baby visitors—she who had a baby brother, who wrote her postcards through his dear papa? She had promised not to tell about him—she knew not why —and she told. And one girl told another, and one girl told her mother, and the thing was out.

"Yes, it is all very sad," Mrs Herriton kept saying. "My daughter-in-law made a very unhappy marriage, as I dare say you know. I suppose that the child will be educated in Italy. Possibly his grandmother may be doing something, but I have not heard of it. I do not expect that she will have him over. She disapproves of the father. It is altogether a painful business for her."

She was careful only to scold Irma for disobedience—that eighth deadly sin, so convenient to parents and guardians. Harriet would have plunged into needless explanations and abuse. The child was ashamed, and talked about the baby less. The end of the school year was at hand, and she hoped to get another prize. But she also had put her hand to the wheel.

It was several days before they saw Miss Abbott. Mrs

Herriton had not come across her much since the kiss of reconciliation, nor Philip since the journey to London. She had, indeed, been rather a disappointment to him. Her creditable display of originality had never been repeated; he feared she was slipping back. Now she came about the Cottage Hospital—her life was devoted to dull acts of charity—and though she got money out of him and out of his mother she still sat tight in her chair, looking graver and more wooden than ever.

"I dare say you have heard," said Mrs Herriton, well knowing what the matter was.

"Yes, I have. I came to ask you: have any steps been taken?"

Philip was astonished. The question was impertinent in the extreme. He had a regard for Miss Abbott, and regretted that she had been guilty of it.

"About the baby?" asked Mrs Herriton pleasantly.

"Yes."

"As far as I know, no steps. Mrs Theobald may have decided on something, but I have not heard of it."

"I was meaning, had you decided on anything?"

"The child is no relation of ours," said Philip. "It is therefore scarcely for us to interfere."

His mother glanced at him nervously. "Poor Lilia was almost a daughter to me once. I know what Miss Abbott means. But now things have altered. Any initiative would naturally come from Mrs Theobald."

"But does not Mrs Theobald always take any initiative from you?" asked Miss Abbott.

Mrs Herriton could not help colouring. "I sometimes have given her advice in the past. I should not presume to do so now."

"Then is nothing to be done for the child at all?"

"It's extraordinarily good of you to take this unexpected interest," said Philip.

"The child came into the world through my negligence," replied Miss Abbott. "It is natural I should take an interest in it."

66

"My dear Caroline," said Mrs Herriton, "you must not brood over the thing. Let bygones be bygones. The child should worry you even less than it worries us. We never even mention it. It belongs to another world."

Miss Abbott got up without replying, and turned to go. Her extreme gravity made Mrs Herriton uneasy. "Of course," she added, "if Mrs Theobald decides on any plan that seems at all practicable—I must say I don't see any such—I shall ask if I may join her in it, for Irma's sake, and share in any possible expenses."

"Please would you let me know if she decides on anything. I should like to join as well."

"My dear, how you throw about your money! We would never allow it."

"And if she decides on nothing please also let me know. Let me know in any case."

Mrs Herriton made a point of kissing her.

"Is the young person mad?" burst out Philip as soon as she had departed. "Never in my life have I seen such colossal impertinence. She ought to be well smacked, and sent back to Sunday-school."

His mother said nothing.

"But don't you see—she is practically threatening us? You can't put her off with Mrs Theobald; she knows as well as we do that she is a nonentity. If we won't do anything she's going to raise a scandal—that we neglect our relatives, etc., which is, of course, a lie. Still, she'll say it. Oh, dear, sweet, sober Caroline Abbott has a screw loose! We knew it at Monteriano. I had my suspicions last year one day in the train; and here it is again. The young person is mad."

She still said nothing.

"Shall I go round at once and give it her well? I'd really enjoy it."

In a low, serious voice—such a voice as she had not used to him for months—Mrs Herriton said: "Caroline has been extremely impertinent. Yet there may be something in what she says after all. Ought the child to grow up in that place —and with that father?"

Philip started and shuddered. He saw that his mother was not sincere. Her insincerity to others had amused him, but it was disheartening when used against himself.

"Let us admit frankly," she continued, "that after all we may have responsibilities."

"I don't understand you, mother. You are turning absolutely round. What are you up to?"

In one moment an impenetrable barrier had been erected between them. They were no longer in smiling confidence. Mrs Herriton was off on tactics of her own—tactics which might be beyond or beneath him.

His remark offended her. "Up to? I am wondering whether I ought not to adopt the child. Is that sufficiently plain?"

"And this is the result of half a dozen idiocies of Miss Abbott?"

"It is. I repeat, she has been extremely impertinent. None the less she is showing me my duty. If I can rescue poor Lilia's baby from that horrible man, who will bring it up either as Papist or infidel—who will certainly bring it up to be vicious—I shall do it."

"You talk like Harriet."

"And why not?" said she, flushing at what she knew to be an insult. "Say, if you choose, that I talk like Irma. That child has seen the thing more clearly than any of us. She longs for her little brother. She shall have him. I don't care if I am impulsive."

He was sure that she was not impulsive, but did not dare to say so. Her ability frightened him. All his life he had been her puppet. She had let him worship Italy, and reform Sawston—just as she had let Harriet be Low Church. She had let him talk as much as he liked. But when she wanted a thing she always got it.

And, though she was frightening him, she did not inspire him with reverence. Her life, he saw, was without meaning. To what purpose was her diplomacy, her insincerity, her continued repression of vigour? Did they make anyone better or happier? Did they even bring happiness to herself?

Harriet with her gloomy peevish creed, Lilia with her clutches after pleasure, were after all more divine than this well-ordered, active, useless machine.

Now that his mother had wounded his vanity he could criticize her thus. But he could not rebel. To the end of his days he would probably go on doing what she wanted. He watched with a cold interest the duel between her and Miss Abbott. Mrs Herriton's policy only appeared gradually. It was to prevent Miss Abbott interfering with the child at all costs, and if possible to prevent her at a small cost. Pride was the only solid element in her disposition. She could not bear to seem less charitable than others.

"I am planning what can be done," she would tell people, "and that kind Caroline Abbott is helping me. It is no business of either of us, but we are getting to feel that the baby must not be left entirely to that horrible man. It would be unfair to little Irma; after all, he is her half-brother. No, we have come to nothing definite."

Miss Abbott was equally civil, but not to be appeased by good intentions. The child's welfare was a sacred duty to her, not a matter of pride or even of sentiment. By it alone, she felt, could she undo a little of the evil that she had permitted to come into the world. To her imagination Monteriano had become a magic city of vice, beneath whose towers no person could grow up happy or pure. Sawston, with its semi-detached houses and snobby schools, its book-teas and bazaars, was certainly petty and dull; at times she found it even contemptible. But it was not a place of sin, and at Sawston, either with the Herritons or with herself, the baby should grow up.

As soon as it was inevitable, Mrs Herriton wrote a letter for Waters & Adamson to send to Gino—the oddest letter; Philip saw a copy of it afterwards. Its ostensible purpose was to complain of the picture-postcards. Right at the end, in a few nonchalant sentences, she offered to adopt the child, provided that Gino would undertake never to come near it, and would surrender some of Lilia's money for its education.

"What do you think of it?" she asked her son. "It would not do to let him know that we are anxious for it."

"Certainly he will never suppose that."

"But what effect will the letter have on him?"

"When he gets it he will do a sum. If it is less expensive in the long run to part with a little money and to be clear of the baby, he will part with it. If he would lose, he will adopt the tone of the loving father."

"Dear, you're shockingly cynical." After a pause she added, "How would the sum work out?"

"I don't know, I'm sure. But if you wanted to ensure the baby being posted by return you should have sent a little sum to *him*. Oh, I'm not cynical—at least I only go by what I know of him. But I am weary of the whole show. Weary of Italy. Weary, weary, weary. Sawston's a kind, pitiful place, isn't it? I will go walk in it and seek comfort."

He smiled as he spoke, for the sake of not appearing serious. When he had left her she began to smile also.

It was to the Abbotts' that he walked. Mr Abbott offered him tea, and Caroline, who was keeping up her Italian in the next room, came in to pour it out. He told them that his mother had written to Signor Carella, and they both uttered fervent wishes for her success.

"Very fine of Mrs Herriton, very fine indeed," said Mr Abbott, who, like everyone else, knew nothing of his daughter's exasperating behaviour. "I'm afraid it will mean a lot of expense. She will get nothing out of Italy without paying."

"There are sure to be incidental expenses," said Philip cautiously. Then he turned to Miss Abbott and said, "Do you suppose we shall have difficulty with the man?"

"It depends," she replied, with equal caution.

"From what you saw of him, should you conclude that he would make an affectionate parent?"

"I don't go by what I saw of him, but by what I know of him."

"Well, what do you conclude from that?"

"That he is a thoroughly wicked man."

"Yet thoroughly wicked men have loved their children. Look at Rodrigo Borgia, for example."

"I have also seen examples of that in my district."

With this remark the admirable young woman rose, and returned to keep up her Italian. She puzzled Philip extremely. He could understand enthusiasm, but she did not seem the least enthusiastic. He could understand pure cussedness, but it did not seem to be that either. Apparently she was deriving neither amusement nor profit from the struggle. Why, then, had she undertaken it? Perhaps she was not sincere. Perhaps, on the whole, that was most likely. She must be professing one thing and aiming at another. What the other thing could be he did not stop to consider. Insincerity was becoming his stock explanation for anything unfamiliar, whether that thing was a kindly action or a high ideal.

"She fences well," he said to his mother afterwards.

"What had you to fence about?" she said suavely. Her son might know her tactics, but she refused to admit that he knew. She still pretended to him that the baby was the one thing she wanted, and had always wanted, and that Miss Abbott was her valued ally.

And when, next week, the reply came from Italy, she showed him no face of triumph. "Read the letters," she said. "We have failed."

Gino wrote in his own language, but the solicitors had sent a laborious English translation, where "Pregiatissima Signora" was rendered as "Most Praiseworthy Madam", and every delicate compliment and superlative—superlatives are delicate in Italian—would have felled an ox. For a moment Philip forgot the matter in the manner; this grotesque memorial of the land he had loved moved him almost to tears. He knew the originals of these lumbering phrases; he also had sent "sincere auguries"; he also had addressed letters—who writes at home?—from the Caffè Garibaldi. "I didn't know I was still such an ass," he thought. "Why can't I realize that it's merely tricks of expression? A bounder's a bounder, whether he lives in Sawston or Monteriano."

"Isn't it disheartening?" said his mother.

He then read that Gino could not accept the generous offer. His paternal heart would not permit him to abandon this symbol of his deplored spouse. As for the picture-postcards, it displeased him greatly that they had been obnoxious. He would send no more. Would Mrs Herriton, with her notorious kindness, explain this to Irma, and thank her for those which Irma (courteous Miss!) had sent to him?

"The sum works out against us," said Philip. "Or perhaps he is putting up the price."

"No," said Mrs Herriton decidedly. "It is not that. For some perverse reason he will not part with the child. I must go and tell poor Caroline. She will be equally distressed."

She returned from the visit in the most extraordinary condition. Her face was red, she panted for breath, there were dark circles round her eyes.

"The impudence!" she shouted. "The cursed impudence! Oh, I'm swearing. I don't care. That beastly woman—how dare she interfere—I'll—Philip, dear, I'm sorry. It's no good. You must go."

"Go where? Do sit down. What's happened?" This outburst of violence from his elegant ladylike mother pained him dreadfully. He had not known that it was in her.

"She won't accept—won't accept the letter as final. You must go to Monteriano!"

"I won't!" he shouted back. "I've been and I've failed. I'll never see the place again. I hate Italy."

"If you don't go, she will."

"Abbott?"

"Yes. Going alone; would start this evening. I offered to write; she said it was 'too late'! Too late! The child, if you please—Irma's brother—to live with her, to be brought up by her and her father at our very gates, to go to school like a gentleman, she paying. Oh, you're a man! It doesn't matter for you. You can laugh. But I know what people say; and that woman goes to Italy this evening."

He seemed to be inspired. "Then let her go! Let her mess with Italy by herself. She'll come to grief somehow. Italy's too dangerous, too—"

"Stop that nonsense, Philip. I will not be disgraced by her. I *will* have the child. Pay all we've got for it. I will have it."

"Let her go to Italy!" he cried. "Let her meddle with what she doesn't understand! Look at this letter! The man who wrote it will marry her, or murder her, or do for her somehow. He's a bounder, but he's not an English bounder. He's mysterious and terrible. He's got a country behind him that's upset people from the beginning of the world."

"Harriet!" exclaimed his mother. "Harriet shall go too. Harriet, now, will be invaluable!" And before Philip had stopped talking nonsense she had planned the whole thing and was looking out the trains.

# Chapter 6

Italy, Philip had always maintained, is only her true self in the height of the summer, when the tourists have left her, and her soul awakes under the beams of a vertical sun. He now had every opportunity of seeing her at her best, for it was nearly the middle of August before he went out to meet Harriet in the Tirol.

He found his sister in a dense cloud five thousand feet above the sea, chilled to the bone, overfed, bored, and not at all unwilling to be fetched away.

"It upsets one's plans terribly," she remarked, as she squeezed out her sponges, "but obviously it is my duty."

"Did mother explain it all to you?" asked Philip.

"Yes, indeed! Mother has written me a really beautiful letter. She describes how it was that she gradually got to feel that we must rescue the poor baby from its terrible surroundings, how she has tried by letter, and it is no good —nothing but insincere compliments and hypocrisy came back. Then she says, 'There is nothing like personal influence; you and Philip will succeed where I have failed.' She says, too, that Caroline Abbott has been wonderful."

Philip assented.

"Caroline feels it as keenly almost as us. That is because she knows the man. Oh, he must be loathsome! Goodness me! I've forgotten to pack the ammonia! . . . It has been a terrible lesson for Caroline, but I fancy it is her turning-point. I can't help liking to think that out of all this evil good will come."

Philip saw no prospect of good, nor of beauty either. But the expedition promised to be highly comic. He was not averse to it any longer; he was simply indifferent to all in it except the humours. These would be wonderful. Harriet,

74

worked by her mother; Mrs Herriton, worked by Miss Abbott; Gino, worked by a cheque—what better entertainment could he desire? There was nothing to distract him this time; his sentimentality had died, so had his anxiety for the family honour. He might be a puppet's puppet, but he knew exactly the disposition of the strings.

They travelled for thirteen hours downhill, whilst the streams broadened and the mountains shrank, and the vegetation changed, and the people ceased being ugly and drinking beer, and began instead to drink wine and to be beautiful. And the train which had picked them at sunrise out of a waste of glaciers and hotels was waltzing at sunset round the walls of Verona.

"Absurd nonsense they talk about the heat," said Philip, as they drove from the station. "Supposing we were here for pleasure, what could be more pleasurable than this?"

"Did you hear, though, they are remarking on the cold?" said Harriet nervously. "I should never have thought it cold."

And on the second day the heat struck them, like a hand laid over the mouth, just as they were walking to see the tomb of Juliet. From that moment everything went wrong. They fled from Verona. Harriet's sketch-book was stolen, and the bottle of ammonia in her trunk burst over her prayerbook, so that purple patches appeared on all her clothes. Then, as she was going through Mantua at four in the morning, Philip made her look out of the window because it was Virgil's birthplace, and a smut flew in her eye, and Harriet with a smut in her eye was notorious. At Bologna they stopped twenty-four hours to rest. It was a *festa*, and children blew bladder whistles night and day. "What a religion!" said Harriet. The hotel smelt, two puppies were asleep on her bed, and her bedroom window looked into a belfry, which saluted her slumbering form every quarter of an hour. Philip left his walking-stick, his socks and the Baedeker at Bologna; she only left her sponge-bag. Next day they crossed the Apennines with a train-sick child and a hot lady who told them that never, never before had she sweated so profusely. "Foreigners are a filthy nation," said Harriet. "I don't care if there are tunnels; open the window." He obeyed, and she got another smut in her eye. Nor did Florence improve matters. Eating, walking, even a cross word would bathe them both in boiling water. Philip, who was slighter of build, and less conscientious, suffered less. But Harriet had never been to Florence, and between the hours of eight and eleven she crawled like a wounded creature through the streets, and swooned before various masterpieces of art. It was an irritable couple who took tickets to Monteriano.

"Singles or returns?" said he.

"A single for me," said Harriet peevishly; "I shall never get back alive."

"Sweet creature!" said her brother, suddenly breaking down. "How helpful you will be when we come to Signor Carella!"

"Do you suppose," said Harriet, standing still among a whirl of porters—"do you suppose I am going to enter that man's house?"

"Then what have you come for, pray? For ornament?"

"To see that you do your duty."

"Oh, thanks!"

"So mother told me. For goodness' sake get the tickets; here comes that hot woman again! She has the impudence to bow."

"Mother told you, did she?" said Philip wrathfully, as he went to struggle for tickets at a slit so narrow that they were handed to him edgeways. Italy was beastly, and Florence station is the centre of beastly Italy. But he had a strange feeling that he was to blame for it all; that a little influx into him of virtue would make the whole land not beastly but amusing. For there was enchantment, he was sure of that; solid enchantment, which lay behind the porters and the screaming and the dust. He could see it in the terrific blue sky beneath which they travelled, in the whitened plain which gripped life tighter than a frost, in the exhausted reaches of the Arno, in the ruins of brown castles which stood quivering upon the hills. He could see it, though his head ached and his skin was twitching, though he was here as a puppet, and though his sister knew how he was here. There was nothing pleasant in that journey to Monteriano station. But nothing—not even the discomfort—was commonplace.

"But do people live inside?" asked Harriet. They had exchanged the railway carriage for the *legno*, and the *legno* had emerged from the withered trees, and had revealed to them their destination.

Philip, to be annoying, answered: "No."

"What do they do there?" continued Harriet, with a frown.

"There is a *caffè*. A prison. A theatre. A church. Walls. A view."

"Not for me, thank you," said Harriet, after a weighty pause.

"Nobody asked you, miss, you see. Now Lilia was asked by such a nice young gentleman, with curls all over his forehead, and teeth just as white as father makes them." Then his manner changed. "But, Harriet, do you see nothing wonderful or attractive in that place—nothing at all?"

"Nothing at all. It's frightful."

"I know it is. But it's old—awfully old."

"Beauty is the only test." said Harriet. "At least so you told me when I sketched old buildings—for the sake, I suppose, of making yourself unpleasant."

"Oh, I'm perfectly right. But at the same time—I don't know—so many things have happened here—people have lived so hard and so splendidly—I can't explain."

"I shouldn't think you could. It doesn't seem the best moment to begin your Italy mania. I thought you were cured of it by now. Instead, will you kindly tell me what you are going to do when you arrive. I do beg you will not be taken unawares this time."

"First, Harriet, I shall settle you at the Stella d'Italia, in the comfort that befits your sex and disposition. Then I shall make myself some tea. After tea I shall take a book into

77

Santa Deodata's, and read there. It is always fresh and cool."

The martyred Harriet exclaimed: "I'm not clever, Philip. I don't go in for it, as you know. But I know what's rude. And I know what's wrong."

"Meaning—?"

"You!" she shouted, bouncing on the cushions of the *legno* and startling all the fleas. "What's the good of cleverness if a man's murdered a woman?"

"Harriet, I am hot. To whom do you refer?"

"He. Her. If you don't look out he'll murder you. I wish he would."

"Tut, tut, tutlet! You'd find a corpse extraordinarily inconvenient." Then he tried to be less aggravating. "I heartily dislike the fellow, but we know he didn't murder her. In that letter, though she said a lot, she never said he was physically cruel."

"He has murdered her. The things he did—things one can't even mention—"

"Things which one must mention if one's to talk at all. And things which one must keep in their proper place. Because he was unfaithful to his wife, it doesn't follow that in every way he's absolutely vile." He looked at the city. It seemed to approve his remark.

"It's the supreme test. The man who is unchivalrous to a woman—"

"Oh, stow it! Take it to the Back Kitchen. It's no more a supreme test than anything else. The Italians never were chivalrous from the first. If you condemn him for that, you'll condemn the whole lot."

"I condemn the whole lot."

"And the French as well?"

"And the French as well."

"Things aren't so jolly easy," said Philip, more to himself than to her.

But for Harriet things were easy, though not jolly, and she turned upon her brother yet again. "What about the baby, pray? You've said a lot of smart things and whittled away morality and religion and I don't know what; but what about the baby? You think me a fool, but I've been noticing you all today, and you haven't mentioned the baby once. You haven't thought about it, even. You don't care. Philip! I shall not speak to you. You are intolerable."

She kept her promise, and never opened her lips all the rest of the way. But her eyes glowed with anger and resolution. For she was a straight, brave woman, as well as a peevish one.

Philip acknowledged her reproof to be true. He did not care about the baby one straw. Nevertheless, he meant to do his duty, and he was fairly confident of success. If Gino would have sold his wife for a thousand lire, for how much less would he not sell his child? It was just a commercial transaction. Why should it interfere with other things? His eyes were fixed on the towers again, just as they had been fixed when he drove with Miss Abbott. But this time his thoughts were pleasanter, for he had no such grave business on his mind. It was in the spirit of the cultivated tourist that he approached his destination.

One of the towers, rough as any other, was topped by a cross—the tower of the Collegiate Church of Santa Deodata. She was a holy maiden of the Dark Ages, the city's patron saint, and sweetness and barbarity mingle strangely in her story. So holy was she that all her life she lay upon her back in the house of her mother, refusing to eat, refusing to play, refusing to work. The devil, envious of such sanctity, tempted her in various ways. He dangled grapes above her, he showed her fascinating toys, he pushed soft pillows beneath her aching head. When all proved vain he tripped up the mother and flung her downstairs before her very eyes. But so holy was the saint that she never picked her mother up, but lay upon her back through all, and thus assured her throne in Paradise. She was only fifteen when she died, which shows how much is within the reach of any schoolgirl. Those who think her life was unpractical need only think of the victories upon Poggibonsi, San Gimignano, Volterra, Siena itself—all gained through the invocation of

her name; they need only look at the church which rose
over her grave. The grand schemes for a marble façade
were never carried out, and it is brown unfinished stone
until this day. But for the inside Giotto was summoned to
decorate the walls of the nave. Giotto came—that is to say,
he did not come, German research having decisively
proved—but at all events the nave is covered with frescoes,
and so are two chapels in the left transept, and the arch
into the choir, and there are scraps in the choir itself. There
the decoration stopped, till in the full spring of the Renaissance a great painter came to pay a few weeks' visit to his
friend the Lord of Monteriano. In the intervals between
the banquets and the discussions on Latin etymology and the
dancing, he would stroll over to the church, and there in
the fifth chapel to the right he has painted two frescoes of the
death and burial of Santa Deodata. That is why Baedeker
gives the place a star.

Santa Deodata was better company than Harriet, and
she kept Philip in a pleasant dream until the *legno* drew up
at the hotel. Everyone there was asleep, for it was still the
hour when only idiots were moving. There were not even
any beggars about. The cabman put their bags down in the
passage—they had left heavy luggage at the station—and
strolled about till he came on the landlady's room and woke
her, and sent her to them.

Then Harriet pronounced the monosyllable "Go!"

"Go where?" asked Philip, bowing to the landlady, who
was swimming down the stairs.

"To the Italian. Go."

"Buona sera, signora padrona. Si ritorna volontieri a
Monteriano! (Don't be a goose. I'm not going now. You're
in the way, too.) Vorrei due camere—"

"Go. This instant. Now. I'll stand it no longer. Go!"

"I'm damned if I'll go. I want my tea."

"Swear if you like!" she cried. "Blaspheme! Abuse me!
But understand, I'm in earnest."

"Harriet, don't act. Or act better."

"We've come here to get the baby back, and for nothing

80

else. I'll not have this levity and slackness, and talk about pictures and churches. Think of mother; did she send you out for *them*?"

"Think of mother and don't straddle across the stairs. Let the cabman and the landlady come down, and let me go up and choose rooms."

"I shan't."

"Harriet, are you mad?"

"If you like. But you will not come up till you have seen the Italian."

"La signorina si sente male," said Philip. "È il sole."

"Poveretta!" cried the landlady and the cabman.

"Leave me alone!" said Harriet, snarling round at them. "I don't care for the lot of you. I'm English, and neither you'll come down nor he up till he goes for the baby."

"La prego—piano—piano—c'è un' altra signorina che dorme—"

"We shall probably be arrested for brawling, Harriet. Have you the very slightest sense of the ludicrous?"

Harriet had not; that was why she could be so powerful. She had concocted this scene in the carriage, and nothing should baulk her of it. To the abuse in front and the coaxing behind she was equally indifferent. How long she would have stood like a glorified Horatius, keeping the staircase at both ends, was never to be known. For the young lady whose sleep they were disturbing awoke, and opened her bedroom door, and came out onto the landing. She was Miss Abbott.

Philip's first coherent feeling was one of indignation. To be run by his mother and hectored by his sister was as much as he could stand. The intervention of a third female drove him suddenly beyond politeness. He was about to say exactly what he thought about the thing from beginning to end. But before he could do so Harriet also had seen Miss Abbott. She uttered a shrill cry of joy.

"You, Caroline, here of all people!" And in spite of the heat she darted up the stairs and imprinted an affectionate kiss upon her friend.

Philip had an inspiration. "You will have a lot to tell

Miss Abbott, Harriet, and she may have as much to tell you. So I'll pay my call on Signor Carella, as you suggested, and see how things stand."

Miss Abbott uttered some noise of greeting or alarm. He did not reply to it or approach nearer to her. Without even paying the cabman, he escaped into the street.

"Tear each other's eyes out!" he cried, gesticulating at the façade of the hotel. "Give it her, Harriet! Teach her to leave us alone. Give it her, Caroline! Teach her to be grateful to you. Go it, ladies; go it!"

Such people as observed him were interested, but did not conclude that he was mad. This aftermath of conversation is not unknown in Italy.

He tried to think how amusing it was; but it would not do—Miss Abbott's presence affected him too personally. Either she suspected him of dishonesty, or else she was being dishonest herself. He preferred to suppose the latter. Perhaps she had seen Gino, and they had prepared some elaborate mortification for the Herritons. Perhaps Gino had sold the baby cheap to her for a joke; it was just the kind of joke that would appeal to him. Philip still remembered the laughter that had greeted his fruitless journey, and the uncouth push that had toppled him onto the bed. And, whatever it might mean, Miss Abbott's presence spoiled the comedy: she would do nothing funny.

During this short meditation he had walked through the city, and was out on the other side. "Where does Signor Carella live?" he asked the men at the *dogana*.

"I'll show you!" cried a little girl, springing out of the ground as Italian children will.

"She will show you," said the *dogana* men, nodding reassuringly. "Follow her always, always, and you will come to no harm. She is a trustworthy guide. She is my

{ daughter."
  cousin."
  sister."

Philip knew these relatives well; they ramify, if need be, all over the peninsula.

"Do you chance to know whether Signor Carella is in?"
he asked her.

She had just seen him go in. Philip nodded. He was
looking forward to the interview this time; it would be an
intellectual duel with a man of no great intellect. What was
Miss Abbott up to? That was one of the things he was going
to discover. While she had it out with Harriet, he would
have it out with Gino. He followed the *dogana*'s relative
softly, like a diplomatist.

He did not follow her long, for this was the Volterra gate,
and the house was exactly opposite to it. In half a minute
they had scrambled down the mule-track and reached the
only practicable entrance. Philip laughed, partly at the
thought of Lilia in such a building, partly in the confidence
of victory. Meanwhile the *dogana*'s relative lifted up her
voice and gave a shout.

For an impressive interval there was no reply. Then the
figure of a woman appeared high up on the loggia.

"That is Perfetta," said the girl.

"I want to see Signor Carella," cried Philip.

"Out!"

"Out," echoed the girl complacently.

"Why on earth did you say he was in?" He could have
strangled her for temper. He had been just ripe for an
interview—just the right combination of indignation and
acuteness: blood hot, brain cool. But nothing ever did go
right in Monteriano. "When will he be back?" he called to
Perfetta. It really was too bad.

She did not know. He was away on business. He might be
back this evening, he might not. He had gone to Poggibonsi.

At the sound of this word the little girl put her fingers to
her nose and swept them at the plain. She sang as she did so,
even as her foremothers had sung seven hundred years back—

> Poggibonizzi, fatti in là,
> Che Monteriano si fa città!

Then she asked Philip for a halfpenny. A German lady,
friendly to the Past, had given her one that very spring.

"I shall have to leave a message," he called.

"Now Perfetta has gone for her basket," said the little girl. "When she returns she will lower it—so. Then you will put your card into it. Then she will raise it—thus. By this means—"

When Perfetta returned, Philip remembered to ask after the baby. It took longer to find than the basket, and he stood perspiring in the evening sun, trying to avoid the smell of the drains and to prevent the little girl from singing against Poggibonsi. The olive-trees beside him were draped with the weekly—or more probably the monthly—wash. What a frightful spotty blouse! He could not think where he had seen it. Then he remembered that it was Lilia's. She had bought it "to hack about in" at Sawston, and had taken it to Italy because "in Italy anything does". He had rebuked her for the sentiment.

"Beautiful as an angel!" bellowed Perfetta, holding out something which must be Lilia's baby. "But who am I addressing?"

"Thank you—here is my card." He had written on it a civil request to Gino for an interview next morning. But before he placed it in the basket and revealed his identity he wished to find something out. "Has a young lady happened to call here lately—a young English lady?"

Perfetta begged his pardon: she was a little deaf.

"A young lady—pale, large, tall."

She did not quite catch.

"A YOUNG LADY!"

"Perfetta is deaf when she chooses," said the *dogana*'s relative. At last Philip admitted the peculiarity and strode away. He paid off the detestable child at the Volterra gate. She got two nickel pieces and was not pleased, partly because it was too much, partly because he did not look pleased when he gave it to her. He caught her fathers and cousins winking at each other as he walked past them. Monteriano seemed in one vast conspiracy to make him look a fool. He felt tired and anxious and muddled, and not sure of anything except that his temper was lost. In this mood he

84

returned to the Stella d'Italia, and there, as he was ascending the stairs, Miss Abbott popped out of the dining-room on the first floor and beckoned to him mysteriously.

"I was going to make myself some tea," he said, with his hand still on the banisters.

"I should be grateful—"

So he followed her into the dining-room and shut the door.

"You see," she began, "Harriet knows nothing."

"No more do I. He was out."

"But what's that to do with it?"

He presented her with an unpleasant smile. She fenced well, as he had noticed before. "He was out. You find me as ignorant as you have left Harriet."

"What do you mean? Please, please, Mr Herriton, don't be mysterious; there isn't the time. Any moment Harriet may be down, and we shan't have decided how to behave to her. Sawston was different: we had to keep up appearances. But here we must speak out, and I think I can trust you to do it. Otherwise we'll never start clear."

"Pray let us start clear," said Philip, pacing up and down the room. "Permit me to begin by asking you a question. In which capacity have you come to Monteriano—spy or traitor?"

"Spy!" she answered, without a moment's hesitation. She was standing by the little Gothic window as she spoke —the hotel had been a palace once—and with her finger she was following the curves of the moulding as if they might feel beautiful and strange. "Spy," she repeated, for Philip was bewildered at learning her guilt so easily, and could not answer a word. "Your mother has behaved dishonourably all through. She never wanted the child; no harm in that; but she is too proud to let it come to me. She has done all she could to wreck things; she did not tell you everything; she has told Harriet nothing at all; she has lied or acted lies everywhere. I cannot trust your mother. So I have come here alone—all across Europe; no one knows it; my father thinks I am in Normandy—to spy on Mrs Herriton. Don't let's argue!" For he had begun, almost mechanically, to rebuke her for impertinence. "If you are here to get the child, I will help you; if you are here to fail, I shall get it instead of you."

"It is hopeless to expect you to believe me," he stammered. "But I can assert that we are here to get the child, even if it costs us all we've got. My mother has fixed no money limit whatever. I am here to carry out her instructions. I think that you will approve of them, as you have practically dictated them. I do not approve of them. They are absurd."

She nodded carelessly. She did not mind what he said. All she wanted was to get the baby out of Monteriano.

"Harriet also carries out your instructions," he continued. "She, however, approves of them, and does not know that they proceed from you. I think, Miss Abbott, you had better take entire charge of the rescue-party. I have asked for an interview with Signor Carella tomorrow morning. Do you acquiesce?"

She nodded again.

"Might I ask for details of your interview with him? They might be helpful to me."

He had spoken at random. To his delight she suddenly collapsed. Her hand fell from the window. Her face was red with more than the reflection of evening.

"My interview—how do you know of it?"

"From Perfetta, if it interests you."

"Who ever is Perfetta?"

"The woman who must have let you in."

"In where?"

"Into Signor Carella's house."

"Mr Herriton!" she exclaimed. "How could you believe her? Do you suppose that I would have entered that man's house, knowing about him all that I do? I think you have very odd ideas of what is possible for a lady. I hear you wanted Harriet to go. Very properly she refused. Eighteen months ago I might have done such a thing. But I trust I have learned how to behave by now."

Philip began to see that there were two Miss Abbotts—

the Miss Abbott who could travel alone to Monteriano, and the Miss Abbott who could not enter Gino's house when she got there. It was an amusing discovery. Which of them would respond to his next move?

"I suppose I misunderstood Perfetta. Where did you have your interview, then?"

"Not an interview—an accident—I am very sorry—I meant you to have the chance of seeing him first. Though it is your fault. You are a day late. You were due here yesterday. So I came yesterday, and, not finding you, went up to the Rocca—you know that kitchen-garden where they let you in, and there is a ladder up to a broken tower, where you can stand and see all the other towers below you and the plain and all the other hills?"

"Yes, yes. I know the Rocca; I told you of it."

"So I went up in the evening for the sunset; I had nothing to do. He was in the garden; it belongs to a friend of his."

"And you talked."

"It was very awkward for me. But I had to talk; he seemed to make me. You see, he thought I was here as a tourist; he thinks so still. He intended to be civil, and I judged it better to be civil also."

"And of what did you talk?"

"The weather—there will be rain, he says, by tomorrow evening—the other towns, England, myself, about you a little, and he actually mentioned Lilia. He was perfectly disgusting; he pretended he loved her; he offered to show me her grave—the grave of the woman he has murdered!"

"My dear Miss Abbott, he is not a murderer. I have just been driving that into Harriet. And when you know the Italians as well as I do you will realize that in all that he said to you he was perfectly sincere. The Italians are essentially dramatic: they look on death and love as spectacles. I don't doubt that he persuaded himself, for the moment, that he had behaved admirably, both as husband and widower."

"You may be right," said Miss Abbott, impressed for the first time. "When I tried to pave the way, so to speak—to

87

hint that he had not behaved as he ought—well, it was no good at all. He couldn't or wouldn't understand."

There was something very humorous in the idea of Miss Abbott approaching Gino, on the Rocca, in the spirit of a district visitor. Philip, whose temper was returning, laughed.

"Harriet would say he has no sense of sin."

"Harriet may be right, I am afraid."

"If so, perhaps he isn't sinful!"

Miss Abbott was not one to encourage levity. "I know what he has done," she said. "What he says and what he thinks is of very little importance."

Philip smiled at her crudity. "I should like to hear, though, what he said about me. Is he preparing a warm reception?"

"Oh no, not that. I never told him that you and Harriet were coming. You could have taken him by surprise if you liked. He only asked after you, and wished he hadn't been so rude to you eighteen months ago."

"What a memory the fellow has for little things!" He turned away as he spoke, for he did not want her to see his face. It was suffused with pleasure. For an apology, which would have been intolerable eighteen months ago, was gracious and agreeable now.

She would not let this pass. "You did not think it a little thing at the time. You told me he had assaulted you."

"I lost my temper," said Philip lightly. His vanity had been appeased, and he knew it. This tiny piece of civility had changed his mood. "Did he really—what exactly did he say?"

"He said he was sorry—pleasantly, as Italians do say such things. But he never mentioned the baby once."

What did the baby matter when the world was suddenly right way up? Philip smiled, and was shocked at himself for smiling, and smiled again. For romance had come back to Italy; there were no cads in her; she was beautiful, courteous, lovable, as of old. And Miss Abbott—she, too, was beautiful in her way, for all her gaucheness and conventionality. She really cared about life, and tried to live it properly. And Harriet—even Harriet tried.

This admirable change in Philip proceeds from nothing admirable, and may therefore provoke the gibes of the cynical. But angels and other practical people will accept it reverently, and write it down as good.

"The view from the Rocca (small gratuity) is finest at sunset," he murmured, more to himself than to her.

"And he never mentioned the baby once," Miss Abbott repeated. But she had returned to the window, and again her finger pursued the delicate curves. He watched her in silence, and was more attracted to her than he had ever been before. She really was the strangest mixture.

"The view from the Rocca—wasn't it fine?"

"What isn't fine here?" she answered gently, and then added, "I wish I was Harriet," throwing an extraordinary meaning into the words.

"Because Harriet—"

She would not go further, but he believed that she had paid homage to the complexity of life. For her, at all events, the expedition was neither easy nor jolly. Beauty, evil, charm, vulgarity, mystery—she also acknowledged this tangle, in spite of herself. And her voice thrilled him when she broke silence with "Mr Herriton—come here—look at this!"

She removed a pile of plates from the Gothic window, and they leant out of it. Close opposite, wedged between mean houses, there rose up one of the great towers. It is your tower: you stretch a barricade between it and the hotel, and the traffic is blocked in a moment. Farther up, where the street empties out by the church, your connections, the Merli and the Capocchi, do likewise. They command the Piazza, you the Siena gate. No one can move in either but he shall be instantly slain, either by bows or by cross-bows, or by Greek fire. Beware, however, of the back bedroom windows. For they are menaced by the tower of the Aldobrandeschi, and before now arrows have stuck quivering over the washstand. Guard these windows well, lest there be a repetition of the events of February 1338, when the hotel was surprised from the rear, and your dearest friend

—you could just make out that it was he—was thrown at you over the stairs.

"It reaches up to heaven," said Philip, "and down to the other place." The summit of the tower was radiant in the sun, while its base was in shadow and pasted over with advertisements. "Is it to be a symbol of the town?"

She gave no hint that she understood him. But they remained together at the window because it was a little cooler and so pleasant. Philip found a certain grace and lightness in his companion which he had never noticed in England. She was appallingly narrow, but her consciousness of wider things gave to her narrowness a pathetic charm. He did not suspect that he was more graceful too. For our vanity is such that we hold our own characters immutable, and we are slow to acknowledge that they have changed, even for the better.

Citizens came out for a little stroll before dinner. Some of them stood and gazed at the advertisements on the tower.

"Surely that isn't an opera-bill?" said Miss Abbott.

Philip put on his pince-nez. " '*Lucia di Lammermoor*. By the Master Donizetti. Unique representation. This evening.' "

"But is there an opera? Right up here?"

"Why, yes. These people know how to live. They would sooner have a thing bad than not have it at all. That is why they have got to have so much that is good. However bad the performance is tonight, it will be alive. Italians don't love music silently, like the beastly Germans. The audience takes its share—sometimes more."

"Can't we go?"

He turned on her, but not unkindly. "But we're here to rescue a child!"

He cursed himself for the remark. All the pleasure and the light went out of her face, and she became again Miss Abbott of Sawston—good, oh, most undoubtedly good, but most appallingly dull. Dull and remorseful: it is a deadly combination, and he strove against it in vain, till he was interrupted by the opening of the dining-room door.

They started as guiltily as if they had been flirting. Their interview had taken such an unexpected course. Anger, cynicism, stubborn morality—all had ended in a feeling of goodwill towards each other and towards the city which had received them. And now Harriet was here—acrid, indissoluble, large; the same in Italy as in England—changing her disposition never, and her atmosphere under protest.

Yet even Harriet was human, and the better for a little tea. She did not scold Philip for finding Gino out, as she might reasonably have done. She showered civilities on Miss Abbott, exclaiming again and again that Caroline's visit was one of the most fortunate coincidences in the world. Caroline did not contradict her.

"You see him tomorrow at ten, Philip. Well, don't forget the blank cheque. Say an hour for the business. No, Italians are so slow; say two. Twelve o'clock. Lunch. Well—then it's no good going till the evening train. I can manage the baby as far as Florence—"

"My dear sister, you can't run on like that. You don't buy a pair of gloves in two hours, much less a baby."

"Three hours, then, or four; or make him learn English ways. At Florence we get a nurse—"

"But, Harriet," said Miss Abbott, "what if at first he was to refuse?"

"I don't know the meaning of the word," said Harriet impressively. "I've told the landlady that Philip and I only want our rooms one night, and we shall keep to it."

"I dare say it will be all right. But, as I told you, I thought the man I met on the Rocca a strange, difficult man."

"He's insolent to ladies, we know. But my brother can be trusted to bring him to his senses. That woman, Philip, whom you saw will carry the baby to the hotel. Of course you must tip her for it. And try, if you can, to get poor Lilia's silver bangles. They were nice quiet things, and will do for Irma. And there is an inlaid box I lent her—lent, not gave—to keep her handkerchiefs in. It's of no real value; but this is our only chance. Don't ask for it; but if you see it lying about, just say—"

"No, Harriet; I'll try for the baby, but for nothing else. I promise to do that tomorrow, and to do it in the way you wish. But tonight, as we're all tired, we want a change of topic. We want relaxation. We want to go to the theatre."

"Theatre? Here? And at such a moment?"

"We should hardly enjoy it, with the great interview impending," said Miss Abbott, with an anxious glance at Philip.

He did not betray her, but said, "Don't you think it's better than sitting in all the evening and getting nervous?"

His sister shook her head. "Mother wouldn't like it. It would be most unsuitable—almost irreverent. Besides all that, foreign theatres are notorious. Don't you remember those letters in the *Church Family Newspaper*?"

"But this is an opera—*Lucia di Lammermoor*—Sir Walter Scott—classical, you know."

Harriet's face grew resigned. "Certainly one has so few opportunities of hearing music. It is sure to be very bad. But it might be better than sitting idle all the evening. We have no books, and I lost my crochet at Florence."

"Good. Miss Abbott, you are coming too?"

"It is very kind of you, Mr Herriton. In some ways I should enjoy it; but—excuse the suggestion—I don't think we ought to go to cheap seats."

"Good gracious me!" cried Harriet, "I should never have thought of that. As likely as not, we should have tried to save money and sat among the most awful people. One keeps on forgetting this is Italy."

"Unfortunately I have no evening dress; and if the seats—"

"Oh, that'll be all right," said Philip, smiling at his timorous, scrupulous womenkind. "We'll go as we are, and buy the best we can get. Monteriano is not formal."

So this strenuous day of resolutions, plans, alarms, battles, victories, defeats, truces, ended at the opera. Miss Abbott and Harriet were both a little shamefaced. They thought of their friends at Sawston, who were supposing them to be now tilting against the powers of evil. What would Mrs

Herriton, or Irma, or the curates at the Back Kitchen say if they could see the rescue-party at a place of amusement on the very first day of its mission? Philip, too, marvelled at his wish to go. He began to see that he was enjoying his time in Monteriano, in spite of the tiresomeness of his companions and the occasional contrariness of himself.

He had been to this theatre many years before, on the occasion of a performance of *La Zia di Carlo*. Since then it had been thoroughly done up, in the tints of the beetroot and the tomato, and was in many other ways a credit to the little town. The orchestra had been enlarged, some of the boxes had terracotta draperies, and over each box was now suspended an enormous tablet, neatly framed, bearing upon it the number of that box. There was also a drop-scene, representing a pink and purple landscape, wherein sported many a lady lightly clad, and two more ladies lay along the top of the proscenium to steady a large and pallid clock. So rich and so appalling was the effect that Philip could scarcely suppress a cry. There is something majestic in the bad taste of Italy; it is not the bad taste of a country which knows no better; it has not the nervous vulgarity of England, or the blinded vulgarity of Germany. It observes beauty, and chooses to pass it by. But it attains to beauty's confidence. This tiny theatre of Monteriano spraddled and swaggered with the best of them, and these ladies with their clock would have nodded to the young men on the ceiling of the Sistine.

Philip had tried for a box, but all the best were taken; it was rather a grand performance, and he had to be content with stalls. Harriet was fretful and insular. Miss Abbott was pleasant, and insisted on praising everything; her only regret was that she had no pretty clothes with her.

"We do all right," said Philip, amused at her unwonted vanity.

"Yes, I know; but pretty things pack as easily as ugly ones. We had no need to come to Italy like guys."

This time he did not reply, "But we're here to rescue a baby." For he saw a charming picture, as charming a picture as he had seen for years—the hot red theatre; outside the theatre, towers and dark gates and medieval walls; beyond the walls, olive-trees in the starlight and white winding roads and fireflies and untroubled dust; and here in the middle of it all Miss Abbott, wishing she had not come looking like a guy. She had made the right remark. Most undoubtedly she had made the right remark. This stiff suburban woman was unbending before the shrine.

"Don't you like it all?" he asked her.

"Most awfully." And by this bald interchange they convinced each other that Romance was here.

Harriet, meanwhile, had been coughing ominously at the drop-scene, which presently rose on the grounds of Ravenswood, and the chorus of Scotch retainers burst into cry. The audience accompanied with tappings and drummings, swaying in the melody like corn in the wind. Harriet, though she did not care for music, knew how to listen to it. She uttered an acid "Shish!"

"Shut it," whispered her brother.

"We must make a stand from the beginning. They're talking."

"It is tiresome," murmured Miss Abbott; "but perhaps it isn't for us to interfere."

Harriet shook her head and shished again. The people were quiet, not because it is wrong to talk during a chorus, but because it is natural to be civil to a visitor. For a little time she kept the whole house in order, and could smile at her brother complacently.

Her success annoyed him. He had grasped the principle of opera in Italy—it aims not at illusion but at entertainment—and he did not want this great evening party to turn into a prayer-meeting. But soon the boxes began to fill, and Harriet's power was over. Families greeted each other across the auditorium. People in the pit hailed their brothers and sons in the chorus, and told them how well they were singing. When Lucia appeared by the fountain there was loud applause, and cries of "Welcome to Monteriano!"

"Ridiculous babies!" said Harriet, settling down in her stall.

"Why, it is the famous hot lady of the Apennines," cried Philip; "the one who had never, never before—"

"Ugh! Don't. She will be very vulgar. And I'm sure it's even worse here than in the tunnel. I wish we'd never—"

Lucia began to sing, and there was a moment's silence. She was stout and ugly; but her voice was still beautiful, and as she sang the theatre murmured like a hive of happy bees. All through the coloratura she was accompanied by sighs, and its top note was drowned in a shout of universal joy.

So the opera proceeded. The singers drew inspiration from the audience, and the two great sextets were rendered not unworthily. Miss Abbott fell into the spirit of the thing. She, too, chatted and laughed and applauded and encored, and rejoiced in the existence of beauty. As for Philip, he forgot himself as well as his mission. He was not even an enthusiastic visitor. For he had been in this place always. It was his home.

Harriet, like M. Bovary on a more famous occasion, was trying to follow the plot. Occasionally she nudged her companions, and asked them what had become of Walter Scott. She looked round grimly. The audience sounded drunk, and even Caroline, who never took a drop, was swaying oddly. Violent waves of excitement, all arising from very little, went sweeping round the theatre. The climax was reached in the mad scene. Lucia, clad in white, as befitted her malady, suddenly gathered up her streaming hair and bowed her acknowledgements to the audience. Then from the back of the stage—she feigned not to see it—there advanced a kind of bamboo clothes-horse, stuck all over with bouquets. It was very ugly, and most of the flowers in it were false. Lucia knew this, and so did the audience; and they all knew that the clothes-horse was a piece of stage property, brought in to make the performance go year after year. None the less did it unloose the great deeps. With a scream of amazement and joy she embraced the animal, pulled out one or two practicable blossoms, pressed them to her lips, and flung them into her admirers. They flung them back, with loud melodious cries, and a little boy in one of the stage-boxes snatched up his sister's carnations and offered them. "Che carino!" exclaimed the singer. She darted at the little boy and kissed him. Now the noise became tremendous. "Silence! Silence!" shouted many old gentlemen behind. "Let the divine creature continue!" But the young men in the adjacent box were imploring Lucia to extend her civility to them. She refused, with a humorous expressive gesture. One of them hurled a bouquet at her. She spurned it with her foot. Then, encouraged by the roars of the audience, she picked it up and tossed it to them. Harriet was always unfortunate. The bouquet struck her full in the chest, and a little *billet-doux* fell out of it into her lap.

"Call this classical?" she cried, rising from her seat. "It's not even respectable! Philip! Take me out at once."

"Whose is it?" shouted her brother, holding up the bouquet in one hand and the *billet-doux* in the other. "Whose is it?"

The house exploded, and one of the boxes was violently agitated, as if someone was being hauled to the front. Harriet moved down the gangway, and compelled Miss Abbott to follow her. Philip, still laughing and calling "Whose is it?" brought up the rear. He was drunk with excitement. The heat, the fatigue and the enjoyment had mounted into his head.

"To the left!" the people cried. "The innamorato is to the left."

He deserted his ladies and plunged towards the box. A young man was flung stomach downwards across the balustrade. Philip handed him up the bouquet and the note. Then his own hands were seized affectionately. It all seemed quite natural.

"Why have you not written?" cried the young man. "Why do you take me by surprise?"

"Oh, I've written," said Philip hilariously. "I left a note this afternoon."

"Silence! Silence!" cried the audience, who were be-

ginning to have enough. "Let the divine creature continue."
Miss Abbott and Harriet had disappeared.

"No! No!" cried the young man. "You don't escape me
now." For Philip was trying feebly to disengage his hands.
Amiable youths bent out of the box and invited him to
enter it.

"Gino's friends are ours—"

"Friends?" cried Gino. "A relative! A brother! Fra
Filippo, who has come all the way from England and never
written."

"I left a message."

The audience began to hiss.

"Come in to us."

"Thank you—ladies—there is not time—"

The next moment he was swinging by his arms. The
moment after he shot over the balustrade into the box.
Then the conductor, seeing that the incident was over,
raised his baton. The house was hushed, and Lucia di
Lammermoor resumed her song of madness and death.

Philip had whispered introductions to the pleasant people
who had pulled him in—tradesmen's sons perhaps they
were, or medical students, or solicitors' clerks, or sons of
other dentists. There is no knowing who is who in Italy.
The guest of the evening was a private soldier. He shared
the honour now with Philip. The two had to stand side by
side in the front, and exchange compliments, whilst Gino
presided, courteous, but delightfully familiar. Philip would
have a spasm of horror at the muddle he had made. But
the spasm would pass, and again he would be enchanted by
the kind, cheerful voices, the laughter that was never vapid,
and the light caress of the arm across his back.

He could not get away till the play was nearly finished,
and Edgardo was singing amongst the tombs of his ancestors. His new friends hoped to see him at the Garibaldi
tomorrow evening. He promised; then he remembered that
if they kept to Harriet's plan he would have left Monteriano.
"At ten o'clock, then," he said to Gino. "I want to speak to
you alone. At ten."

"Certainly!" laughed the other.

Miss Abbott was sitting up for him when he got back. Harriet, it seemed, had gone straight to bed.

"That was he, wasn't it?" she asked.

"Yes, rather."

"I suppose you didn't settle anything?"

"Why, no; how could I? The fact is—well, I got taken by surprise, but after all, what does it matter? There's no earthly reason why we shouldn't do the business pleasantly. He's a perfectly charming person, and so are his friends. I'm his friend now—his long-lost brother. What's the harm? I tell you, Miss Abbott, it's one thing for England and another for Italy. There we plan and get on high moral horses. Here we find what asses we are, for things go off quite easily, all by themselves. My hat, what a night! Did you ever see a really purple sky and really silver stars before? Well, as I was saying, it's absurd to worry; he's not a pawky father. He wants that baby as little as I do. He's been ragging my dear mother—just as he ragged me eighteen months ago, and I've forgiven him. Oh, but he has a sense of humour!"

Miss Abbott, too, had had a wonderful evening, nor did she ever remember such stars or such a sky. Her head, too, was full of music, and that night when she opened the window her room was filled with warm sweet air. She was bathed in beauty within and without; she could not go to bed for happiness. Had she ever been so happy before? Yes, once before, and here, a night in March, the night Gino and Lilia had told her of their love—the night whose evil she had come now to undo.

She gave a sudden cry of shame. "This time—the same place—the same thing"—and she began to beat down her happiness, knowing it to be sinful. She was here to fight against this place, to rescue a little soul who was innocent as yet. She was here to champion morality and purity, and the holy life of an English home. In the spring she had sinned through ignorance; she was not ignorant now. "Help me!" she cried, and shut the window as if there was magic in the

98

encircling air. But the tunes would not go out of her head, and all night long she was troubled by torrents of music, and by applause and laughter, and angry young men who shouted the distich out of Baedeker:

> Poggibonizzi, fatti in là,
> Che Monteriano si fa città!

Poggibonsi was revealed to her as they sang—a joyless, straggling place, full of people who pretended. When she woke up she knew that it had been Sawston.

# Chapter 7

At about nine o'clock next morning Perfetta went out onto the loggia, not to look at the view, but to throw some dirty water at it. "Scuse tante!" she wailed, for the water spattered a tall young lady who had for some time been tapping at the lower door.

"Is Signor Carella in?" the young lady asked. It was no business of Perfetta's to be shocked, and the style of the visitor seemed to demand the reception-room. Accordingly she opened its shutters, dusted a round patch on one of the horsehair chairs, and bade the lady do herself the inconvenience of sitting down. Then she ran into Monteriano and shouted up and down its streets until such time as her young master should hear her.

The reception-room was sacred to the dead wife. Her shiny portrait hung upon the wall—similar, doubtless, in all respects to the one which would be pasted on her tombstone. A little piece of black drapery had been tacked above the frame to lend a dignity to woe. But two of the tacks had fallen out, and the effect was now rakish, as of a drunkard's bonnet. A coon song lay open on the piano, and of the two tables one supported Baedeker's *Central Italy*, the other Harriet's inlaid box. And over everything there lay a deposit of heavy white dust, which was only blown off one memento to thicken on another. It is well to be remembered with love. It is not so very dreadful to be forgotten entirely. But, if we shall resent anything on earth at all, we shall resent the consecration of a deserted room.

Miss Abbott did not sit down, partly because the antimacassars might harbour fleas, partly because she had suddenly felt faint, and was glad to cling onto the funnel of the stove. She struggled with herself, for she had need to be very calm; only if she was very calm might her behaviour be justified. She had broken faith with Philip and Harriet: she was going to try for the baby before they did. If she failed she could scarcely look them in the face again.

"Harriet and her brother," she reasoned, "don't realize what is before them. She would bluster and be rude; he would be pleasant and take it as a joke. Both of them— even if they offered money—would fail. But I begin to understand the man's nature: he does not love the child, but he will be touchy about it—and that is quite as bad for us. He's charming, but he's no fool; he conquered me last year; he conquered Mr Herriton yesterday, and if I am not careful he will conquer us all today, and the baby will grow up in Monteriano. He is terribly strong; Lilia found that out, but only I remember it now."

This attempt, and this justification of it, were the results of the long and restless night. Miss Abbott had come to believe that she alone could do battle with Gino, because she alone understood him; and she had put this, as nicely as she could, in a note which she had left for Philip. It distressed her to write such a note, partly because her education inclined her to reverence the male, partly because she had got to like Philip a good deal after their last strange interview. His pettiness could be dispersed, and as for his "unconventionality", which was so much gossiped about at Sawston, she began to see that it did not differ greatly from certain familiar notions of her own. If only he would forgive her for what she was doing now, there might perhaps lie before them a long and profitable friendship. But she must succeed. No one would forgive her if she did not succeed. She prepared to do battle with the powers of evil.

The voice of her adversary was heard at last, singing fearlessly from his expanded lungs, like a professional. Herein he differed from Englishmen, who always have a little feeling against music, and sing only from the throat, apologetically. He padded upstairs, and looked in at the open door of the reception-room without seeing her. Her heart leapt and her throat was dry when he turned away and passed, still singing, into the room opposite. It is alarming not to be seen.

He had left the door of this room open, and she could see into it, right across the landing. It was in a shocking mess. Food, bedclothes, patent-leather boots, dirty plates and knives, lay strewn over a large table and on the floor. But it was the mess that comes of life, not of desolation. It was preferable to the charnel-chamber in which she was standing now, and the light in it was soft and large, as from some gracious noble opening.

He stopped singing, and cried, "Where is Perfetta?"

His back was turned and he was lighting a cigar. He was not speaking to Miss Abbott. He could not even be expecting her. The vista of the landing and the two open doors made him both remote and significant, like an actor on the stage, intimate and unapproachable at the same time. She could no more call out to him than if he was Hamlet.

"You know!" he continued. "But you will not tell me. Exactly like you." He reclined on the table and blew a fat smoke-ring. "And why won't you tell me the numbers? I have dreamt of a red hen—that is two hundred and five, and a friend unexpected—he means eighty-two. But I try for the *terno* this week. So tell me another number."

Miss Abbott did not know of the *tombola*. His speech terrified her. She felt those subtle restrictions which come upon us in fatigue. Had she slept well she would have greeted him as soon as she saw him. Now it was impossible. He had got into another world.

She watched his smoke-ring. The air had carried it slowly away from him, and brought it out intact upon the landing.

"Two hundred and five—eighty-two. In any case I shall put them on Bari, not on Florence. I cannot tell you why; I have a feeling this week for Bari." Again she tried to speak. But the ring mesmerized her. It had become vast and elliptical, and floated in at the reception-room door.

"Ah! you don't care, if you get the profits. You won't even say, 'Thank you, Gino.' Say it, or I'll drop hot, red-hot ashes on you. 'Thank you, Gino—' "

The ring had extended its pale blue coils towards her. She lost self-control. It enveloped her. As if it was a breath from the pit, she screamed.

There he was, wanting to know what had frightened her, how she had got here, why she had never spoken. He made her sit down. He brought her wine, which she refused. She had not one word to say to him.

"What is it?" he repeated. "What has frightened you?"

He, too, was frightened, and perspiration came starting through the tan. For it is a serious thing to have been watched. We all radiate something curiously intimate when we believe ourselves to be alone.

"Business—" she said at last.

"Business with me?"

"Most important business." She was lying, white and limp, in the dusty chair.

"Before business you must get well; this is the best wine."

She refused it feebly. He poured out a glass. She drank it. As she did so she became self-conscious. However important the business, it was not proper of her to have called on him, or to accept his hospitality.

"Perhaps you are engaged," she said. "And as I am not very well—"

"You are not well enough to go back. And I am not engaged."

She looked nervously at the other room.

"Ah, now I understand," he exclaimed. "Now I see what frightened you. But why did you never speak?" And taking her into the room where he lived, he pointed to—the baby.

She had thought so much about this baby, of its welfare, its soul, its morals, its probable defects. But, like most unmarried people, she had only thought of it as a word —just as the healthy man only thinks of the word death, not of death itself. The real thing, lying asleep on a dirty rug, disconcerted her. It did not stand for a principle any longer. It was so much flesh and blood, so many inches and ounces of life—a glorious, unquestionable fact, which a man and another woman had given to the world. You could talk to it; in time it would answer you; in time it would not answer you unless it chose, but would secrete, within the compass of its body, thoughts and wonderful passions of its own. And this was the machine on which she and Mrs Herriton and Philip and Harriet had for the last month been exercising their various ideals—had determined that in time it should move this way or that way, should accomplish this and not that. It was to be Low Church, it was to be high-principled, it was to be tactful, gentlemanly, artistic—excellent things all. Yet now that she saw this baby, lying asleep on a dirty rug, she had a great disposition not to dictate one of them, and to exert no more influence than there may be in a kiss or in the vaguest of the heartfelt prayers.

But she had practised self-discipline, and her thoughts and actions were not yet to correspond. To recover her self-esteem she tried to imagine that she was in her district, and to behave accordingly.

"What a fine child, Signor Carella. And how nice of you to talk to it. Though I see that the ungrateful little fellow is asleep! Seven months? No, eight; of course eight. Still, he is a remarkably fine child for his age."

Italian is a bad medium for condescension. The patronizing words came out gracious and sincere, and he smiled with pleasure.

"You must not stand. Let us sit on the loggia, where it is cool. I am afraid the room is very untidy," he added, with the air of a hostess who apologizes for a stray thread on the drawing-room carpet. Miss Abbott picked her way to the chair. He sat near her, astride the parapet, with one foot in the loggia and the other dangling into the view. His face was in profile, and its beautiful contours drove artfully against the misty green of the opposing hills. "Posing!" said Miss Abbott to herself. "A born artist's model."

"Mr Herriton called yesterday," she began, "but you were out."

He started an elaborate and graceful explanation. He had gone for the day to Poggibonsi. Why had the Herritons not written to him, so that he could have received them properly? Poggibonsi would have done any day; not but what his business there was fairly important. What did she suppose that it was?

Naturally she was not greatly interested. She had not come from Sawston to guess why he had been to Poggibonsi. She answered politely that she had no idea, and returned to her mission.

"But guess!" he persisted, clapping the balustrade between his hands.

She suggested, with gentle sarcasm, that perhaps he had gone to Poggibonsi to find something to do.

He intimated that it was not as important as all that. Something to do—an almost hopeless quest! "E manca questo!" He rubbed his thumb and forefinger together, to indicate that he had no money. Then he sighed, and blew another smoke-ring. Miss Abbott took heart and turned diplomatic.

"This house," she said, "is a large house."

"Exactly," was his gloomy reply. "And when my poor wife died—" He got up, went in, and walked across the landing to the reception-room door, which he closed reverently. Then he shut the door of the living-room with his foot, returned briskly to his seat, and continued his sentence. "When my poor wife died I thought of having my relatives to live here. My father wished to give up his practice at Empoli; my mother and sisters and two aunts were also willing. But it was impossible. They have their ways of doing things, and when I was younger I was content with them. But now I am a man. I have my own ways. Do you understand?"

"Yes, I do," said Miss Abbott, thinking of her own dear father, whose tricks and habits, after twenty-five years spent in their company, were beginning to get on her nerves. She remembered, though, that she was not here to sympathize with Gino—at all events, not to show that she sympathized. She also reminded herself that he was not worthy of sympathy. "It is a large house," she repeated.

"Immense; and the taxes! But it will be better when—Ah! but you have never guessed why I went to Poggibonsi—why it was that I was out when he called."

"I cannot guess, Signor Carella. I am here on business."

"But try."

"I cannot; I hardly know you."

"But we are old friends," he said, "and your approval will be grateful to me. You gave it me once before. Will you give it now?"

"I have not come as a friend this time," she answered stiffly. "I am not likely, Signor Carella, to approve of anything you do."

"Oh, Signorina!" He laughed, as if he found her piquante and amusing. "Surely you approve of marriage?"

"Where there is love," said Miss Abbott, looking at him hard. His face had altered in the last year, but not for the worse, which was baffling.

"Where there is love," said he, politely echoing the English view. Then he smiled on her, expecting congratulations.

"Do I understand that you are proposing to marry again?"

He nodded.

"I forbid you, then!"

He looked puzzled, but took it for some foreign banter, and laughed.

"I forbid you!" repeated Miss Abbott, and all the indignation of her sex and her nationality went thrilling through the words.

"But why?" He jumped up, frowning. His voice was squeaky and petulant, like that of a child who is suddenly forbidden a toy.

"You have ruined one woman; I forbid you to ruin another. It is not a year since Lilia died. You pretended to me the other day that you loved her. It is a lie. You wanted her money. Has this woman money too?"

"Why, yes!" he said irritably. "A little."

"And I suppose you will say that you love her."

"I shall not say it. It will be untrue. Now my poor wife—" He stopped, seeing that the comparison would involve him in difficulties. And indeed he had often found Lilia as agreeable as anyone else.

Miss Abbott was furious at this final insult to her dead acquaintance. She was glad that after all she could be so angry with the boy. She glowed and throbbed; her tongue moved nimbly. At the finish, if the real business of the day had been completed, she could have swept majestically from the house. But the baby still remained, asleep on a dirty rug.

Gino was thoughtful, and stood scratching his head. He respected Miss Abbott. He wished that she would respect him. "So you do not advise me?" he said dolefully. "But why should it be a failure?"

Miss Abbott tried to remember that he was really a child still—a child with the strength and the passions of a disreputable man. "How can it succeed," she said solemnly, "where there is no love?"

"But she does love me! I forgot to tell you that."

"Indeed."

"Passionately." He laid his hand upon his own heart.

"Then God help her!"

He stamped impatiently. "Whatever I say displeases you, signorina. God help you, for you are most unfair. You say that I ill-treated my dear wife. It is not so. I have never ill-treated anyone. You complain that there is no love in this marriage. I prove that there is, and you become still more angry. What do you want? Do you suppose she will not be contented? Glad enough she is to get me, and she will do her duty well."

"Her duty!" cried Miss Abbott, with all the bitterness of which she was capable.

"Why, of course. She knows why I am marrying her."

"To succeed where Lilia failed! To be your housekeeper, your slave, your—" The words she would like to have said were too violent for her.

"To look after the baby, certainly," said he.

"The baby—?" She had forgotten it.

"It is an English marriage," he said proudly. "I do not care about the money. I am having her for my son. Did you not understand that?"

"No," said Miss Abbott, utterly bewildered. Then for a moment, she saw light. "It is not necessary, Signor Carella. Since you are tired of the baby—"

Ever after she remembered it to her credit that she saw her mistake at once. "I don't mean that," she added quickly.

"I know," was his courteous response. "Ah, in a foreign language (and how perfectly you speak Italian) one is certain to make slips."

She looked at his face. It was apparently innocent of satire.

"You meant that we could not always be together yet, he and I. You are right. What is to be done? I cannot afford a nurse, and Perfetta is too rough. When he was ill I dare not let her touch him. When he has to be washed, which happens now and then, who does it? I. I feed him, or settle what he shall have. I sleep with him and comfort him when he is unhappy in the night. No one talks, no one may sing to him but I. Do not be unfair this time; I like to do these things. But nevertheless" (his voice became pathetic) "they take up a great deal of time, and are not all suitable for a young man."

"Not at all suitable," said Miss Abbott, and closed her eyes wearily. Each moment her difficulties were increasing. She wished that she was not so tired, so open to contradictory impressions. She longed for Harriet's burly obtuseness or for the soulless diplomacy of Mrs Herriton.

"A little more wine?" asked Gino kindly.

"Oh no, thank you! But marriage, Signor Carella, is a very serious step. Could you not manage more simply? Your relatives, for example—"

"Empoli! I would as soon have him in England!"

"England, then—"

He laughed.

"He has a grandmother there, you know—Mrs Theobald."

"He has a grandmother here. No, he is troublesome, but I must have him with me. I will not even have my father and mother too. For they would separate us," he added.

"How?"

"They would separate our thoughts."

She was silent. This cruel, vicious fellow knew of strange refinements. The horrible truth, that wicked people are capable of love, stood naked before her, and her moral being was abashed. It was her duty to rescue the baby, to save it from contagion, and she still meant to do her duty. But the comfortable sense of virtue left her. She was in the presence of something greater than right or wrong.

Forgetting that this was an interview, he had strolled back into the room, driven by the instinct she had aroused in him. "Wake up!" he cried to his baby, as if it was some grown-up friend. Then he lifted his foot and trod lightly on its stomach.

Miss Abbott cried, "Oh, take care!" She was unaccustomed to this method of awakening the young.

"He is not much longer than my boot, is he? Can you believe that in time his own boots will be as large? And that he also—"

"But ought you to treat him like that?"

He stood with one foot resting on the little body, suddenly musing, filled with the desire that his son should be like him, and should have sons like him, to people the earth. It is the strongest desire that can come to a man—if it comes to him at all—stronger even than love or the desire for personal immortality. All men vaunt it, and declare that it is theirs; but the hearts of most are set elsewhere. It is the exception who comprehends that physical and spiritual life may stream out of him for ever. Miss Abbott, for all her goodness, could not comprehend it, though such a thing is more within the comprehension of women. And when Gino pointed first to himself and then to his baby, and said "Father—son," she still took it as a piece of nursery prattle, and smiled mechanically.

The child, the first-fruits, woke up and glared at her.

Gino did not greet it, but continued the exposition of his policy.

"This woman will do exactly what I tell her. She is fond of children. She is clean; she has a pleasant voice. She is not beautiful; I cannot pretend that to you for a moment. But she is what I require."

The baby gave a piercing yell.

"Oh, do take care!" begged Miss Abbott. "You are squeezing it."

"It is nothing. If he cries silently then you may be frightened. He thinks I am going to wash him, and he is quite right."

"Wash him!" she cried. "You? Here?" The homely piece of news seemed to shatter all her plans. She had spent a long half-hour in elaborate approaches, in high moral attacks; she had neither frightened her enemy nor made him angry, nor interfered with the least detail of his domestic life.

"I had gone to the *farmacia*," he continued, "and was sitting there comfortably, when suddenly I remembered that Perfetta had heated water an hour ago—over there, look, covered with a cushion. I came away at once, for really he must be washed. You must excuse me. I can put it off no longer."

"I have wasted your time," she said feebly.

He walked sternly to the loggia and drew from it a large earthenware bowl. It was dirty inside; he dusted it with a tablecloth. Then he fetched the hot water, which was in a copper pot. He poured it out. He added cold. He felt in his pocket and brought out a piece of soap. Then he took up the baby, and, holding his cigar between his teeth, began to unwrap it. Miss Abbott turned to go.

"But why are you going? Excuse me if I wash him while we talk."

"I have nothing more to say," said Miss Abbott. All she could do now was to find Philip, confess her miserable defeat, and bid him go in her stead and prosper better. She cursed her feebleness; she longed to expose it, without apologies or tears.

"Oh, but stop a moment!" he cried. "You have not seen him yet."

"I have seen as much as I want, thank you."

The last wrapping slid off. He held out to her in his two hands a little kicking image of bronze.

"Take him!"

She would not touch the child.

"I must go at once," she cried; for the tears—the wrong tears—were hurrying to her eyes.

"Who would have believed his mother was blonde? For he is brown all over—brown every inch of him. Ah, but how beautiful he is! And he is mine; mine for ever. Even if he hates me he will be mine. He cannot help it; he is made out of me; I am his father."

It was too late to go. She could not tell why, but it was too late. She turned away her head when Gino lifted his son to his lips. This was something too remote from the prettiness of the nursery. The man was majestic; he was a part of Nature; in no ordinary love scene could he ever be so great. For a wonderful physical tie binds the parents to the children; and—by some sad, strange irony—it does not bind us children to our parents. For if it did, if we could answer their love not with gratitude but with equal love, life would lose much of its pathos and much of its squalor, and we might be wonderfully happy. Gino passionately embracing, Miss Abbott reverently averting her eyes—both of them had parents whom they did not love so very much.

"May I help you to wash him?" she asked humbly.

He gave her his son without speaking, and they knelt side by side, tucking up their sleeves. The child had stopped crying, and his arms and legs were agitated by some overpowering joy. Miss Abbott had a woman's pleasure in cleaning anything—more especially when the thing was human. She understood little babies from long experience in a district, and Gino soon ceased to give her directions, and only gave her thanks.

"It is very kind of you," he murmured, "especially in your beautiful dress. He is nearly clean already. Why, I take the whole morning! There is so much more of a baby than one expects. And Perfetta washes him just as she washes clothes. Then he screams for hours. My wife is to have a light hand. Ah, how he kicks! Has he splashed you? I am very sorry."

"I am ready for a soft towel now," said Miss Abbott, who was strangely exalted by the service.

"Certainly! Certainly!" He strode in a knowing way to a cupboard. But he had no idea where the soft towel was. Generally he dabbed the baby on the first dry thing he found.

"And if you had any powder."

He struck his forehead despairingly. Apparently the stock of powder was just exhausted.

She sacrificed her own clean handkerchief. He put a chair for her on the loggia, which faced westward, and was still pleasant and cool. There she sat, with twenty miles of view behind her, and he placed the dripping baby on her knee. It shone now with health and beauty; it seemed to reflect light, like a copper vessel. Just such a baby Bellini sets languid on his mother's lap, or Signorelli flings wriggling on pavements of marble, or Lorenzo di Credi, more reverent but less divine, lays carefully among flowers, with his head upon a wisp of golden straw. For a time Gino contemplated them standing. Then, to get a better view, he knelt by the side of the chair, with his hands clasped before him.

So they were when Philip entered, and saw, to all intents and purposes, the Virgin and Child, with Donor.

"Hallo!" he exclaimed; for he was glad to find things in such cheerful trim.

She did not greet him, but rose up unsteadily and handed the baby to his father.

"No, do stop!" whispered Philip. "I got your note. I'm not offended; you're quite right. I really want you; I could never have done it alone."

No words came from her, but she raised her hands to her mouth, like one who is in sudden agony.

"Signorina, do stop a little—after all your kindness."

She burst into tears.

"What is it?" said Philip kindly.

She tried to speak, and then went away, weeping bitterly.

The two men stared at each other. By a common impulse they ran onto the loggia. They were just in time to see Miss Abbott disappear among the trees.

"What is it?" asked Philip again. There was no answer, and somehow he did not want an answer. Some strange thing had happened which he could not presume to understand. He would find out from Miss Abbott, if ever he found out at all.

"Well, our business," said Gino, after a puzzled sigh.

"Our business—Miss Abbott has told you of that."

"No."

"But surely—"

"She came for business. But she forgot about it; so did I."

Perfetta, who had a genius for missing people, now returned, loudly complaining of the size of Monteriano and the intricacies of its streets. Gino told her to watch the baby. Then he offered Philip a cigar, and they proceeded to the business.

# Chapter 8

"Mad!" screamed Harriet—"absolutely stark, staring, raving mad!"

Philip judged it better not to contradict her.

"What's she here for? Answer me that. What's she doing in Monteriano in August? Why isn't she in Normandy? Answer that. She won't. I can: she's come to thwart us; she's betrayed us—got hold of mother's plans. Oh, goodness, my head!"

He was unwise enough to reply: "You mustn't accuse her of that. Though she is exasperating, she hasn't come here to betray us."

"Then why has she come here? Answer me that."

He made no answer. But fortunately his sister was too much agitated to wait for one. "Bursting in on me—crying and looking a disgusting sight—and says she has been to see the Italian. Couldn't even talk properly; pretended she had changed her opinions. What are her opinions to us? I was very calm. I said: 'Miss Abbott, I think there is a little misapprehension in this matter. My mother, Mrs Herriton—' Oh, goodness, my head! Of course you've failed—don't trouble to answer—I know you've failed. Where's the baby, pray? Of course you haven't got it. Dear sweet Caroline won't let you. Oh yes, and we're to go away at once and trouble the father no more. Those are her commands. Commands! COMMANDS!" And Harriet also burst into tears.

Philip governed his temper. His sister was annoying, but quite reasonable in her indignation. Moreover, Miss Abbott had behaved even worse than she supposed.

"I've not got the baby, Harriet, but at the same time I haven't exactly failed. I and Signor Carella are to have

114

another interview this afternoon, at the Caffè Garibaldi. He is perfectly reasonable and pleasant. Should you be disposed to come with me, you would find him quite willing to discuss things. He is desperately in want of money, and has no prospect of getting any. I discovered that. At the same time, he has a certain affection for the child." For Philip's insight, or perhaps his opportunities, had not been equal to Miss Abbott's.

Harriet would only sob, and accuse her brother of insulting her; how could a lady speak to such a horrible man? That, and nothing else, was enough to stamp Caroline. Oh, poor Lilia!

Philip drummed on the bedroom window-sill. He saw no escape from the deadlock. For though he spoke cheerfully about his second interview with Gino he felt at the bottom of his heart that it would fail. Gino was too courteous; he would not break off negotiations by a sharp denial; he loved this civil, half-humorous bargaining. And he loved fooling his opponent, and did it so nicely that his opponent did not mind being fooled.

"Miss Abbott has behaved extraordinarily," he said at last; "but at the same time—"

His sister would not hear him. She burst forth again on the madness, the interference, the intolerable duplicity of Caroline.

"Harriet, you must listen. My dear, you must stop crying. I have something quite important to say."

"I shall not stop crying," said she. But in time, finding that he would not speak to her, she did stop.

"Remember that Miss Abbott has done us no harm. She said nothing to him about the matter. He assumes that she is working with us; I gathered that."

"Well, she isn't."

"Yes; but if you're careful she may be. I interpret her behaviour thus: she went to see him, honestly intending to get the child away. In the note she left me she says so, and I don't believe she'd lie."

"I do."

"When she got there, there was some pretty domestic scene between him and the baby, and she has got swept off in a gush of sentimentalism. Before very long, if I know anything about psychology, there will be a reaction. She'll be swept back."

"I don't understand your long words. Say plainly—"

"When she's swept back, she'll be invaluable. For she has made quite an impression on him. He thinks her so nice with the baby. You know, she washed it for him."

"Disgusting!"

Harriet's ejaculations were more aggravating than the rest of her. But Philip was averse to losing his temper. The access of joy that had come to him yesterday in the theatre promised to be permanent. He was more anxious than heretofore to be charitable towards the world.

"If you want to carry off the baby, keep your peace with Miss Abbott. For if she chooses she can help you better than I can."

"There can be no peace between me and her," said Harriet gloomily.

"Did you—?"

"Oh, not all I wanted. She went away before I had finished speaking—just like those cowardly people!—into the church."

"Into Santa Deodata's?"

"Yes; I'm sure she needs it. Anything more unchristian—"

In time Philip went to the church also, leaving his sister a little calmer and a little disposed to think over his advice. What had come over Miss Abbott? He had always thought her both stable and sincere. That conversation he had had with her last Christmas in the train to Charing Cross—that alone furnished him with a parallel. For the second time, Monteriano must have turned her head. He was not angry with her, for he was quite indifferent to the outcome of their expedition. He was only extremely interested.

It was now nearly midday, and the streets were clearing. But the intense heat had broken, and there was a pleasant suggestion of rain. The Piazza with its three great attractions

—the Palazzo Pubblico, the Collegiate Church, and the Caffè Garibaldi: the intellect, the soul, and the body—had never looked more charming. For a moment Philip stood in its centre, much inclined to be dreamy, and thinking how wonderful it must feel to belong to a city, however mean. He was here, however, as an emissary of civilization and as a student of character, and, after a sigh, he entered Santa Deodata's to continue his mission.

There had been a *festa* two days before, and the church still smelt of incense and of garlic. The little son of the sacristan was sweeping the nave, more for amusement than for cleanliness, sending great clouds of dust over the frescoes and the scattered worshippers. The sacristan himself had propped a ladder in the centre of the Deluge—which fills one of the nave spandrels—and was freeing a column from its wealth of scarlet calico. Much scarlet calico also lay upon the floor—for the church can look as fine as any theatre— and the sacristan's little daughter was trying to fold it up. She was wearing a tinsel crown. The crown really belonged to St Augustine. But it had been cut too big: it fell down over his cheeks like a collar—you never saw anything so absurd. One of the canons had unhooked it just before the *festa* began, and had given it to the sacristan's daughter.

"Please," cried Philip, "is there an English lady here?"

The man's mouth was full of tin-tacks, but he nodded cheerfully towards a kneeling figure. In the midst of this confusion Miss Abbott was praying.

He was not much surprised; a spiritual breakdown was quite to be expected. For though he was growing more charitable towards mankind he was still a little jaunty, and too apt to stake out beforehand the course that will be pursued by the wounded soul. It did surprise him, however, that she should greet him naturally, with none of the sour self-consciousness of a person who had just risen from her knees. This was indeed the spirit of Santa Deodata's, where a prayer to God is thought none the worse of because it comes next to a pleasant word to a neighbour. "I am sure that I need it," said she; and he, who had expected her to be ashamed, became confused, and knew not what to reply.

"I've nothing to tell you," she continued. "I have simply changed straight round. If I had planned the whole thing out, I could not have treated you worse. I can talk it over now; but please believe that I have been crying."

"And please believe that I have not come to scold you," said Philip. "I know what has happened."

"What?" asked Miss Abbott. Instinctively she led the way to the famous chapel, the fifth chapel on the right, wherein Giovanni da Empoli has painted the death and burial of the saint. Here they could sit out of the dust and the noise, and proceed with a discussion which promised to be important.

"What might have happened to me—he has made you believe that he loves the child."

"Oh yes; he has. He will never give it up."

"At present it is still unsettled."

"It will never be settled."

"Perhaps not. Well, as I said, I know what has happened, and I am not here to scold you. But I must ask you to withdraw from the thing for the present. Harriet is furious. But she will calm down when she realizes that you have done us no harm, and will do none."

"I can do no more," she said. "But I tell you plainly I have changed sides."

"If you do no more, that is all we want. You promise not to prejudice our cause by speaking to Signor Carella?"

"Oh, certainly. I don't want to speak to him again; I shan't ever see him again."

"Quite nice, wasn't he?"

"Quite."

"Well, that's all I wanted to know. I'll go and tell Harriet of your promise, and I think things'll quiet down now."

But he did not move, for it was an increasing pleasure to him to be near her, and her charm was at its strongest today. He thought less of psychology and feminine reaction. The gush of sentimentalism which had carried her away had only made her more alluring. He was content to observe her beauty and to profit by the tenderness and the wisdom that dwelt within her.

"Why aren't you angry with me?" she asked, after a pause.

"Because I understand you—all sides, I think—Harriet, Signor Carella, even my mother."

"You do understand wonderfully. You are the only one of us who has a general view of the muddle."

He smiled with pleasure. It was the first time she had ever praised him. His eyes rested agreeably on Santa Deodata, who was dying in full sanctity, upon her back. There was a window open behind her, revealing just such a view as he had seen that morning, and on her widowed mother's dresser there stood just such another copper pot. The saint looked neither at the view nor at the pot, and at her widowed mother still less. For lo! she had a vision: the head and shoulders of St Augustine were sliding like some miraculous enamel along the roughcast wall. It is a gentle saint who is content with half another saint to see her die. In her death, as in her life, Santa Deodata did not accomplish much.

"So what are you going to do?" said Miss Abbott.

Philip started, not so much at the words as at the sudden change in the voice. "Do?" he echoed, rather dismayed. "This afternoon I have another interview."

"It will come to nothing. Well?"

"Then another. If that fails I shall wire home for instructions. I dare say we may fail altogether, but we shall fail honourably."

She had often been decided. But now behind her decision there was a note of passion. She struck him not as different, but as more important, and he minded it very much when she said:

"That's not doing anything! You would be doing something if you kidnapped the baby, or if you went straight away. But that! To fail honourably! To come out of the thing as well as you can! Is that all you are after?"

"Why, yes," he stammered. "Since we talk openly, that

is all I am after just now. What else is there? If I can persuade Signor Carella to give in, so much the better. If he won't, I must report the failure to my mother, and then go home. Why, Miss Abbott, you can't expect me to follow you through all these turns—"

"I don't! But I do expect you to settle what is right and to follow that. Do you want the child to stop with his father, who loves him and will bring him up badly, or do you want him to come to Sawston, where no one loves him, but where he will be brought up well? There is the question put dispassionately enough even for you. Settle it. Settle which side you'll fight on. But don't go talking about an 'honourable failure', which means simply not thinking and not acting at all."

"Because I understand the position of Signor Carella and of you, it's no reason that—"

"None at all. Fight us if you think us wrong. Oh, what's the use of your fairmindedness if you never decide for yourself? Anyone gets hold of you and makes you do what they want. And you see through them and laugh at them—and do it. It's not enough to see clearly; I'm muddle-headed and stupid, and not worth a quarter of you, but I have tried to do what seemed right at the time. And you—your brain and your insight are splendid. But when you see what's right you're too idle to do it. You told me once that we shall be judged by our intentions, not by our accomplishments. I thought it a grand remark. But we must intend to accomplish—not sit intending on a chair."

"You are wonderful!" he said gravely.

"Oh, you appreciate me!" she burst out again. "I wish you didn't. You appreciate us all—see good in all of us. And all the time you are dead—dead—dead. Look, why aren't you angry?" She came up to him, and then her mood suddenly changed, and she took hold of both his hands. "You are so splendid, Mr Herriton, that I can't bear to see you wasted. I can't bear—she has not been good to you—your mother."

"Miss Abbott, don't worry over me. Some people are born

120

not to do things. I'm one of them; I never did anything at school or at the Bar. I came out to stop Lilia's marriage, and it was too late. I came out intending to get the baby, and I shall return an 'honourable failure'. I never expect anything to happen now, and so I am never disappointed. You would be surprised to know what my great events are. Going to the theatre yesterday, talking to you now—I don't suppose I shall ever meet anything greater. I seem fated to pass through the world without colliding with it or moving it —and I'm sure I can't tell you whether the fate's good or evil. I don't die—I don't fall in love. And if other people die or fall in love they always do it when I'm not there. You are quite right: life to me is just a spectacle, which—thank God, and thank Italy, and thank you—is now more beautiful and heartening than it has ever been before."

She said solemnly, "I wish something would happen to you, my dear friend; I wish something would happen to you."

"But why?" he asked, smiling. "Prove to me why I don't do as I am."

She also smiled, very gravely. She could not prove it. No argument existed. Their discourse, splendid as it had been, resulted in nothing, and their respective opinions and policies were exactly the same when they left the church as when they had entered it.

Harriet was rude at lunch. She called Miss Abbott a turncoat and a coward to her face. Miss Abbott resented neither epithet, feeling that one was justified and the other not unreasonable. She tried to avoid even the suspicion of satire in her replies. But Harriet was sure that she was satirical because she was so calm. She got more and more violent, and Philip at one time feared that she would come to blows.

"Look here!" he cried, with something of the old manner, "it's too hot for this. We've been talking and interviewing each other all the morning, and I have another interview this afternoon. I do stipulate for silence. Let each lady retire to her bedroom with a book."

"I retire to pack," said Harriet. "Please remind Signor

Carella, Philip, that the baby is to be here by half-past eight this evening."

"Oh, certainly, Harriet. I shall make a point of reminding him."

"And order a carriage to take us to the evening train."

"And please," said Miss Abbott, "would you order a carriage for me too?"

"You going!" he exclaimed.

"Of course," she replied, suddenly flushing. "Why not?"

"Why, of course you would be going. Two carriages, then. Two carriages for the evening train." He looked at his sister hopelessly. "Harriet, what ever are you up to? We shall never be ready."

"Order my carriage for the evening train," said Harriet, and departed.

"Well, I suppose I shall. And I shall also have my interview with Signor Carella."

Miss Abbott gave a little sigh.

"But why should you mind? Do you suppose that I shall have the slightest influence over him?"

"No. But—I can't repeat all that I said in the church. You ought never to see him again. You ought to bundle Harriet into a carriage, not this evening, but now, and drive her straight away."

"Perhaps I ought. But it isn't a very big 'ought'. Whatever Harriet and I do, the issue is the same. Why, I can see the splendour of it—even the humour. Gino sitting up here on the mountain top with his cub. We come and ask for it. He welcomes us. We ask for it again. He is equally pleasant. I'm agreeable to spend the whole week bargaining with him. But I know that at the end of it I shall descend empty-handed to the plains. It might be finer of me to make up my mind. But I'm not a fine character. And nothing hangs on it."

"Perhaps I am extreme," she said humbly. "I've been trying to run you, just like your mother. I feel you ought to fight it out with Harriet. Every little trifle, for some reason, does seem incalculably important today, and when you say of a thing that 'nothing hangs on it' it sounds like blasphemy. There's never any knowing—how am I to put it?—which of our actions, which of our idlenesses won't have things hanging on it for ever."

He assented, but her remark had only an aesthetic value. He was not prepared to take it to his heart. All the afternoon he rested—worried, but not exactly despondent. The thing would jog out somehow. Probably Miss Abbott was right. The baby had better stop where it was loved. And that, probably, was what the fates had decreed. He felt little interest in the matter, and he was sure that he had no influence.

It was not surprising, therefore, that the interview at the Caffè Garibaldi came to nothing. Neither of them took it very seriously. And before long Gino had discovered how things lay, and was ragging his companion hopelessly. Philip tried to look offended, but in the end he had to laugh. "Well, you are right," he said. "The affair *is* being managed by the ladies."

"Ah, the ladies—the ladies!" cried the other, and then he roared like a millionaire for two cups of black coffee, and insisted on treating his friend, as a sign that their strife was over.

"Well, I have done my best," said Philip, dipping a long slice of sugar into his cup, and watching the brown liquid ascend into it. "I shall face my mother with a good conscience. Will you bear me witness that I've done my best?"

"My poor fellow, I will!" He laid a sympathetic hand on Philip's knee.

"And that I have—" The sugar was now impregnated with coffee, and he bent forward to swallow it. As he did so his eyes swept the opposite side of the Piazza, and he saw there, watching them, Harriet. "Mia sorella!" he exclaimed. Gino, much amused, laid his head upon the little table, and beat the marble humorously with his fists. Harriet turned away and began gloomily to inspect the Palazzo Pubblico.

"Poor Harriet!" said Philip, swallowing the sugar. "One more wrench and it will all be over for her; we are leaving this evening."

Gino was sorry for this. "Then you will not be here this evening as you promised us. All three leaving?"

"All three," said Philip, who had not revealed the secession of Miss Abbott; "by the night train; at least, that is my sister's plan. So I'm afraid I shan't be here."

They watched the departing figure of Harriet, and then entered upon the final civilities. They shook each other warmly by both hands. Philip was to come again next year, and to write beforehand. He was to be introduced to Gino's wife, for he was told of the marriage now. He was to be god-father to his next baby. As for Gino, he would remember some time that Philip liked vermouth. He begged him to give his love to Irma. Mrs Herriton—should he send her his sympathetic regards? No; perhaps that would hardly do.

So the two young men parted with a good deal of genuine affection. For the barrier of language is sometimes a blessed barrier, which only lets pass what is good. Or—to put the thing less cynically—we may be better in new clean words, which have never been tainted by our pettiness or vice. Philip, at all events, lived more graciously in Italian, the very phrases of which entice one to be happy and kind. It was horrible to think of the English of Harriet, whose every word would be as hard, as distinct and as unfinished as a lump of coal.

Harriet, however, talked little. She had seen enough to know that her brother had failed again, and with unwonted dignity she accepted the situation. She did her packing, she wrote up her diary, she made a brown paper cover for the new Baedeker. Philip, finding her so amenable, tried to discuss their future plans. But she only said that they would sleep in Florence, and told him to telegraph for rooms. They had supper alone. Miss Abbott did not come down. The landlady told them that Signor Carella had called on Miss Abbott to say goodbye, but she, though in, had not been able to see him. She also told them that it had begun to rain. Harriet sighed, but indicated to her brother that he was not responsible.

The carriages came round at a quarter past eight. It was

not raining much, but the night was extraordinarily dark, and one of the drivers wanted to go slowly to the station. Miss Abbott came down and said that she was ready, and would start at once.

"Yes, do," said Philip, who was standing in the hall. "Now that we have quarrelled we scarcely want to travel in procession all the way down the hill. Well, goodbye; it's all over at last; another scene in my pageant has shifted."

"Goodbye; it's been a great pleasure to see you. I hope that won't shift, at all events." She gripped his hand.

"You sound despondent," he said, laughing. "Don't forget that you return victorious."

"I suppose I do," she replied, more despondently than ever, and got into the carriage. He concluded that she was thinking of her reception at Sawston, whither her fame would doubtless precede her. What ever would Mrs Herriton do? She could make things quite unpleasant when she thought it right. She might think it right to be silent, but then there was Harriet. Who could bridle Harriet's tongue? Between the two of them Miss Abbott was bound to have a bad time. Her reputation, both for consistency and for moral enthusiasm, would be lost for ever.

"It's hard luck on her," he thought. "She is a good person. I must do for her anything I can." Their intimacy had been very rapid, but he too hoped that it would not shift. He believed that he understood her, and that she, by now, had seen the worst of him. What if after a long time —if after all—he flushed like a boy as he looked after her carriage.

He went into the dining-room to look for Harriet. Harriet was not to be found. Her bedroom, too, was empty. All that was left of her was the purple prayerbook which lay open on the bed. Philip took it up aimlessly, and saw—"Blessed be the Lord my God, who teacheth my hands to war, and my fingers to fight." He put the book in his pocket, and began to brood over more profitable themes.

Santa Deodata gave out half past eight. All the luggage was on, and still Harriet had not appeared. "Depend upon it," said the landlady, "she has gone to Signor Carella's to say goodbye to her little nephew." Philip did not think it likely. They shouted all over the house and still there was no Harriet. He began to be uneasy. He was helpless without Miss Abbott; her grave kind face had cheered him wonderfully, even when it looked displeased. Monteriano was sad without her; the rain was thickening; the scraps of Donizetti floated tunelessly out of the wineshops, and of the great tower opposite he could only see the base, fresh papered with the advertisements of quacks.

A man came up the street with a note. Philip read: "Start at once. Pick me up outside the gate. Pay the bearer. H. H."

"Did the lady give you this note?" he cried.

The man was unintelligible.

"Speak up!" exclaimed Philip. "Who gave it you—and where?"

Nothing but horrible sighings and bubblings came out of the man.

"Be patient with him," said the driver, turning round on the box. "It is the poor idiot." And the landlady came out of the hotel and echoed: "The poor idiot. He cannot speak. He takes messages for us all."

Philip then saw that the messenger was a ghastly creature, quite bald, with trickling eyes and gray twitching nose. In any other country he would have been shut up; here he was accepted as a public institution, and part of Nature's scheme.

"Ugh!" shuddered the Englishman. "Signora padrona, find out from him; this note is from my sister. What does it mean? Where did he see her?"

"It is no good," said the landlady. "He understands everything, but he can explain nothing."

"He has visions of the saints," said the man who drove the cab.

"But my sister—where has she gone? How has she met him?"

"She has gone for a walk," asserted the landlady. It was a nasty evening, but she was beginning to understand the

English. "She has gone for a walk—perhaps to wish good-bye to her little nephew. Preferring to come back another way, she has sent you this note by the poor idiot and is waiting for you outside the Siena gate. Many of my guests do this."

There was nothing to do but to obey the message. He shook hands with the landlady, gave the messenger a nickel piece, and drove away. After a dozen yards the carriage stopped. The poor idiot was running and whimpering behind.

"Go on," cried Philip, "I have paid him plenty."

A horrible hand pushed three soldi into his lap. It was part of the idiot's malady only to receive what was just for his services. This was the change out of the nickel piece.

"Go on!" shouted Philip, and flung the money into the road. He was frightened at the episode; the whole of life had become unreal. It was a relief to be out of the Siena gate. They drew up for a moment on the terrace. But there was no sign of Harriet. The driver called to the *dogana* men. But they had seen no English lady pass.

"What am I to do?" he cried; "it is not like the lady to be late. We shall miss the train."

"Let us drive slowly," said the driver, "and you shall call her by name as we go."

So they started down into the night, Philip calling "Harriet! Harriet! Harriet!" And there she was, waiting for them in the wet, at the first turn of the zigzag.

"Harriet, why don't you answer?"

"I heard you coming," said she, and got quickly in. Not till then did he see that she carried a bundle.

"What's that?"

"Hush—"

"What ever is that?"

"Hush—sleeping."

Harriet had succeeded where Miss Abbott and Philip had failed. It was the baby.

She would not let him talk. The baby, she repeated, was asleep, and she put up an umbrella to shield it and her from the rain. He should hear all later. So he had to conjecture

127

the course of the wonderful interview—an interview between the South Pole and the North. It was quite easy to conjecture: Gino crumpling up suddenly before the intense conviction of Harriet; being told, perhaps, to his face that he was a villain; yielding his only son, perhaps for money, perhaps for nothing. "Poor Gino," he thought. "He's no greater than I am, after all."

Then he thought of Miss Abbott, whose carriage must be descending the darkness some mile or two below them, and his easy self-accusation failed. She, too, had conviction; he had felt its force; he would feel it again when she knew this day's sombre and unexpected close.

"You have been pretty secret," he said; "you might tell me a little now. What do we pay for him? All we've got?"

"Hush!" answered Harriet, and dandled the bundle laboriously, like some bony prophetess—Judith, or Deborah, or Jael. He had last seen the baby sprawling on the knees of Miss Abbott, shining and naked, with twenty miles of view behind him, and his father kneeling by his feet. And that remembrance, together with Harriet, and the darkness, and the poor idiot, and the silent rain, filled him with sorrow and with the expectation of sorrow to come.

Monteriano had long disappeared, and he could see nothing but the occasional wet stem of an olive, which their lamp illumined as they passed it. They travelled quickly, for this driver did not care how fast he went to the station, and would dash down each incline and scuttle perilously round the curves.

"Look here, Harriet," he said at last, "I feel bad; I want to see the baby."

"Hush!"

"I don't mind if I do wake him up. I want to see him. I've as much right in him as you."

Harriet gave in. But it was too dark for him to see the child's face. "Wait a minute," he whispered, and before she could stop him he had lit a match under the shelter of her umbrella. "But he's awake!" he exclaimed. The match went out.

"Good ickle quiet boysey, then."

Philip winced. "His face, do you know, struck me as all wrong."

"All wrong?"

"All puckered queerly."

"Of course—with the shadows—you couldn't see him."

"Well, hold him up again." She did so. He lit another match. It went out quickly, but not before he had seen that the baby was crying.

"Nonsense," said Harriet sharply. "We should hear him if he cried."

"No, he's crying hard; I thought so before, and I'm certain now."

Harriet touched the child's face. It was bathed in tears. "Oh, the night air, I suppose," she said, "or perhaps the wet of the rain."

"I say, you haven't hurt it, or held it the wrong way, or anything; it is too uncanny—crying and no noise. Why didn't you get Perfetta to carry it to the hotel instead of muddling with the messenger? It's a marvel he understood about the note."

"Oh, he understands." And he could feel her shudder. "He tried to carry the baby—"

"But why not Gino or Perfetta?"

"Philip, don't talk. Must I say it again? Don't talk. The baby wants to sleep." She crooned harshly as they descended, and now and then she wiped up the tears which welled inexhaustibly from the little eyes. Philip looked away, winking at times himself. It was as if they were travelling with the whole world's sorrow, as if all the mystery, all the persistency of woe were gathered to a single fount. The roads were now coated with mud, and the carriage went more quietly but not less swiftly, sliding by long zigzags into the night. He knew the landmarks pretty well: here was the cross-road to Poggibonsi; and the last view of Monteriano, if they had light, would be from here. Soon they ought to come to that little wood where violets were so plentiful in spring. He wished the weather had not changed; it was not cold, but the air was extraordinarily damp. It could not be good for the child.

"I suppose he breathes, and all that sort of thing?" he said.

"Of course," said Harriet, in an angry whisper. "You've started him again. I'm certain he was asleep. I do wish you wouldn't talk; it makes me so nervous."

"I'm nervous too. I wish he'd scream. It's too uncanny. Poor Gino! I'm terribly sorry for Gino."

"Are you?"

"Because he's weak—like most of us. He doesn't know what he wants. He doesn't grip onto life. But I like that man, and I'm sorry for him."

Naturally enough, she made no answer.

"You despise him, Harriet, and you despise me. But you do us no good by it. We fools want someone to set us on our feet. Suppose a really decent woman had set up Gino—I believe Caroline Abbott might have done it—mightn't he have been another man?"

"Philip," she interrupted, with an attempt at non-chalance, "do you happen to have those matches handy? We might as well look at the baby again if you have."

The first match blew out immediately. So did the second. He suggested that they should stop the carriage and borrow the lamp from the driver.

"Oh, I don't want all that bother. Try again."

They entered the little wood as he tried to strike the third match. At last it caught. Harriet poised the umbrella rightly, and for a full quarter-minute they contemplated the face that trembled in the light of the trembling flame. Then there was a shout and a crash. They were lying in the mud in darkness. The carriage had overturned.

Philip was a good deal hurt. He sat up and rocked himself to and fro, holding his arm. He could just make out the outline of the carriage above him, and the outlines of the carriage cushions and of their luggage upon the gray road. The accident had taken place in the wood, where it was even darker than in the open.

"Are you all right?" he managed to say. Harriet was screaming, the horse was kicking, the driver was cursing some other man.

Harriet's screams became coherent. "The baby—the baby—it slipped—it's gone from my arms! I stole it!"

"God help me!" said Philip. A cold circle came round his mouth, and he fainted.

When he recovered, it was still the same confusion. The horse was kicking, the baby had not been found, and Harriet still screamed like a maniac: "I stole it! I stole it! I stole it! It slipped out of my arms!"

"Keep still!" he commanded the driver. "Let no one move. We may tread on it. Keep still."

For a moment they all obeyed him. He began to crawl through the mud, touching first this, then that, grasping the cushions by mistake, listening for the faintest whisper that might guide him. He tried to light a match, holding the box in his teeth and striking at it with the uninjured hand. At last he succeeded, and the light fell upon the bundle which he was seeking.

It had rolled off the road into the wood a little way, and had fallen across a great rut. So tiny it was that had it fallen lengthways it would have disappeared, and he might never have found it.

"I stole it! I and the idiot—no one was there." She burst out laughing.

He sat down and laid it on his knee. Then he tried to cleanse the face from the mud and the rain and the tears. His arm, he supposed, was broken, but he could still move it a little, and for the moment he forgot all pain. He was listening—not for a cry, but for the tick of a heart or the slightest tremor of breath.

"Where are you?" called a voice. It was Miss Abbott, against whose carriage they had collided. She had re-lit one of the lamps, and was picking her way towards him.

"Silence!" he called again, and again they obeyed. He shook the bundle; he breathed into it; he opened his coat and pressed it against him. Then he listened, and heard nothing but the rain and the panting horses, and Harriet, who was somewhere chuckling to herself in the dark.

Miss Abbott approached, and took it gently from him. The face was already chilly, but thanks to Philip it was no longer wet. Nor would it again be wetted by any tear.

# Chapter 9

The details of Harriet's crime were never known. In her illness she spoke more of the inlaid box that she had lent to Lilia—lent, not given—than of recent troubles. It was clear that she had gone prepared for an interview with Gino, and, finding him out, she had yielded to a grotesque temptation. But how far this was the result of ill-temper, to what extent she had been fortified by her religion, when and how she had met the poor idiot—these questions were never answered, nor did they interest Philip greatly. Detection was certain: they would have been arrested by the police of Florence or Milan, or at the frontier. As it was, they had been stopped in a simpler manner a few miles out of the town.

As yet he could scarcely survey the thing. It was too great. Round the Italian baby who had died in the mud there centred deep passions and high hopes. People had been wicked or wrong in the matter; no one save himself had been trivial. Now the baby had gone, but there remained this vast apparatus of pride and pity and love. For the dead, who seem to take away so much, really take with them nothing that is ours. The passion they have aroused lives after them, easy to transmute or to transfer, but well-nigh impossible to destroy. And Philip knew that he was still voyaging on the same magnificent, perilous sea, with the sun or the clouds above him, and the tides below.

The course of the moment—that, at all events, was certain. He and no one else must take the news to Gino. It was easy to talk of Harriet's crime—easy also to blame the negligent Perfetta or Mrs Herriton at home. Everyone had contributed—even Miss Abbott and Irma. If one chose, one might consider the catastrophe composite or the work of fate. But Philip did not so choose. It was his own fault, due to acknowledged weakness in his own character. Therefore he, and no one else, must take the news of it to Gino.

Nothing prevented him. Miss Abbott was engaged with Harriet, and people had sprung out of the darkness and were conducting them towards some cottage. Philip had only to get into the uninjured carriage and order the driver to return. He was back at Monteriano after a two hours' absence. Perfetta was in the house now, and greeted him cheerfully. Pain, physical and mental, had made him stupid. It was some time before he realized that she had never missed the child.

Gino was still out. The woman took him to the reception-room, just as she had taken Miss Abbott in the morning, and dusted a circle for him on one of the horsehair chairs. But it was dark now, so she left the guest a little lamp.

"I will be as quick as I can," she told him. "But there are many streets in Monteriano; he is sometimes difficult to find. I could not find him this morning."

"Go first to the Caffè Garibaldi," said Philip, remembering that this was the hour appointed by his friends of yesterday.

He occupied the time he was left alone not in thinking —there was nothing to think about; he simply had to tell a few facts—but in trying to make a sling for his broken arm. The trouble was in the elbow-joint, and as long as he kept this motionless he could go on as usual. But inflammation was beginning, and the slightest jar gave him agony. The sling was not fitted before Gino leapt up the stairs, crying—

"So you are back! How glad I am! We are all waiting—"

Philip had seen too much to be nervous. In low, even tones, he told what had happened; and the other, also perfectly calm, heard him to the end. In the silence Perfetta called up that she had forgotten the baby's evening milk; she must fetch it. When she had gone Gino took up the lamp without a word, and they went into the other room.

"My sister is ill," said Philip, "and Miss Abbott is guilt-less. I should be glad if you did not have to trouble them."

Gino had stooped down by the rug, and was feeling the

place where his son had lain. Now and then he frowned a little and glanced at Philip.

"It is through me," he continued. "It happened because I was cowardly and idle. I have come to know what you will do."

Gino had left the rug, and began to pat the table from the end, as if he was blind. The action was so uncanny that Philip was driven to intervene.

"Gently, man, gently; he is not here."

He went up and touched him on the shoulder.

He twitched away, and began to pass his hands over things more rapidly—over the table, the chairs, the entire floor, the walls, as high as he could reach them. Philip had not presumed to comfort him. But now the tension was too great—he tried.

"Break down, Gino; you must break down. Scream and curse and give in for a little; you must break down."

There was no reply, and no cessation of the sweeping hands.

"It is time to be unhappy. Break down, or you will be ill like my sister. You will go—"

The tour of the room was over. He had touched everything in it except Philip. Now he approached him. His face was that of a man who has lost his old reason for life and seeks a new one.

"Gino!"

He stopped for a moment; then he came nearer. Philip stood his ground.

"You are to do what you like with me, Gino. Your son is dead, Gino. He died in my arms, remember. It does not excuse me; but he did die in my arms."

The left hand came forward, slowly this time. It hovered before Philip like an insect. Then it descended and gripped him by his broken elbow.

Philip struck out with all the strength of his other arm. Gino fell to the blow, without a cry or a word.

"You brute!" exclaimed the Englishman. "Kill me if you like! But just you leave my broken arm alone."

Then he was seized with remorse, and knelt beside his adversary and tried to revive him. He managed to raise him up, and propped his body against his own. He passed his arm round him. Again he was filled with pity and tenderness. He awaited the revival without fear, sure that both of them were safe at last.

Gino recovered suddenly. His lips moved. For one blessed moment it seemed that he was going to speak. But he scrambled up in silence, remembering everything, and he made not towards Philip, but towards the lamp.

"Do what you like; but think first—"

The lamp was tossed across the room, out through the loggia. It broke against one of the trees below. Philip began to cry out in the dark.

Gino approached from behind and gave him a sharp pinch. Philip spun round with a yell. He had only been pinched on the back, but he knew what was in store for him. He struck out, exhorting the devil to fight him, to kill him, to do anything but this. Then he stumbled to the door. It was open. He lost his head and, instead of turning down the stairs, he ran across the landing into the room opposite. There he lay down on the floor between the stove and the skirting-board.

His senses grew sharper. He could hear Gino coming in on tiptoe. He even knew what was passing in his mind, how now he was at fault, now he was hopeful, now he was wondering whether after all the victim had not escaped down the stairs. There was a quick swoop above him, and then a low growl like a dog's. Gino had broken his fingernails against the stove.

Physical pain is almost too terrible to bear. We can just bear it when it comes by accident or for our good—as it generally does in modern life, except at school. But when it is caused by the malignity of a man, full-grown, fashioned like ourselves, all our control disappears. Philip's one thought was to get away from that room at whatever sacrifice of nobility or pride.

Gino was now at the farther end of the room, groping by

the little tables. Suddenly the instinct came to him. He crawled quickly to where Philip lay and had him clean by the elbow.

The whole arm seemed red-hot, and the broken bone grated in the joint, sending out shoots of the essence of pain. His other arm was pinioned against the wall, and Gino had trampled in behind the stove and was kneeling on his legs. For the space of a minute he yelled and yelled with all the force of his lungs. Then this solace was denied him. The other hand, moist and strong, began to close round his throat.

At first he was glad, for here, he thought, was death at last. But it was only a new torture; perhaps Gino inherited the skill of his ancestors—the childlike ruffians who flung each other from the towers. Just as the windpipe closed the hand fell off, and Philip was revived by the motion of his arm. And just as he was about to faint, and gain at least one moment of oblivion, the motion stopped, and he would struggle instead against the pressure on his throat.

Vivid pictures came dancing through the pain—Lilia dying some months back in this very house, Miss Abbott bending over the baby, his mother at home, now reading evening prayers to the servants. He felt that he was growing weaker; his brain wandered; the agony did not seem so great. Not all Gino's care could indefinitely postpone the end. His yells and gurgles became mechanical—functions of the tortured flesh rather than true notes of indignation and despair. He was conscious of a horrid tumbling. Then his arm was pulled a little too roughly, and everything was quiet at last.

"But your son is dead, Gino. Your son is dead, dear Gino. Your son is dead."

The room was full of light, and Miss Abbott had Gino by the shoulders, holding him down in a chair. She was exhausted with the struggle, and her arms were trembling.

"What is the good of another death? What is the good of more pain?"

He too began to tremble. Then he turned and looked

curiously at Philip, whose face, covered with dust and foam, was visible by the stove. Miss Abbott allowed him to get up, though she still held him firmly. He gave a loud and curious cry—a cry of interrogation it might be called. Below there was the noise of Perfetta returning with the baby's milk.

"Go to him," said Miss Abbott, indicating Philip. "Pick him up. Treat him kindly."

She released him, and he approached Philip slowly. His eyes were filling with trouble. He bent down, as if he would gently raise him up.

"Help! Help!" moaned Philip. His body had suffered too much from Gino. It could not bear to be touched by him.

Gino seemed to understand. He stopped, crouched above him. Miss Abbott herself came forward and lifted her friend in her arms.

"Oh, the foul devil!" he murmured. "Kill him! Kill him for me."

Miss Abbott laid him tenderly on the couch and wiped his face. Then she said gravely to them both, "This thing stops here."

"Latte! Latte!" cried Perfetta, hilariously ascending the stairs.

"Remember," she continued, "there is to be no revenge. I will have no more intentional evil. We are not to fight with each other any more."

"I shall never forgive him," sighed Philip.

"Latte! Latte freschissimo! Bianco come neve!" Perfetta came in with another lamp and a little jug.

Gino spoke for the first time. "Put the milk on the table," he said. "It will not be wanted in the other room." The peril was over at last. A great sob shook the whole body, another followed, and then he gave a piercing cry of woe, and stumbled towards Miss Abbott like a child and clung to her.

All through the day Miss Abbott had seemed to Philip like a goddess, and more than ever did she seem so now. Many people look younger and more intimate during great emotion. But some there are who look older, and remote, and he could not think that there was little difference in years, and none in composition, between her and the man whose head was laid upon her breast. Her eyes were open, full of infinite pity and full of majesty, as if they discerned the boundaries of sorrow, and saw unimaginable tracts beyond. Such eyes he had seen in great pictures but never in a mortal. Her hands were folded round the sufferer, stroking him lightly, for even a goddess can do no more than that. And it seemed fitting, too, that she should bend her head and touch his forehead with her lips.

Philip looked away, as he sometimes looked away from the great pictures where visible forms suddenly become inadequate for the things they have shown to us. He was happy; he was assured that there was greatness in the world. There came to him an earnest desire to be good through the example of this good woman. He would try henceforward to be worthy of the things she had revealed. Quietly, without hysterical prayers or banging of drums, he underwent conversion. He was saved.

"That milk," said she, "need not be wasted. Take it, Signor Carella, and persuade Mr Herriton to drink."

Gino obeyed her, and carried the child's milk to Philip. And Philip obeyed also and drank.

"Is there any left?"

"A little," answered Gino.

"Then finish it." For she was determined to use such remnants as lie about the world.

"Will you not have some?"

"I do not care for milk; finish it all."

"Philip, have you had enough milk?"

"Yes, thank you, Gino; finish it all."

He drank the milk, and then, either by accident or in some spasm of pain, broke the jug to pieces. Perfetta exclaimed in bewilderment. "It does not matter," he told her. "It does not matter. It will never be wanted any more."

# Chapter 10

"He will have to marry her," said Philip. "I heard from him this morning, just as we left Milan. He finds he has gone too far to back out. It would be expensive. I don't know how much he minds—not as much as we suppose, I think. At all events there's not a word of blame in the letter. I don't believe he even feels angry. I never was so completely forgiven. Ever since you stopped him killing me, it has been a vision of perfect friendship. He nursed me, he lied for me at the inquest, and at the funeral, though he was crying, you would have thought it was my son who had died. Certainly I was the only person he had to be kind to; he was so distressed not to make Harriet's acquaintance, and that he scarcely saw anything of you. In his letter he says so again."

"Thank him, please, when you write," said Miss Abbott, "and give him my kindest regards."

"Indeed I will." He was surprised that she could slide away from the man so easily. For his own part, he was bound by ties of almost alarming intimacy. Gino had the southern knack of friendship. In the intervals of business he would pull out Philip's life, turn it inside out, remodel it, and advise him how to use it for the best. The sensation was pleasant, for he was a kind as well as a skilful operator. But Philip came away feeling that he had not a secret corner left. In that very letter Gino had again implored him, as a refuge from domestic difficulties, "to marry Miss Abbott, even if her dowry is small". And how Miss Abbott herself, after such tragic intercourse, could resume the conventions and send calm messages of esteem, was more than he could understand.

"When will you see him again?" she asked. They were

standing together in the corridor of the train, slowly ascending out of Italy towards the St Gotthard tunnel.

"I hope next spring. Perhaps we shall paint Siena red for a day or two with some of the new wife's money. It was one of the arguments for marrying her."

"He has no heart," she said severely. "He does not really mind about the child at all."

"No; you're wrong. He does. He is unhappy, like the rest of us. But he doesn't try to keep up appearances as we do. He knows that the things that have made him happy once will probably make him happy again."

"He said he would never be happy again."

"In his passion. Not when he was calm. We English say it when we are calm—when we do not really believe it any longer. Gino is not ashamed of inconsistency. It is one of the many things I like him for."

"Yes; I was wrong. That is so."

"He's much more honest with himself than I am," continued Philip, "and he is honest without an effort and without pride. But you, Miss Abbott, what about you? Will you be in Italy next spring?"

"No."

"I'm sorry. When will you come back, do you think?"

"I think never."

"For whatever reason?" He stared at her as if she were some monstrosity.

"Because I understand the place. There is no need."

"Understand Italy!" he exclaimed.

"Perfectly."

"Well, I don't. And I don't understand you," he murmured to himself, as he paced away from her up the corridor. By this time he loved her very much, and he could not bear to be puzzled. He had reached love by the spiritual path: her thoughts and her goodness and her nobility had moved him first, and now her whole body and all its gestures had become transfigured by them. The beauties that are called obvious—the beauties of her hair and her voice and her limbs—he had noticed these last; Gino, who never traversed

141

any path at all, had commended them dispassionately to his friend.

Why was she so puzzling? He had known so much about her once—what she thought, how she felt, the reasons for her actions. And now he only knew that he loved her, and all the other knowledge seemed passing from him just as he needed it most. Why would she never come to Italy again? Why had she avoided himself and Gino ever since the evening that she had saved their lives? The train was nearly empty. Harriet slumbered in a compartment by herself. He must ask her these questions now, and he returned quickly to her down the corridor.

She greeted him with a question of her own. "Are your plans decided?"

"Yes. I can't live at Sawston."

"Have you told Mrs Herriton?"

"I wrote from Monteriano. I tried to explain things; but she will never understand me. Her view will be that the affair is settled—sadly settled since the baby is dead. Still, it's over; our family circle need be vexed no more. She won't even be angry with you. You see, you have done us no harm in the long run. Unless, of course, you talk about Harriet and make a scandal. So that is my plan—London and work. What is yours?"

"Poor Harriet!" said Miss Abbott. "As if I dare judge Harriet! Or anybody." And without replying to Philip's question she left him, to visit the other invalid.

Philip gazed after her mournfully, and then he looked mournfully out of the window at the decreasing streams. All the excitement was over—the inquest, Harriet's short illness, his own visit to the surgeon. He was convalescent, both in body and spirit, but convalescence brought no joy. In the looking-glass at the end of the corridor he saw his face haggard, and his shoulders pulled forward by the weight of the sling. Life was greater than he had supposed, but it was even less complete. He had seen the need for strenuous work and for righteousness. And now he saw what a very little way those things would go.

"Is Harriet going to be all right?" he asked. Miss Abbott had come back to him.

"She will soon be her old self," was the reply. For Harriet, after a sharp paroxysm of illness and remorse, was quickly returning to her normal state. She had been "thoroughly upset", as she phrased it, but she soon ceased to realize that anything was wrong beyond the death of a poor little child. Already she spoke of "this unlucky accident", and "the mysterious frustration of one's attempts to make things better". Miss Abbott had seen that she was comfortable, and had given her a kind kiss. But she returned feeling that Harriet, like her mother, considered the affair as settled.

"I'm clear enough about Harriet's future, and about parts of my own. But I ask again, What about yours?"

"Sawston and work," said Miss Abbott.

"No."

"Why not?" she asked, smiling.

"You've seen too much. You've seen as much and done more than I have."

"But it's so different. Of course I shall go to Sawston. You forget my father; and even if he wasn't there I've a hundred ties: my district—I'm neglecting it shamefully— my evening classes, the St. James's—"

"Silly nonsense!" he exploded, suddenly moved to have the whole thing out with her. "You're too good—about a thousand times better than I am. You can't live in that hole; you must go among people who can hope to under- stand you. I mind for myself: I want to see you often—again and again."

"Of course we shall meet whenever you come down; and I hope that will mean often."

"It's not enough; it'll only be in the old horrible way, each with a dozen relatives round us. No, Miss Abbott; it's not good enough."

"We can write at all events."

"You will write?" he cried, with a flush of pleasure. At times his hopes seemed so solid.

"I will indeed."

143

"But I say it's not enough—you can't go back to the old life if you wanted to. Too much has happened."

"I know that," she said sadly.

"Not only pain and sorrow, but wonderful things: that tower in the sunlight—do you remember it, and all you said to me? The theatre, even. And the next day—in the church; and our times with Gino."

"All the wonderful things are over," she said. "That is just where it is."

"I don't believe it. At all events, not for me. The most wonderful things may be to come—"

"The wonderful things are over," she repeated, and looked at him so mournfully that he dare not contradict her. The train was crawling up the last ascent towards the Campanile of Airolo and the entrance of the tunnel.

"Miss Abbott," he murmured, speaking quickly, as if their free intercourse might soon be ended, "what is the matter with you? I thought I understood you, and I don't. All those two great first days at Monteriano I read you as clearly as you read me still. I saw why you had come, and why you changed sides, and afterwards I saw your wonderful courage and pity. And now you're frank with me one moment, as you used to be, and the next moment you shut me up. You see, I owe too much to you—my life, and I don't know what besides. I won't stand it. You've gone too far to turn mysterious. I'll quote what you said to me: 'Don't be mysterious; there isn't the time.' I'll quote something else: 'I and my life must be where I live.' You can't live at Sawston."

He had moved her at last. She whispered to herself hurriedly. "It is tempting—" And those three words threw him into a tumult of joy. What was tempting to her? After all, was the greatest of things possible? Perhaps, after long estrangement, after much tragedy, the South had brought them together in the end. That laughter in the theatre, those silver stars in the purple sky, even the violets of a departed spring, all had helped, and sorrow had helped also, and so had tenderness to others.

"It is tempting," she repeated, "not to be mysterious. I've wanted often to tell you, and then been afraid. I could never tell anyone else, certainly no woman, and I think you're the one man who might understand and not be disgusted."

"Are you lonely?" he whispered. "Is it anything like that?"

"Yes." The train seemed to shake him towards her. He was resolved that though a dozen people were looking he would yet take her in his arm. "I'm terribly lonely, or I wouldn't speak. I think you must know already." Their faces were crimson, as if the same thought was surging through them both.

"Perhaps I do." He came close to her. "Perhaps I could speak instead. But if you will say the word plainly you'll never be sorry; I will thank you for it all my life."

She said plainly, "That I love him." Then she broke down. Her body was shaken with sobs, and lest there should be any doubt she cried between the sobs for Gino! Gino! Gino!

He heard himself remark: "Rather! I love him too! When I can forget how he hurt me that evening. Though whenever we shake hands—" One of them must have moved a step or two, for when she spoke again she was already a little way apart.

"You've upset me." She stifled something that was perilously near hysterics. "I thought I was past all this. You're taking it wrongly. I'm in love with Gino—don't pass it off—I mean it crudely—you know what I mean. So laugh at me."

"Laugh at love?" asked Philip.

"Yes. Pull it to pieces. Tell me I'm a fool or worse—that he's a cad. Say all you said when Lilia fell in love with him. That's the help I want. I dare tell you this because I like you—and because you're without passion; you look on life as a spectacle; you don't enter it; you only find it funny or beautiful. So I can trust you to cure me. Mr Herriton, isn't it funny?" She tried to laugh herself, but became frightened and had to stop. "He's not a gentleman, nor a Christian, nor good in any way. He's never flattered me nor honoured me. But because he's handsome, that's been enough. The son of an Italian dentist, with a pretty face." She repeated the phrase as if it was a charm against passion. "Oh, Mr Herriton, isn't it funny!" Then, to his relief, she began to cry. "I love him, and I'm not ashamed of it. I love him and I'm going to Sawston, and if I mayn't speak about him to you sometimes, I shall die."

In that terrible discovery Philip managed to think not of himself but of her. He did not lament. He did not even speak to her kindly, for he saw that she could not stand it. A flippant reply was what she asked and needed—something flippant and a little cynical. And indeed it was the only reply he could trust himself to make.

"Perhaps it is what the books call 'a passing fancy'?"

She shook her head. Even this question was too pathetic. For, as far as she knew anything about herself, she knew that her passions, once aroused, were sure. "If I saw him often," she said, "I might remember what he is like. Or he might grow old. But I dare not risk it, so nothing can alter me now."

"Well, if the fancy does pass, let me know." After all, he could say what he wanted.

"Oh, you shall know quick enough."

"But before you retire to Sawston—are you so mighty sure?"

"What of?" She had stopped crying. He was treating her exactly as she had hoped.

"That you and he—" He smiled bitterly at the thought of them together. Here was the cruel antique malice of the gods, such as they once sent forth against Pasiphaë. Centuries of aspiration and culture—and the world could not escape it. "I was going to say—what ever have you got in common?"

"Nothing except the times we have seen each other." Again her face was crimson. He turned his own face away.

"Which—which times?"

"The time I thought you weak and heedless, and went

instead of you to get the baby. That began it, as far as I know the beginning. Or it may have begun when you took us to the theatre, and I saw him mixed up with music and light. But I didn't understand till the morning. Then you opened the door—and I knew why I had been so happy. Afterwards, in the church, I prayed for us all; not for anything new, but that we might just be as we were—he with the child he loved, you and I and Harriet safe out of the place—and that I might never see him or speak to him again. I could have pulled through then—the thing was only coming near, like a wreath of smoke; it hadn't wrapped me round."

"But through my fault," said Philip solemnly, "he is parted from the child he loves. And because my life was in danger you came and saw him and spoke to him again." For the thing was even greater than she imagined. Nobody but himself would ever see round it now. And to see round it he was standing at an immense distance. He could even be glad that she had once held the beloved in her arms.

"Don't talk of 'faults'. You're my friend for ever, Mr Herriton, I think. Only don't be charitable and shift or take the blame. Get over supposing I'm refined. That's what puzzles you. Get over that."

As she spoke she seemed to be transfigured, and to have indeed no part with refinement or unrefinement any longer. Out of this wreck there was revealed to him something indestructible—something which she, who had given it, could never take away.

"I say again, don't be charitable. If he had asked me, I might have given myself body and soul. That would have been the end of my rescue-party. But all through he took me for a superior being—a goddess. I who was worshipping every inch of him, and every word he spoke. And that saved me."

Philip's eyes were fixed on the Campanile of Airolo. But he saw instead the fair myth of Endymion. This woman was a goddess to the end. For her no love could be degrading: she stood outside all degradation. This episode, which she thought so sordid, and which was so tragic for him, remained supremely beautiful. To such a height was he lifted that without regret he could now have told her that he was her worshipper too. But what was the use of telling her? For all the wonderful things had happened.

"Thank you," was all that he permitted himself. "Thank you for everything."

She looked at him with great friendliness, for he had made her life endurable. At that moment the train entered the St Gotthard tunnel. They hurried back to the carriage to close the windows lest the smuts should get into Harriet's eyes.

# appendix a
# An Exchange between Forster and R. C. Trevelyan

*Forster to Trevelyan, 28 October 1905*

Your letter was rather what I expected, and very much what I feel about my book myself, though on the whole I am less severe, and inclined, I think, to view my work too complacently. The object of the book is the improvement of Philip, and I did really want the improvement to be a surprise. Therefore in chapters 1–2 I never hinted at the possibility, but at the same time did not demonstrate the impossibility, or did not mean to. In ch. 5 he has got into a mess, through trying to live only by a sense of humour and by a sense of the beautiful. The knowledge of the mess embitters him, and this is the improvement's beginning. From that time I exhibit new pieces of him—pieces that he did not know of, or at all events had never used. He grows large enough to appreciate Miss Abbott, and in the final scene he exceeds her.

All this is what I intended.

But I do begin to think (—I will say "to fear" for it is a pity it should be so—) that this "surprise" method is artistically wrong, and that from the first one must suggest the possibility, not merely the non-impossibility, of improvement. I disliked and do dislike finger posts, and couldn't bear in the earlier scenes the thought of inserting "Philip has other things in him besides these: watch him", however well the insertion had been made. And, when I wrote Monteriano I pushed this dislike to an extreme and should have felt the suggestion that a book must have one atmosphere to be pedantic. Life hasn't any, and the hot and cold of its changes are fascinating to me. I determined to imitate in this and let the result be artistic if it liked. Naturally it did not like.

I too would like to have a talk, and can't get what I want to say on paper. You can gather however that I know I am not a real artist, and at the same time am fearfully serious over my work and willing to sweat at atmosphere it if helps me to

149

[achieve??] what I want. What I want, I think, is the sentimental, but the sentimental reached by no easy beaten track—I cannot explain myself properly, for you must remember (I forget it myself) that though "clever" I have a small and cloudy brain, and cannot clear it by talking or reading philosophy. In fact my equipment is frightfully limited, but so good in parts that I want to do with it what I can.

Miss Abbott comes to grief for archaeological reasons. She was originally meant to turn out smaller and different. About the scene between Philip and Gino I don't, however, quite concur. (Less important than the death of the baby, which is the real crisis.) P. is a person who has scarcely ever felt the physical forces that are banging about in the world, and he couldn't get good and understand by spiritual suffering alone. Bodily punishment, however unjust superficially, was necessary too: in fact the scene—to use a heavy word, and one that I have only just thought of—was sacramental. Nor do I lose interest in Gino after it: here the possibility was hinted at during his intercourse with Lilia.

If you are good enough to write again, I wish you'd tell me on which pages I am unduly facetious. That is an awful evil, and only you have warned me against it. And I wish, if it was only two or three lines, you would say something about my style. It is scarcely fair though, after all your goodness, to bother you again. You're the only person who has troubled to criticize me in any detail.

### Trevelyan to Forster, *undated*

. . . Your letter was very interesting, and made me feel I had been too severe in my strictures, even from my point of view. But though I exaggerated my objections, I still feel them to be real. It is largely no doubt, as you suggest, a question of atmosphere, whatever exactly that vaguest of words may mean. The story no doubt necessitated several different atmospheres, Sawston and the various other non-Sawston atmospheres, i.e. Philip's, Gino's, Miss Abbott's. But I think you should have contrasted Philip and Miss Abbott more with Sawston from the beginning, and made one feel that however much they were *in* Sawston for the time being, they were yet not *of* it, and would eventually rise superior to it. This would at once have gained them our sympathies, and our interest in Philip's development, besides making Sawston more amusing, as seen through Philip's gradually enlightened eyes. But this won't help you much, and I don't feel sure I am right either. No doubt what I suppose one must call style is at the bottom of much that I object to. In the more comic parts it is often right enough, and, in much of the more serious parts, at any rate unobjectionable. But I find it often far too conversational and even slangy, e.g. p. [76], where "beastly Italy" is merely beastly indeed, and what you gain in expressiveness does not compensate for what you lose in something far more important. For the purely narrative part of a story, where the author himself speaks, should surely keep throughout a certain sameness of quality, and also a certain dignity, and if possible, beauty, even in a slight or comic narrative, at least it does in all the books I really care about. The dialogue, if necessary, should be more unequal, either in the emotional or the slangy direction, or in any other direction. This is why I also do not like p. [75], the whole paragraph from "They travelled" down to "Verona" with its "people ceasing being ugly" etc., and its "*waltzing* train *picking* them out etc." Besides I think you ought always to try deliberately to write beautifully, I do not mean poetically—all beauty is not poetry, and Jane Austin [*sic*] and Petronius are often quite beautiful, to say nothing of Apuleius and Cervantes, in their most sublimely amusing moments. Turgenef [*sic*], being when at his best a great sentimentalist, has to be beautiful in the most deliberate way, and when you are sentimental, you will find you have to be so no less. What beauty of style consists in, who can say. But no doubt simplicity and economy of expression are negative elements, as well as the almost complete avoidance of jarring modern notes, and journalistic idiom, which to my mind partly spoils the writing of even such skilful writers as MacCarthy and Roger Fry. The positive elements each must find out for himself by practice; no doubt the rhythm of the sentences, which should be both beautiful in themselves, and as expressive as possible, and also the perfect choice and placing of expressive words, that must be neither exaggerated nor weak nor ugly—these things and many others are what make up style now, just as they did in the time of the Greeks: but you know all these things as well as I do, and practise them too; only, it seems to me, not uncompromisingly enough as yet. To take another instance of a different kind, I do not think p. [18] succeeds.

You seem to have felt rightly that the scene, as it was beautiful, should be described beautifully, but your method seems to me ingenious where it should be simple. The elaborate metaphor of the sea and rocks is surely not appropriate to convey the emotion, and is too much in the nature of an Elizabethan or Henry-Jacobean conceit. Tourgenef [*sic*] would have made it a thing one could never forget; but he would not have talked of "Art" and "painter's courage". That is conversation, not art, and even the writing of modern novels is an art, and may be a very great one, though MacCarthy to my amazement tells me it can never be so. Yet I am very glad indeed that MacCarthy liked your book, for his judgement is very valuable, and he never likes anything without very good reasons, and is the best critic of modern novels I know. To be that, one should be rather more modern than I am, and less enamoured of the classics; and I should not have ventured on these long lectures, if I had not thought you wished it, and if I did not like your work a great deal already. I am glad people appreciate it as much as it seems they do, as it is so much more interesting than other people's in that line, at least so it seems to me. We have just been to Cambridge and seen Dickinson, Kanes (sic?), and Dent, who all liked your book a great deal. . . .

# appendix b
# Manuscript and Proofs

After the death in 1940 of Nathaniel Wedd, Fellow of King's College, Cambridge, papers which he had bequeathed to the College were found to include a complete manuscript of *Where Angels Fear to Tread*—a gift, thirty-five years earlier, from Forster to the man who, more than any other, had encouraged him to write. It remained at King's College until 1971, when the College, taking the view that Forster should be represented at national level by the manuscript of one of his novels, selected this one for presentation to the British Museum, where it forms Additional MSS 57472–3.

Unlike the manuscripts for *The Longest Journey*, *Howards End* and *A Passage to India*, this one consists only of the complete version sent or delivered by Forster to the typist. Moreover, of the 273 leaves—98 of which have been truncated to remove unwanted matter—only eleven contain rejected draft material on their versos; and the entire manuscript is, by Forster's later standards, unusually free from corrections.[1] This may be partly because, with the possible exception of *Maurice*, this was the novel whose writing gave him least trouble; partly, perhaps, because at this stage of his career he was more ready to make fresh copies of messy pages than he later became. Whatever the reason, the net result of all these factors is to make the manuscript much less rich a quarry than, say, that for *Howards End*, and much less deserving of what would have been a decidedly slim volume of its own.

Instead, the following pages contain a selection of the more interesting variants, keyed to the final version by page and line wherever possible (some of the fragments on the versos defy such treatment). No startling changes of plan are revealed, and the

[1] Forster's writing habits are described in *The Manuscripts of Howards End* (Abinger Edition, vol. 4a), pp. vii–ix, and in *Aspects of E. M. Forster*, edited by Oliver Stallybrass (London, Arnold, and New York, Harcourt, Brace, 1969), pp. 143–54. Further details of the present manuscript are given by Ineko Kondo in the *Tsuda Review* (published by Tsuda College, Tokyo), no. 15, November 1970, pp. 71–8.

only incontrovertible generalization to be made about the verbal changes is that most of them are incontrovertible improvements. Many give greater vividness or immediacy or liveliness, as when Lilia is made to *sprawl* rather than peep out of her carriage (p. 1), or the citizens of medieval Monteriano to *fling* each other from towers (p. 137) instead of merely fighting each other from them, or "an Irish lady" blossoms into Miss M'Gee, Maida Vale, *and* an Equerry to the Queen of Peru (p. 21); or, in the dialogue, they express more forcibly the characters' feelings and personalities, as when Lilia speaks of "your beastly family" (p. 27) instead of "the family", or Mrs Herriton of *that place* (p. 67) instead of Italy, or Philip of Miss Abbott's *idiocies* (p. 68) instead of her remarks. A number of changes, however, are in the direction of restraint, as when Mr Kingcroft consoles himself with "someone else" (p. 56) rather than "a young lady from Wales", or some reported antics by Gino (p. 59) and a comment on Philip by one Lady Camberwell (p. 54) are omitted, or a small sick joke jettisoned ("they all obeyed him *save the horse*"—see note to p. 131). And in certain instances what is being restrained is not mere exuberance but a tendency towards staginess or sentimentality or both. Twice, for example, the word "worthlessness" is eliminated: once (p. 47) by the substitution of "infidelity", once (p. 70) by the omission of the passage in which it occurs. Eliminated, also, are references, in the account of Philip's cab-journey with Caroline, to his licking his lips, gasping, coughing, shuddering all over, and edging away from her "as if she was something foul"; the statement, at the height of the opera scene, that "it was the finest rag in the world. He had never felt so jolly nor among so many friends"; a reference to Gino's slipping his arm into Philip's (instead—p. 113—he offers him a cigar); and, when Philip breaks the grim news to Gino, the apostrophes "dear man . . . dear fellow". Most striking of all is the omission of an embarrassingly arch page-long invocation of the "friends, dear friends of mine, whom I have made in Italy!" (see note to p. 23).

This last well-advised omission was effected only in proof—as were several other omissions and insertions such as publishers rightly deplore at proof stage. Here the need to avoid a blank page at the end of the chapter has necessitated much re-setting; and even so the last four pages of the chapter, in the first edition, are each a line short. Elsewhere, conversely, the printer has increased the number of lines on two facing pages to accommodate fresh copy (the account, on p. 48, of how Italians and Germans strike their hats). The heftiest insertion at proof stage occurs in Mrs Herriton's outburst at the end of chapter 5—where, luckily, there was room and to spare.

This not quite complete[2] set of corrected proofs, now at King's College, Cambridge, is unique in Forster's work, and the sole indication of how much revision he was accustomed to doing at this stage. For this reason all changes made in them (mere corrections of misprints apart) are included in the following selection. They are readily distinguished by the signal "[$p$]". For similar reasons I have drawn attention to two substantial bits of rewriting which must have occurred at typescript stage; see notes to pp. 140 and 144. Otherwise the conventions are the same as those used, and explained in greater detail, in *The Manuscripts of Howards End* (Abinger Edition, vol. 4a), i.e. the following; in each case the three dots represent one or more words.

(1) ...←...     words preceding the arrow substituted by Forster for words following it.

(2) \.../     words between oboli inserted by Forster.

(3) ⟨...⟩     words within angle brackets deleted by Forster.

(4) {...}     words within brace brackets inserted, then deleted, by Forster.

(5) ⟨...⟩\.../     (*a*) words deleted, then reinserted, by Forster; or (*b*) words between oboli substituted by Forster for words within angle brackets.

(6) ≪...⟨...⟩...≫     deleted passage (within double angle brackets) within which a deletion (single angle brackets) has already occurred.

(7) \\...\.../...//     inserted passage (between double oboli) within which a further insertion (between single oboli) has later been made.

(8) [...]     words (or letters) clearly intended by Forster and supplied by the editor: or—*if italicized*—interpolated editorial comment.

(9) [...?]     words (or letters) conjectured to have been intended by Forster, or to have been on a missing or mutilated sheet.

[2] Signature T is missing: from the beginning of the seventh new paragraph on p. 134 to "moved" on p. 141, line 34.

| 1 | 2 | Harriet←Georgina [*and similarly at* 5:29 *and* 7:25] |
| | 9 | sprawling←peeping |
| | 18 | San Gimignano←San Gemignano [*only the first and American editions retain this incorrect spelling*], Volterra |
| 3 | 19 | late←[*p*] so very late |
| 4 | 18 | being←[*p*] making himself |
| | 23 | No.←[*p*] Well, |
| | 28 | My←[*p*] Oh, my |
| 6 | 11 | existed←existed in good society |
| | 12 | good←[*p*] very good |
| 7 | 26 | of Philip←[*p*] Philip |
| | 30 | anxious←[*p*] hastening |
| 8 | 2 | [*p*] \all day/ |
| 9 | 5 | some early←[*p*] the spring |
| | 8 | her elderly daughter←[*p*] Harriet |
| | 28 | the duller vegetables first←[*p*] onions, carrots, turnips, lettuces |
| | 32 | pointed←[*p*] piece of |
| 10 | 1 | was very careful to let those peas←[*p*] often thought afterwards of those peas, and of the complacency with which she sowed them. She was very careful to let them |
| | 3 | expensive←[*p*] expensive peas |
| | 10 | "Her letters never did."←"Give it me then." |
| | | But Harriet in stupid heavy tones began to read as |
| | 14 | indulgently←[*p*] indulgently and then read it from beginning to end |
| | 15 | [*p*] \long/ |
| | 22 | a hotel←[*p*] the hotel |
| | 32 | This←[*p*] A hundred things. This |
| 11 | 14 | whose team are you in this afternoon \—Miss Edith's or Miss May's/←what news of the verb 'To Be' |
| | 17 | took out the large atlas ... and read [*line 31*]←looked out Monteriano in the Atlas. It was too small to be marked there. Then for the first time in her life, she opened 'Central Italy' by Baedeker, and read |
| 12 | 11 | \, and seat of the district prison/ |
| | 18 | dull. Whereas←[*p*] dull, whereas←dull. Whereas |
| 13 | 2 | has←[*p*] is |
| | 35 | had←[*p*] was full of |
| 14 | 11 | voice. It was the first time he had had anything to do←voice, "but—it is the first time I have ever done anything." |
| | 14 | March←[*p*] February |
| | 28 | ground←[*p*] ground. And paper is the most indestructible of things |
| 15 | 8 | be as quick as Baedeker←[*p*] be as quick as Mr Baedeker←do an Italian hill town between the trains |

15 in a dream he watched the train depart←[*p*] he watched the train depart in a dream

20 lire←[*p*] lira

31 He had known . . . for Philip [16:21]←He could gather little from her face, which naturally scarred [?] with her terrible jolting. She made room for him

**16** 17 , solitary, dusty, frightened,←[*p*]—solitary, dusty, frightened — ←, solitary, dusty, frightened

32 his←[*p*] such

**17** 1 "Are we to talk it over now?" he asked. . . . She entered [*line 9*]←[*p*] He licked his lips once or twice, gave a cough, and said—

"Are we to talk it over now?" . . . She entered←He licked his lips once or twice, gasped, coughed, and said "How long has she been engaged?"
Miss Abbott entered

16 "Oh! Who is he?"←[*p*] "Oh!" Then, with another cough and swallow, "Who is he?"

18 The second←[*p*] Monteriano is not a fashionable residential centre. The second

24 mistake←[*p*] misunderstanding

**18** 6 gathering sarcasm←[*p*] a tinge of sarcasm in his voice

13 "May . . . him?"←[*p*] "May . . . him?" he said.

27 March←[*p*] February

**19** 7 hour←[*p*] hour. No other qualification is necessary

13 Meanwhile [*see p. 173*]

21 "His father," said . . . pain [20:12]←⟨"A dentist [?]," she replied and suddenly covered her face with⟩ Miss Abbott screamed "A dentist!" ⟨The⟩ \and the/ thing was ⟨out⟩ \clear/ at last. Philip shuddered all over, and edged away from his companion as if she was something foul

31 my sister-in-law←[*p*] she

**21** 20 his two cards of recommendation—one from Miss M'Gee, Maida Vale, the other, less valuable, from an Equerry to the Queen of Peru←a card of recommendation given him by an Irish lady six years before

**22** 12 Carella←Vannucci [*and similarly at* 22:37, 23:21 *and* 29, 24:38, 27:26, *and* 28:20]

30 was←[*p*] sat

34 Behind him loomed←[*p*] The only other noteworthy object was

37 The face . . . spaghetti [23:11]←Signor Vannucci was ⟨terribly nervous⟩ \grimacing with nervousness/ [*lacuna*] Spaghetti came first. He was hungry

**23** 15 beautiful←[*p*] handsome

19 Conversation←[*p*] Let us have the truth, though it is the saddest truth in all the world. O friends, dear friends of mine, whom I have made in Italy!—cabmen, waiters, sacristans, shop assistants, soldiers, friars, porters at wayside stations, lighthouse-keepers, boatmen at Syracuse, muleteers in the Sabines, stokers on Adriatic steamers!—we had been friends for years, I think, when we first met, for the stress went out of life and we understood each other's gestures, and talked or were silent as we chose. You told me everything, and I told you more than I shall ever tell my true and tried acquaintance here. Then we parted with warm hand-grasp, wondering why we had been kept apart so long. And, thank goodness, oh, thank goodness, I shall never see one of you again!

So it was with Philip, my true and tried acquaintance, who, on this occasion, as on so many others, feels and behaves as I do.

Conversation

23 19 that←[*p*] the

22 Miss Abbott←[*p*] Philip and Miss Abbott

23 interpreter←[*p*] interpreters

24 3 nostra←[*p*] questa

7 glanced←[*p*] glanced significantly

7 to see whether he noticed that←[*p*] as much as to say that at all events

10 , it appeared,←[*p*] it appeared←, it appeared,

15 did not expect to love←never loved

24 "But may not the fish die?" said Miss Abbott. "They have no air."←[*p*] "But surely," said Miss Abbott, "the fish will die. They have no air."←"But surely," said Philip, "the fish will die. They have no air."

31 you are ready for bye-bye←you're ready for bye-bye←you must be tired

32 we don't meet←[*p*] not

25 3 strengthened←[*p*] overcame

26 10 lady,←[*p*] lady←lady,

12 the son of the servants' dentist in Coronation Place←the Bulmers' [?] at Sawston, for I do not suppose his father has so large a custom

18 [*p*] \we expected her to/

27 10 your beastly←the

12 spoilt←[*p*] were spoilt

13 'Bully'? 'Insolent boy'? Who's that, pray, but you?←[*p*] It was you who were a bully, you who were insolent and frightened me and made me be cowardly.

14 But, thank goodness,←[*p*] But thank goodness

23 our←your

23 There is going to be such a row←There's going to be such a row←There shall be such a confusion, such an uproar

26 Carella, and I shall tell him so now←Signor Vannucci: now go and speak to him

28 "Do," she cried . . . Philip, not [28:9]←[*p*] "Do," she cried . . . Philip, who was not←"Yes, do," she cried, "speak to him! speak to him! Gino! Gino! Signor ⟨Vannucci⟩ \Herriton/ wants to speak to you! He has so much to say. Quick! He is waiting." And before Philip could stop her she had left the room.

And in a few minutes Gino did appear, striving to look defiant but with twitching lips and eyes.

"Pray sit down," said Philip. He refused, and stood in the full glare of the gas jet, while Philip, who was not

29 11 and let us hope←[*p*] and, let us hope,←and let us hope

35 me. I could prosecute him. But←[*p*] me: I could prosecute him, but←me: I could prosecute him: but

30 4 suggest a gentleman's garden←[*p*] give the idea of a gentleman's garden←give an imposing air of privacy

4 in its middle a large hole←[*p*] a large hole in its middle

13 This house←This door is always shut, and the door key is a quarter of a yard long. The house

31 12 him,←[*p and editions*] him←him,

38 Lilia. Then←[*p*] Lilia, upon which

32 8 ⟨their⟩ \the/ acceptance of a cheque. They took the cheque not to Poggibonsi, after all, but to Empoli—a ⟨ga[y?]⟩ lively, dusty town some twenty miles off ⟨, where⟩ \. There/ they settled down in ⟨great⟩ comfort ⟨,⟩ \;/ and \the sisters/ said they had been driven ⟨to it⟩ {there} \to it/ by Gino←⟨the⟩ \their/ possession of the cheque which was ⟨the⟩ \a/ price of their departure. He had never known a marriage cause disunion before

11 off. There←[*p*] off, where

12 to it←[*p*] there

33 22 effect←[*p*] effect at all ←effect

32 or sitting astride it disconsolately←[*p*] and spitting into the view

34 12 woke←[*p*] waked

24 his silly self←himself alone

30 \If they are poor and have to work for their living I may see them—but not otherwise./

35 23 Low-class men.←[*p*] "Low-class men."←Low class men.

38 socialism which←[*p*] Socialism—which←socialism, which

36 3 our life←[*p*] the age

37 2 reflected←[*p*] murmured

37 [p] \own/

38 8 possible!←[p] possible?←possible!

9 If←[p] As

16 beg←[p] beseech

19 he←[p] Gino

22 whether you love it or hate it←[p] whether you love or hate
it←where people are not ashamed to be kind

39 23 understands us←[p] understands one←understands you

23 irritates us←[p] irritates one←irritates←irritates you

24 we←[p] one←you

40 1 Then he spoke of his exciting and←[p] This introduced the
delightful joke of the

2 made fun of←[p] alternately mocked and pitied

5 toppled←[p] pushed

41 9 "What am I to do about it?"
"Do nothing. Or ask me!"←"Had she been presented at
her court she might perhaps have commanded people and they
would have come. But no lady would accept such an
invitation."
"You'd better ask me!"

16 Waiter←[p] Waiter, the bill

32 like.←[p] like——←like.

42 1 humming←[p] decrepid [sic]

2 sang,←[p] sang←sang,

43 8 meant sitting in the farmacia←was purely fictitious

31 forgot her nature and began to reflect←[p] forgot herself and
began to think←frequently thought←began to think

44 1 She reflected chiefly←[p] She thought chiefly←First of all
she thought

45 21 He looked horrified.
Now was the moment to assert herself. She made the statement again. He got up from his chair←He jumped up

46 5 "Hardly anything," said Lilia, and crossed herself also. Thus
did the two women pay homage to their outraged male.
←"Hardly anything."
"I have heard it said that men become like beasts when
they are wronged too deeply for words. There are sceptics
who say we are descended from beasts, and that is the proof.
That of course is a lie. But guard your tongue well, signora,
guard it well, for it was lucky I came in."

28 should←[p] would←should

47 7 infidelity←worthlessness

25 despite herself, for there are some situations in which
⟨disposition⟩ \vulgarity/ counts no longer←despite herself.
There are some situations so simple that every man and

woman ⟨, great or small,⟩ ‖who ⟨enters⟩ \enter/ them‖
⟨becomes⟩ \become/ tragic \and alike/, their personalities
born [*sic*] away by the levelling if not the ennobling power of
sorrow

**48** 5 felt hat, strike it in the right place as infallibly as a
German strikes his in the wrong place, and leave her←[*p*]
hat

11 and←and ⟨autumn⟩ \University Extension/ lectures, and
tea parties, and

31 little←[*p*] nice little

**49** 2 afternoon in March←[*p*] February afternoon

**50** 5 abuse←[*p*] abuse, which broke from English into Italian, and
from Italian into *patois*

29 He has forgiven you!←Ahi! You have hurt ⟨me⟩ \my arm/!
What have I done?

**52** 23 this←[*p*] the←this

24 gave candles to Santa Deodata←[*p*] burnt candles at Santa
Deodata's

25 [*p*] \to her/

**53** 6 But←⟨[*new paragraph*] She did not hear.⟩ But

**54** 11 him.←him. "He would have been a fine man," said Lady
Camberwell, "if only he had kept on as he began."

**55** 24 The disillusion was convenient for Mrs Herriton, who saw a
trying little period ahead of her, and was glad to have her
family united←So at a very trying moment Mrs Herriton
found her family united. Morality, religion, and sentiment
were all against Gino

**56** 16 at last←[*p*] just

17 someone else←[*p*] a young lady from Wales

**58** 15 Charing Cross←Cannon [Street]

**59** 23 He—well, he was willing←One hand went to his heart and
the other flew up in the air and the thing was done

**60** 31 there were things about her I didn't like←silly and vulgar
and sentimental

**61** 9 what is proper←[*p*] 'Sawston'←convention

18 For a moment . . . "I hope you see . . . nonsense." [*line 35*]
←["] [*lacuna*] take the world as we find it [*lacuna*] should be so
invincible! Go against it if you dare! There's nothing despic-
able about it. If puts you on [*sic*] a groove—you hate
metaphors a second time [*sic*], but you must and will have this
one till the ⟨world's end⟩ \world ends/—and if you get off it
you smash. If you try to free yourself you die."

**62** 29 seemed←was

32 gave←[*p*] uttered

35 screamed←[*p*] shouted

65    3    He did not think of his own morals and behaviour any more←
                Now he never gave it a harsher name, even to himself

66    2    nor Philip since the journey to London. She had ⟨proved⟩ \,
                indeed, been/ rather a disappointment to him. Her creditable
                display of originality had never been repeated; he feared she
                was slipping back←and as for Philip he always avoided her if
                he could: her ghastly behaviour at Monteriano and ⟨the
                still more ghastly journey with her⟩ \their still more ghastly
                journey/ over Europe had been too much for him

67   15    know. Let me know in ⟨either⟩ \any/ case←know, as I shall
                then take the initiative myself
     37    that place←Italy

68    6    "I don't ... up to?"←"Mrs Theobald ≪⟨may⟩ has≫ \may
                have/: no one else."
                  "Possibly you are right. But she ⟨will never admit them. I
                cannot⟩ \is practically half-witted now. Nor would I/ dictate
                to her. If anything is done it must be done by us."
                  "I don't ... up to?"
     15    idiocies←remarks
     28    dare to say←[p] say←dare to say

70   19    also←also, and meditated on his worthlessness. Intellect and
                enthusiasm had not helped him much
     21    keeping up her Italian in the next room←giving a music
                lesson

71    4    [p] \of that/
      6    keep up her Italian ⟨again⟩←finish her music lesson
     35    "sincere auguries"←[p] "sincere auguries" to people he had
                not seen

72   10    those←[p] the one
     24    from←[p] in
     25    He had not known that it was in her [see p. 173]
     33    [p] \The child ... this evening. [line 38]/

73    1    Then let←[p] Let
      5    all we've got←[p] what you like
      7    [p] \to Italy/
     13    "Harriet!" exclaimed his mother. "Harriet shall go too.
                Harriet, now, will be invaluable!" And before Philip had
                stopped talking nonsense she had planned the whole thing and
                was looking out the trains.←[p] "But Harriet shall go too!"
                exclaimed his mother, "Harriet, now, will be invaluable!"
                And before Philip's lyrical outcry was over, she had planned
                the whole thing and was looking out the trains.←"Harriet
                shall go ⟨too⟩ \with you/!" exclaimed his mother. "Harriet,
                now, will be invaluable!"

74   25    fancy←[p] think

**76**  8  \like a wounded creature/

**77**  14  a *caffè*. A prison. A theatre. A church. Walls. A view←[*p*] a
*caffè*, a prison, a theatre, a church, walls, a view←a caffè.
A prison. A theatre. A church. Walls. A view

      16  "Not for me, thank you," said Harriet, after a weighty pause.

          "Nobody asked you, miss, you see. Now Lilia was asked by
such a nice young gentleman, with curls all over his forehead,
and teeth ⟨white from his father's shop⟩ \just as white as
father makes them/."←Harriet was not impressed. "⟨Their
lives⟩ \They/ must be fearfully narrow up there ⟨, narrow and
wicked⟩. And we know that they are wicked. Poor Lilia, oh
poor Lilia! What a life! Whatever induced her?"

          "The young gentleman was handsome you know" said
Philip relentlessly. "⟨Full of blood: a butcher's son.⟩ He has
nice glossy hair."

**78**  13  a corpse←[*p*] it

**79**  2  You←Am I right, or perhaps I'm mistaken, that we've come
all the way to this den of ⟨thieves⟩ \murderers/ to get the
baby? You

      5  care.←[*p*] care,←care.

     27  such←[*p*] her

     31  the mother←[*p*] her mother

     34  assured←[*p*] secured

**81**  11  [1924] È←[1905] C'è←[*p*] È←C'è [?]

**82**  37  ramify←[*p*] extend

**83**  23  could have strangled her for temper←was furious with the
whole world

     36  [*p*] \A German lady, friendly to the Past, had given her one
that very spring./

**84**  11  What a frightful spotty blouse!←[*p*] A spotty blouse of
peculiar vulgarity caught his eye.

**85**  15  What do you mean?←[*p*] It isn't possible.

**86**  6  [*p*] \, even if it costs us all we've got/

**89**  2  may therefore←[*p*] therefore may

     22  [*passage ending*] broke silence with ⟨the exclamation⟩ "Mr
Herriton—come here—look at this!"←[*passage ending* "..."]
even fight with a thing you don't understand."

          "Most awfully true" he murmured. He was more attracted
to Miss Abbott than he had ever been. She was the strangest
mixture of conventionality and penetration.

          "Harriet will keep us up to the mark; I thought I shouldn't
need keeping up, but I shall. The thing is going to be frightfully difficult: all the evil is mixed up with beauty and mystery
in the most hopeless way. Monteriano is the most wonderful
place I've ever been to, and it is the most wicked. Harriet

sees the wickedness and she will remind us of it. But she sees nothing else. Look here, for instance. Look at this."

**90** **7**  She gave no hint that she understood him.←"If we turn poetical we're done for" said she.←≪She surprised him by picking up his meaning. "I think it is. And the ⟨beautiful⟩ \lovely/ part is \small and/ beyond our reach. It only deludes us, so that we do not see the rest."

"Wait till the morning: then the sun comes down the street and ⟨the tower⟩ lights the tower from top to bottom," adver[ted Philip?]≫ "We mustn't be poetical ⟨.⟩," said she. "It's fatal to success."

**91** **30**  "He's insolent to ladies, we know. But my brother can be trusted to bring him to his senses. That woman, Philip, whom . . ."←He's insolent to ladies, we know. Philip can be trusted to bring him to his senses."

Harriet always exalted her brother in company. He smiled nervously, and suggested that she should accompany him. Miss Abbott supported the suggestion.

"No. He must go alone. Only a man can deal with a man. Besides Philip—you oblige me to say it—his is not a house any lady could enter."

"Yes that is so" said Miss Abbott. "I forgot that."

"That woman whom . . ."

**93** **25**  with the best of them, and ⟨the⟩ \these/ ladies with their clock would have nodded to \the young men on/ the ⟨roof⟩ \ceiling/ of the Sistine←[MS p. 184v] as if it was the Sistine chapel

**26**  ceiling←[p] roof

**27**  Philip \had/ tried . . . swaying in the melody [94:15]←[MS p. 184v] They were a little late, and the chorus of Scotch retainers was [MS p. 178] already in full cry, accompanied by the tappings and drummings of the audience, who swayed with the melody

**37**  charming a picture←[p] charming←charming a picture

**95** **4**  tunnel←[p] train

**25**  theatre. The climax was reached in the mad scene. Lucia, clad in white, ⟨and with streaming hair,⟩ as befitted her malady, suddenly gathered up her streaming hair and bowed her acknowledgements to the audience. Then from←room. Lucia had to stop in the middle of the mad scene and bow her acknowledgements. From

**29**  it—there advanced←him—there advanced one of the stage scene shifters carrying

**31**  It←⟨He⟩ ⟨She started: she could not believe her eyes: she w⟩ It

**36**  embraced the animal←rushed to it

**96**   5   many←[*p*] some

       29   box←stage box. It was the finest rag in the world. He had never felt so jolly ⟨and⟩ \nor/ among so many friends

**97**   2   had←[*p*] had by this time

       8   Fra Filippo, who←The monkey

**98**  28   [*p*] \before/

      28   March←[*p*] spring←[*p*] February

      36   In the spring←[*p*] Last time

**100**  25   dreadful←[*p*] bad

**101**  34   always have a little feeling against music, and sing only from the throat, apologetically←make music with shame

**104**  30   parapet←[*p*] balustrade

      34   "A born artist's model."←"A born artist's model." But the sneer made no difference to his good looks. And ⟨the next⟩ \in a/ moment she was ashamed of it.

**105**   6   guess why he had been to ⟨Siena⟩ \Poggibonsi/←play ⟨a kind of animal vegetable or mineral game⟩ \guessing games/ with him

**106**   8   grateful←gratifying

      13   He←[*p*] he←He←he

      15   "Where there is love," . . . words [*line 29*]←"You marry again!" she exclaimed in cold angry tones. ⟨How dare you!⟩ I forbid it."

**107**   7   boy←boy: at times she had thought of him as a pleasant unmoral creature, whom it was impossible to scold

**110**  18   [*passage ending*] "I had gone . . ."←[*passage ending*] even harder [than she had?] expected. In desperation she opened her mouth. ⟨So did the baby⟩ \The baby did likewise/.

           "I know what is the matter" said Gino. "You think that I am going to wash you, and you are quite right. I had gone . . ."

**111**  10   blonde←[*p*] fair

**112**  35   No words came from her, but she raised her hands to her mouth, like one who is in sudden agony←"It is time for me to go" she replied

**113**   6   "What is it?"←⟨"What is it?" asked Philip again.

           "Whatever is it?" asked the other. "She was faint at first— but she been [*sic*] happier and kinder every moment. She was going to stop a long time. Why, she came to me on some business and we have both forgotten it!"⟩ "What is it?"

      19   offered Philip a cigar←slipped his arm into Philip's

**115**  25   Caroline←Caroline. And she did not even know of Caroline's behaviour in England. She still thought of her as Mrs Herriton's ally

**117**   5   belong to←[*p*] be citizen of

19 crown. The crown really belonged to←–crown—⟨not the crown of the Madonna or Santa Deodata or Sant' Ubaldo or of any one who⟩ which had been originally intended for

23 had given←–[p] given

**118** 10 fifth←–fourth←–fifth

**119** 30 She had ⟨always⟩ \often/ been decided. But now behind her decision there was a note of passion. She struck him not as different, but as more important, and he minded it very much when she said:←–Her excitement grew. She left the chapel and began to walk up and down the nave.

**120** 17 Oh←–I'm preaching but I can't help it. I've seen what I think good, and I can't bear you shouldn't also. Oh

**122** 36 fight←–[p] have

**127** 20 [p] \to be late/

36 [passage ending] She would not let him talk←–[passage ending] salute their retreating lights. The next moment they were out of Monteriano, in the darkness of the winding road.
        Harriet checked his exclamations

**128** 14 [p] \All we've got?/

22 expectation←–[p] belief

**129** 22 understands←–[p] understands. Ugh! Horrible man

**130** 6 started←–[p] woken

21 [p] \those/

26 Try again←–Besides—I don't think he's seen baby yet, and there's no need he should. There's sure to be a lot of gossip: we may as well be out of it

**131** 11 [p] \It slipped out of my arms!/

14 him←–[p] him save the horse

36 obeyed←–obeyed him←–obeyed him ⟨, as well as they could,⟩ ⟨though Harriet had to cover⟩ \. Harriet covered/ her mouth with her handkerchief, ⟨chuckli[ng]⟩ and ⟨walk⟩ \walked/ away a little, chuckling in the dark, till her laughter was no louder than the rain

**133** 1 [Opening of chapter]←–[MS p. 250v] He was waiting in the reception room, ⟨⟨where⟩ just as Miss Abbott had waited in the morning, and Perfetta was again running through the streets calling for Gino. It was scarcely two hours since he had left Monteriano and ⟨the horror was (so far as he was still conscious of horrors) that⟩ no one there yet knew that anything was wrong. Harriet ⟨had⟩ \must have/ simply walked in, found the door open, and taken the baby up, and Perfetta now, on her way down the stairs, ⟨had⟩ bellowed endearments into the room where she supposed ⟨the child⟩ it to be still sleeping.
        They had held no consultation. Miss Abbott and Harriet

had gone to a cottage with one of the drivers, carrying the
body with them. ⟨Philip⟩ They ⟨supposed⟩ \concluded/ that
Philip was coming too, but he had ⟨bribed⟩ \paid/ the man who
drove the second carriage to take him back to Monteriano. For
he saw what he must do at last, even if he were killed in doing
it. No one but he must bring the news to Gino. The mechanism
of this catastrophe had been vast. Lilia had contributed to it,
Mrs Herriton, ⟨Irma⟩ even Irma: Harriet by breaking the
[*space*] commandment, Miss Abbott, Perfetta, Gino himself
who had meant to ⟨sit⟩ \keep/ at home but had been dissuaded
by a friend. The rain had helped: so had a slow horse and a
swift horse and a faulty carriage lamp. If one chose one might
consider ⟨the⟩ it \a composite work or/ the work of Fate. But
Philip did not so choose. It was his own fault ⟨: he thought
it was due to conscious⟩ \, due to achnowledged/ defects in
his own character. And he had come now to take the blame
for it

**134**  30  [*passage ending*] Philip had seen too much to be nervous
          ←[*passage ending, on MS p. 257v*] He had seen too much to be
          nervous. He never trembled when Gino came leaping up the
          stairs. He could even ⟨enjoy the⟩ endure the friendly greeting
          and the sympathy for his bandaged arm

      33  forgotten the baby's evening milk←[*MS p. 257v*] left her
          umbrella ⟨in the town⟩ \at the Farmacia/

      34  it←[*MS p. 257v*] it. Gino did not ⟨stop her⟩ \reply/

**135**   9  man←dear man

      16  Gino←dear fellow

      20  "It is time to be unhappy. Break down, or you will be ill like
          my sister. You will go—"←"Don't man!" said Philip again.
          "Speak, or cry, or curse me. But don't do that."

**137**  14  flung←fought

      35  arms←hands

**138**  37  \and more intimate/

**139**  11  Philip . . . saved [*line 19*]←[*MS p. 252v*] He only looked away
          for an instant. During [*lacuna of perhaps 4 words*] eyes had
          closed. \\⟨Before⟩ \But when/ he looked back she had opened
          them again and her expression was as before//

      32  He←⟨So it was that they returned to life.⟩ He

      33  Perfetta exclaimed in bewilderment. "It does not matter,"
          he told her. "It does not matter. It will never be wanted any
          more."←So it was that they all returned to life.

**140**  31  They . . . ". . . things; [142:17] . . ." [*expanded at typescript
          stage*]←
          "Next spring, I hope. How soon will you be coming
          ⟨out \again/⟩ \back/?" They were standing together in the

corridor of the train, slowly ascending out of Italy towards the San Gothard tunnel.

"I expect never."

"⟨Never come back⟩ \For whatever reason/?" He stared at her as if she was some monstrosity.

"⟨Not if I can help it.⟩ \Because/ I understand the place. There is no need."

"Understand Italy ⟨?⟩ \!/" he exclaimed.

"Perfectly."

"Well I don't. And I don't understand you." He paced thoughtfully up the corridor. The train was nearly empty. Harriet slumbered in a ⟨coupée⟩ \compartment/ by herself. When he returned, Miss Abbott spoke to him on another subject.

"Are your plans ⟨settled⟩ \decided/?"

"I've written to my mother saying that I can't come back to Sawston. I tried to explain why: . . ."

**144** 30  He . . . cry [146:7; *revised at typescript stage*]←She whispered to herself "It is tempting—" And those three words threw him into a tumult of joy. "It is ⟨very⟩ tempting" she repeated, "not to be mysterious. I have wanted to speak to you a dozen times. I could never speak to any one else: certainly not to a woman, and I think you are the one man who might \understand and/ not be disgusted."

"I am certain to understand you" said Philip. But he had ⟨scarcely listened to her⟩ \only listened to the first three/ words. It was tempting to her! After all, the greatest of things was possible. After long estrangement, after much tragedy, the south had brought them together in the end. That laughter in the theatre, those silver stars in the purple sky— even the violets of a departed spring—all had helped, and sorrow had helped also, and so had tenderness to others—

"I can't help this sort of thing!"

He looked at her in alarm. She was apologizing for the crimson colour which had suddenly shot over her neck and face. She must be in a strange ⟨mood⟩ \state/, to be so moved and so scornful of her own emotion.

"Keep looking at me!" she exclaimed, for in his trouble he had lowered his eyes. "Try and think of me as a kind of specimen: that's the help I need. ⟨And don't go⟩ A specimen in love."

The word\spoken/ made him crimson also, and for a moment he had a sublime vision that here ⟨was⟩ \stood/ one of those heroines who are not ashamed to speak it first.

"≪⟨I've got⟩ \I'm in≫ \In/ love with Gino."

He heard himself answer steadily "Rather! So am I, when
I can forget how he hurt me. ⟨But to the end of time,⟩
\Though/ when we shake hands—"
    "In love with him—don't pass it off—I mean it crudely.
You know what I mean. Speak! Laugh at me: pull it to pieces.
That's what I want. Tell me I'm a fool or worse:—that he's
a cad. Say what you said when Lilia ⟨did it⟩ fell in love with
him. I dare tell you this, because I like you—and because
you're dispassionate: you look on life as a spectacle: you don't
enter it: you \only/ find it funny or beautiful— So I can
trust you to laugh at this. Mr Herriton, isn't it funny? Why, I
used to think I'd never 'fall' in love at all. A gentleman should
deserve me first by noble deeds: I would repulse him: more
noble deeds: my love for him should grow. Not a deed—not
a word even: he isn't even a gentleman, or good. Son of an
Italian dentist, with a pretty face." She said the words again,
as if they were a charm against passion. Then her voice broke

[*The four following draft fragments occur on versos of the main manuscript, and correspond to no specific passages in the novel as we know it.
The first three, however, clearly relate to the existing chapter 5, while the
last comes, chronologically, between chapters 9 and 10. The final item
is a chronological outline—which was later modified, in the narrative, by
the consistent alteration of February to March.*]

[*MS p. 237v:* ". . .] will agree."
    "And go alone?" asked Harriet.
    "Of course I should not ⟨ask⟩ want you to do ⟨a thing like⟩ that, dear.
Philip would do the bartering, but I think that ⟨the influence of⟩ a
woman's influence is always a great help."
    Harriet ⟨did not like to⟩ \could not/ deny this.
    "I'm very sorry" repeated Philip. "I'll do all the writing with pleasure,
but I don't feel I could go."
    "I don't pretend it's an easy mission" said his mother quietly. "He
sounds a rough man as well as a bad one."
    "I was not considering that" he answered. The remark annoyed him,
and he did not forget it. It changed his

[*MS p. 243v*] He answered angrily "Very possibly I might have been,
if other things had been different—if he had been better educated, \for
instance,/ or richer, or \if/ I had not had ⟨a personal grievance⟩ \personal
grievances/ against him. I assure you, Harriet, I could easily do worse. At

all events I shouldn't have rejected him because he had a poor ideal of women \, for that wouldn't concern me/."

Much put out, he left the room. Harriet exploded, and Mrs Herriton said quietly "I hope Philip is not going to be tiresome."

[MS p. 236v] Germany. He developed a curious attachment for the English country he had hitherto dispraised and neglected. One summer evening, a few days before he left to join his sister, he was sitting at the bottom of the garden with his mother and Miss Abbott, talking over the approaching expedition. A chance remark of the latter's, about the beauty of England, drew from him a speech of unwonted seriousness.

"I don't want to leave England. I'm English, and I love the English best after all. You can't change your nationality at will. I know at last—I don't understand Italy, and it frightens me. Endless rows of olives and vines—towns like castles—palaces like dungeons—the whole world blue sky or white dust—it's all very wonderful and beautiful, but it's nobody's home."

"I shall always like Italy" said Miss Abbott, poking [MS p. 235v] her parasol into the moist earth.

"Oh so shall I. But I frankly confess I am frightened of it."

"Why?" she asked, alarmingly direct. Mrs Herriton moved uneasily on her chair.

Philip was on the defensive at once. He knew women adored physical force, and ⟨at once⟩ saw a reference to his discomfiture by Gino, and an accusation of personal cowardice. His transient sincerity passed, and he replied "I ⟨am⟩ must apologize for my inaccurate vocabulary. Instead of 'frightened' I should have said 'dislike'. I hoped to be poetical, you see, and I have only succeeded in being obscure. \Will you pardon me?/"

"Certainly," said Miss Abbott, getting up rather wearily to go. "You like it, you dislike it, and you are frightened of it. So am I. Give Italy my love."

"Poor Caroline!" said Mrs Herriton, as soon as they were alone. Philip was murmuring "I forgot I said [. . .]"]

[MS p. 260v] had been through the depths sufficiently, and their thoughts were strangely in accord. They spoke gently and lovingly to each other about matters of business—the inquest, the funeral, Gino's second marriage, the date of the Herriton's [sic] departure, a ⟨doctor to set⟩ \surgeon for/ Philip's arm. For a moment they saw the whole tragedy and saw it alike. They had neither the wish nor the power to be unkind. They could even apportion praise and blame.

[*MS p. 273v*] 1902 November. Lilia goes
          1903 February   P's [?] departure
                        The marriage
            December   Death of Lilia
          1904 July. News ⟨reaches⟩ \over/ Sawston.
          August. Departure
                   The 2nd [?] two days.
                   The return.

# Textual Notes

The text of this edition is, with the exceptions recorded below, that of the 1969 printing (the last in Forster's lifetime) of the Pocket Edition first published by Edward Arnold in 1947 (Kirkpatrick A1*d*). This has been collated word by word with the first edition (Edinburgh, William Blackwood, 1905; Kirkpatrick A1*a*), with the first American edition (Knopf, 1920; Kirkpatrick A1*b*), with the first American paperback edition (Vintage Books, 1958; Kirkpatrick A1*e*), with the first British paperback edition (Penguin Books, 1959; Kirkpatrick A1*f*), and with the manuscript in the British Museum (BM Addit. MSS 57472–3). The following have also been consulted: the first Arnold edition (the Uniform Edition of 1924; Kirkpatrick A1*c*); a Knopf reprint of October 1943; the Pocket Edition of 1947; and the corrected proofs of the first edition, which are described in Appendix B.

The first edition differs substantively at six points from later British editions. In two cases (see below, notes to pp. 10 and 133) I have unhesitatingly adopted the reading of the first edition: the change from "a hotel" (1905) to "an hotel" (1924) looks like the work of a rule-bound compositor, while "have" is clearly a misprint for the earlier "had". The other four substantive changes made in 1924 (see the two notes to p. 81 and those to pp. 100 and 138; mere corrections of spelling have not been recorded) all represent tinkerings with Italian dialogue such as are unlikely to have been the work of anyone but Forster himself. In the first and fourth of these instances the later version is unquestionably more correct; in the third there is not much to choose. In the second (p. 81, line 16), whoever made the change got it wrong: the required sense ("there's another young lady who's sleeping") is given by *c'è* ("there is"), not by *è* ("it is"). Since the mistake is hardly one that an Italian could make, since both manuscript and proofs show Forster in a state of chronic indecision over this distinction, and since it is even possible that the second change from *c'è* to *è* was made by an editor, in the belief that it was a corollary to the first which Forster had overlooked, I have adopted the earlier reading.

The Knopf edition of 1920 shows some thirty significant differences from the first edition, none of which bears the mark of Forster's revising hand—although one variant (see note to p. 139, line 12) is confirmed as correct by the manuscript. The majority are clearly compositors' errors, and a few of the more obvious ones are corrected in the Vintage Books edition, which derives from the Knopf. By contrast, several of the smaller number of fresh variants in the Vintage Books edition (see for example the notes to p. 16, line 30, and p. 47) and in the Arnold-derived Penguin edition (e.g. p. 8, line 18) suggest the work of a copy-editor anxious to justify his or her existence.

Far more revealing than any collation of editions has been that of the published text with the set of corrected proofs and, more particularly, with the manuscript. Of the many corrections indicated by Forster in the proofs, one substantive one was not carried out, while another was carried out in a significantly different way. These proofs might thus appear to furnish grounds for two emendations. In each case, however, I find it more likely that Forster, whether or not he saw revised proofs, subsequently changed his mind in one instance, and corrected his correction in the other. At p. 19, line 13,[1] he requested the replacement of "Meanwhile?" by "And meanwhile?". The correction stands prominently on the page, and could hardly have been overlooked by the printer. It is probable, of course, from the mere fact of these proofs having remained in Forster's possession, that they were a spare set which he never returned to the printer;[2] and possible that he corrected this set as he read them, and that when he later transferred the corrections to the printer's set he overlooked this one. Again, however, it is a curiously conspicuous one for the eye to miss; and it seems more likely that, whether at this stage or subsequently, he noticed that the change would result in a slightly inelegant juxtaposition of two sentences beginning with "And". The other instance occurs on p. 72, where "He had not known that it was in her" has replaced "She had never broken down before"— the "not" being absent from Forster's correction. I believe that the omission was a mere slip of the pen, and that if Forster had intended the sense to be positive he would have written something like ". . . dreadfully, though he had always known that it was in her".

At two points Forster corrected in proof an error that must almost certainly have been present in the typescript.[3] It is almost impossible to imagine a compositor setting "enviously" where his typescript read "curiously" (p. 38), or "waxing" where it read "coaxing" (p. 81); but very easy to see how the typist could have misread Forster's manuscript in these ways. We thus have fresh proof, if such were needed, of Forster's carelessness in reading through typescripts of his work. Neither "enviously" nor "waxing" gives anything remotely resembling the right sense; if, therefore, he was capable of overlooking such errors

[1] Page and line numbers refer throughout to the present edition.

[2] They might, of course, have been sent back to Forster with a set of revised proofs; but in that case one would have expected them to contain printers' marks.

[3] The manuscript being, by Forster's standards, unusually clean, it might conceivably, in 1905, have been accepted by the publisher as copy. The "titlepage", however, contains instructions to an unnamed typist,

once, it is not straining credulity to suppose that he was capable of doing so twice (or more often). From this it follows that where a manuscript reading seems superior to the reading of the published text (i.e. seems to give better sense or to be more characteristic of Forster), and where the former can, in Forster's manuscript, easily be mistaken for the latter (or where the error is one easily made, either by a typist or by a compositor), there is a strong case for regarding the manuscript reading as correct. I have done so in thirty-eight instances (particularly striking are the examples recorded in notes to pp. 32, 120, 123 and 134); in a thirty-ninth (see note to p. 108, line 34) I have made an emendation for which the manuscript offers some support. (The single purely conjectural emendation, a fairly safe one, occurs on p. 98.) Other discrepancies between the published version and the manuscript represent Forster's revision; some of the more interesting examples—including *all* changes made in proof —are recorded in Appendix B.

In the following notes, page and line number are in each case followed by the reading given here, which is separated by an oblique stroke from the variant reading. Wherever "MS" occurs, the reading in question is found *only* in the manuscript. Details of the editions cited are given in the first paragraph above; an unqualified "Arnold" refers to *all* the Edward Arnold editions mentioned there.

| | | |
|---|---|---|
| 5 | 9 | **she** / **he** Knopf |
| | 33 | **Herriton** / **Harriet** Knopf |
| 8 | 18 | **it** / **of it** Penguin |
| | 30 | **tracts** MS / **Tracts** |
| 10 | 22 | **a hotel** Blackwood, Knopf, Vintage / **an hotel** Arnold, Penguin |
| 11 | 12 | **"But why—what—"** / omitted Knopf, Vintage |
| 12 | 6 | **1261** / **'261** Knopf, Vintage |
| 16 | 17 | **with** / **and with** Arnold 1947 |
| | 30 | **olives** / **olive-trees** Vintage |
| 18 | 22 | **hollows** / **hollow** Knopf, Vintage |
| 21 | 15 | **walls** MS / **walk.** A similar emendation based on the manuscript can be found in the Abinger Edition of *Howards End* (p. 218, line 1). |
| 23 | 8 | **why even** MS / **why, even** |
| 24 | 33 | *caffè-latte* / *caffè* **latter** Knopf / *caffè* **later** Vintage |
| 25 | 17 | **pulls out** / **pulls** Knopf, Vintage |
| 26 | 4 | **conciliatory** MS / **conciliating** |
| 30 | 22 | **burden** / **burdens** Knopf, Vintage |
| 31 | 12 | **him,** MS / **him** |
| 32 | 35 | **lent,** MS / **but** |
| | 38 | **unwilling** MS / **omitting** |
| 33 | 29 | **letter** / **letters** Penguin |

| 36 | 4 | **it is** / **is** Knopf, Vintage |
|----|----|----|
| 38 | 22 | **whether** / **where** Knopf, Vintage |
| 40 | 8 | **about with** MS / **about** |
| 42 | 1 | **piano,** MS / **piano** |
| 44 | 11 | **safer. And** MS / **safer, and** |
| 45 | 31 | **the** / **his** Knopf, Vintage |
| 47 | 27 | **deserve** / **deserves** Vintage |
| 51 | 24 | **forget** / **forgot** Knopf, Vintage |
| 54 | 4 | **shoulder** / **shoulders** Knopf, Vintage |
|    | 16 | **It is** / **It's** Arnold 1947 |
| 58 | 28 | **everything.** MS / **everything** |
|    | 34 | **of** / **for** Knopf, Vintage |
| 59 | 17 | **would** MS / **could.** A frequent source of trouble; cf. pp. 101, 125, and *Howards End, passim.* |
| 61 | 4 | **character** MS / **characters** |
| 62 | 14 | **the meeting** / **meeting** Penguin |
| 66 | 34 | **It's** MS / **It is.** Forster has corrected "It is" to "It's"; the typist has mistaken the direction of the change. |
| 75 | 21 | **mouth** / **month** Knopf |
| 76 | 3 | **window** MS / **windows** |
| 81 | 11 | **È** / **C'è** Blackwood, Knopf, Vintage. See also p. 181. |
|    | 16 | **c'è** Blackwood / **è** Arnold, Penguin / **c è** Knopf, Vintage. See also pp. 172, 181. |
|    | 30 | **a third** / **third** Knopf |
| 82 | 8 | **it** / **it to** Knopf, Vintage |
|    | 9 | **it** / **it to** Knopf, Vintage |
|    | 28 | **men** / **man** Knopf |
| 84 | 14 | **bought** MS / **brought** |
|    | 36 | **one vast** MS / **one** |
| 88 | 17 | **after** MS / **for** |
| 92 | 5 | **Theatre? Here?** MS / **Theatres here?** |
|    | 20 | **books** MS / **book** |
| 93 | 36 | **reply,** / **reply.** Knopf, Vintage |
| 94 | 8 | **all** MS / **at all** |
| 95 | 28 | **acknowledgements** / **acknowledgment** Knopf, Vintage |
| 97 | 7 | **ours** / **our** Penguin |
|    | 33 | **his ancestors** / **ancestors** Knopf, Vintage |
| 98 | 18 | **pawky** / **porky** MS and editions. Presumably a spelling mistake—see also p. 181. |
|    | 22 | **had had** MS / **had** |
| 100 | 3 | **Scuse tante** / **Scusì tanto** Blackwood, Knopf, Vintage |
|    | 23 | **memento** / **moment** Knopf, Vintage |
| 101 | 24 | **could** MS / **would** |
|    | 28 | **lie** MS / **be** |
| 102 | 36 | **care,** MS / **care** |

107   36   **slave, your / slave, you** Knopf, Vintage
108   24   **all / at all** is a tempting conjecture in view of Miss Abbott's reply.
      34   **relatives / relative** MS and editions. Forster originally wrote "people", and I have assumed that "relative" was a slip of the pen.
113   11   **our** MS **/ your.** The y is imperfectly deleted.
115   17   **a sharp** MS **/ sharp**
117   32   **did / did not** Knopf, Vintage
118   15   **has / had** Vintage
      16   **loves / loved** Vintage
120   17   **us** MS **/ as**
121   12   **not** MS **/ just not.** Forster appears to have begun writing "just" (the page looks like a fair copy, and his eye may have jumped to the following "just"), and not to have deleted it clearly.
123   17   **The / This** Vintage
      31   **opposite side / opposite** Knopf, Vintage
      33   **head** MS **/ hand**
125   19   **could** MS **/ would**
126   25   **any other** MS **/ another**
127   38   **later. So** MS **/ later, so**
133   15   **had** Blackwood, Knopf, Vintage **/ have** Arnold, Penguin
      19   **seem / seemed** Knopf, Vintage
134   38   **rug** MS **/ way**
137   17   **least** MS **/ last**
      20   **came** MS **/ were**
138   27   **freschissimo! Bianco / freschissima! bianca** Blackwood, Knopf, Vintage. Between 1905 and 1924 Forster discovered that in Italian, as in French, milk is masculine.
139   12   **become** MS, Knopf, Vintage **/ became** Blackwood, Arnold, Penguin
143   4   **sharp / short** Knopf, Vintage
      31   **that** MS **/ that it**
145   10   **arm / arms** Knopf, Vintage. The Knopf copy-editor or compositor presumably forgot that Philip has one arm in a sling. The same "correction" was made by the Blackwood compositor (probably), but spotted by Forster in proof.
147   4   **But I / But** Knopf, Vintage
      24   **As she / As he** Vintage

It will be noticed that a number of the emendations based on the manuscript are matters of punctuation, and that one is a matter of capitalization. Each of these affects the sense, or at least the emphasis or rhythm or tone; as do fifteen corrections to punctuation which Forster has made in proof—most of them reversing a change made, presumably, by the publisher or printer.[4] Over punctuation too, however, Forster was a careless proof-reader: thus on p. 42, lines 1–2, he has reinstated the comma after "sang" but not the one after "piano". In any case, as I have noted elsewhere, his initial punctuation is often exceedingly slap-dash. It follows that neither the punctuation of his manuscripts nor that, probably composite, of his published work need be regarded as sacrosanct; and I have therefore felt free, here as elsewhere, silently to emend the latter (with or without the support of the former) in the interests of clarity or consistency. The same applies to spelling, capitalization and word-division, in all of which consistency is desirable provided it is not achieved at the cost of nuances.

[4] One or the other appears also, at one point, to have made a misguided attempt to correct Forster's grammar: on p. 46, line 28, "should" appears in proof as "would".

# General Notes

Page 1: Gubbio is in Umbria; Pienza, Cortona and San Gimignano are in Tuscany; Monteriano is a thinly disguised version of San Gimignano.

Page 2: the Campanile of Airolo and the other landmarks mentioned in this paragraph lie along the route followed by Forster in October 1901, during his first visit to Italy.

Foot-warmers, for many years the only form of heating on trains, were by 1905 well on the way out. Latterly they consisted of tins filled with soda-acetate crystals, sealed, and heated in great vats. They continued to give out heat as the solution crystallized, and could to some extent be revivified by shaking.

Page 3: "the New Life" is the first of several allusions to *La Vita Nuova*, Dante's celebration of his love for Beatrice.

Page 8: Santa Deodata is Forster's name both for the Collegiate Church at San Gimignano and for the town's saint, Santa Fina. See also notes to pp. 79, 118.

Pages 11–12: the "quotation" from Baedeker bears virtually no relation to the account of San Gimignano given in the 1900 or the 1904 edition of *Central Italy and Rome*—though the latter does mention "the *Rocca* (1353), or the highest part of the old fortifications", which "commands a fine view of the town and neighbourhood". The history, likewise, bears little relationship to that of San Gimignano, which is nowhere mentioned or alluded to by Dante (although he visited the city on official Florentine business in 1299), and whose traditional enemy was Volterra rather than Poggibonsi. The distich may be translated: Men of Poggibonsi, move on—Monteriano is becoming a city!

Page 15: "the station of Monteriano". The usual station for San Gimignano was and is Poggibonsi. *Legno* means both wood and carriage.

Page 19: Philip's information about the Bersaglieri is essentially correct: "For the bersaglieri the height varies between 1·62 m. and 1·75 m. Great care is taken that the men chosen for these celebrated light infantry corps possess good constitutions, are broad and deep in the chest, quick and active in their step. . . . Almost incredible stories are told of the distances traversed by bersaglieri battalions during a few hours. . . ." (Charles Martel [i.e. Repington], *Military Italy*; London, Macmillan, 1884.)

Page 20: the Etruscan League was a loose pre-Roman confederation of cities in an area roughly corresponding to modern Tuscany. The Pax Romana: the peace which reigned for long periods under the Roman Empire. Alaric: chief of the Visigoths and leader of the army that sacked Rome in 410. Countess Matilda: owner of the castle at Canossa where in 1077 Pope Gregory VII received the barefoot penance of the Emperor Henry IV.

The number of structures in San Gimignano that rank as towers ranges from 12 to 15; the number "that had filled the city in her prime" is variously put at 56, 72 and 76. The more cautious guidebooks refer merely to "numerous towers".

Page 21: a card of recommendation from "an Equerry to the Queen of Peru" would be "less valuable" than one from "Miss M'Gee, Maida Vale" since there never was a Queen of Peru. The Siena gate is probably, in San Gimignano terms, the Porta alle Fonti. The *dogana* is the customs-house; "in most Italian towns a tax . . . is levied on comestibles." (Baedeker, 1904.)

Page 24: the Dante quotation reads, in Dorothy Sayers's translation:

Midway this way of life we're bound upon,
I woke to find myself in a dark wood,
Where the right road was wholly lost and gone.

Lilia is thirty-three—near enough "midway"; Forster may have had in mind also the disaster which will occur, literally, "in a dark wood".
*Pallone*: in full, *pallone con bracciale* ("ball with armlet"). The ball resembles a football rather than a tennis-ball. *Caffè-latte* is white coffee.

Page 25: "rising rapidly in his profession". At the period in question Poggibonsi was only marginally bigger than San Gimignano—and we already know the view of the former held by the fictional inhabitants of the latter.

Page 28: a thousand lire were worth, at the then rate of exchange, just under £40; in real terms, considerably more.

Page 30: the Volterra gate is probably, in San Gimignano terms, the Porta S. Matteo.
"Some dark and mostly stuffy": did some friend or enemy of Forster pick on this phrase as an example of his "vulgar style"? The question is prompted by the passage in *Howards End* where Leonard Bast wonders whether he can adapt an orotund sentence of Ruskin to his own use:

"Let us consider a little each of these characters in succession; and first (for of the absence of ventilation enough has been said already), what is very peculiar to this flat, its obscurity."

Something told him that the modifications would not do; and that something, had he known it, was the spirit of English Prose. "My flat is dark as well as stuffy." Those were the words for him.

Page 31: Siena and Leghorn. Gino's preference is for a lively seaport rather than for one of the most beautiful cities in Italy.

Page 37: the *Sindaco* is the mayor. Chiasso, on the Swiss-Italian frontier, was the scene of an "apalling custom house examination" undergone by Forster and his mother on 8 October 1901.

Page 38: Solferino, in Lombardy, where on 24 June 1859, during the second War of Italian Independence, a Franco-Piedmontese army defeated an Austrian one.

Page 39: a word corresponding to the untranslatable *simpatica* exists in many other languages, e.g. French *sympathique*, Norwegian and Danish *sympatisk*. "Non era": he was not. "Sono poco simpatiche le donne": women are not very—the untranslatable word.

Page 40: Palazzo Pubblico (town hall). In San Gimignano the Palazzo Pubblico (originally the Nuovo Palazzo del Podestà, today the Palazzo Comunale) is topped by the highest of the famous towers.

Page 43: a *farmacia* is a chemist's shop.

Page 47: Cordelia and Imogen figure in *King Lear* and *Cymbeline* respectively.

Page 48: C.M.S.: Church Missionary Society.

Page 49: "Non vengo": I'm not coming.

Page 55: "Laughter, he read and believed, was a sign of good moral health." Almost certainly a reference to Meredith's *An Essay on Comedy and the Uses of the Comic Spirit*, e.g.: "One excellent test of the civilization of a country... I take to be the flourishing of the Comic idea and Comedy; and the test of true Comedy is that it shall awaken thoughtful laughter.... the laughter directed by the Comic spirit... enters you like fresh air into a study."

Page 65: for "the unwritten song of Miriam" see Exodus 2: 3–4; for the "written" one see Exodus 15: 20–21.

Page 71: Cardinal Rodrigo Borgia, afterwards Pope Alexander VI (reigned 1492–1503), is generally credited with seven children, the most famous being Cesare and Lucrezia Borgia. The assassination in 1497 of his son Giovanni or Juan is known to have caused him intense grief.

Page 73: "mysterious and terrible". The adjectives were applied, on p. 43, to the Tuscan landscape.

Page 79: "the Collegiate Church of Santa Deodata". La Collegiata in San Gimignano includes a Chapel of Santa Fina, with frescoes of her death and burial by Ghirlandaio, painted in 1475. Santa Fina (Seraphina dei Ciardi, 1238–53), a semi-legendary figure, lay on her back on a hard oak bench from the age of ten after being stricken with what is described in one source as "a complication of painful and repulsive diseases" which she interpreted as punishment for her "sin" in accepting the gift of an orange (in one account an apple) "from a boy too shy to express his feelings in any other way". Forster is just possibly the author excoriated by Jean Carlyle Graham and Elizabeth M. Derbishire in *Sangimignano of Val d'Elsa in Tuscany* (Rome, Ermanno Loescher, 1910) as "a certain writer, the picturesqueness of whose diction is invariably marred by his superficiality of thought and the inaccuracy of his observations and deductions", and who "has read in this record of patience under suffering, simply the view that a young girl was canonised for rotting on a plank".

Page 80: "Buona sera", etc.: Good evening, landlady. It's good to be back in Monteriano. . . . I want two rooms.

Page 81: Philip explains that "the young lady is feeling unwell—it's the sun" and elicits a cry of "Poor little thing!" The landlady tries to quieten Harriet with "Please—quiet—quiet—there's another young lady sleeping—"

Page 89: Forster has drawn freely on his fancy in alluding to the Salvucci and the Ardinghelli, the two families whose feud rent San Gimignano in the thirteenth and fourteenth centuries.

Page 90: "Unique representation" is a deliberate mistranslation of *rappresentazione unica*, i.e. single performance.

Page 93: *La Zia di Carlo* is an Italian version of *Charley's Aunt*, by Brandon Thomas (1892). The theatre at San Gimignano, used as such in the summer months only, is the loggia of the Vecchio Palazzo del Podestà. Possibly "spraddled" (i.e. sprawled; "now chiefly dialect"—*OED*) is a mistake for "straddled", i.e. strutted. The twenty nude youths on the ceiling of the Sistine Chapel were painted by Michelangelo.

Page 94: the audience "swaying in the melody like corn in the wind" prefigures T. S. Eliot's "readers of the *Boston Evening Transcript*" (1915) who "sway in the wind like a field of ripe corn".

Page 95: "the two great sextets": there is only one sextet in *Lucia di Lammermoor*. The "more famous occasion" occurs in *Madame Bovary*, part 2, chapter 15.

Page 96: "Che carino!": The little darling! The statement that "Harriet was always unfortunate" occurred earlier, on p. 12.

Page 98: "pawky" gives so much better sense ("tricky, artful, sly, cunning, crafty, shrewd"—*OED*) than Forster's "porky" that I have assumed the latter to be merely a spelling mistake.

Page 100: "Scuse tante!": I'm *so* sorry! "Tante scuse!" or "Scusi tanto!" (see p. 175) would be more idiomatic.

Page 102: *tombola* is better known, in England, as bingo; a *terno* is a set of three winning numbers.

Page 105: "E manca questo!": And I'm short of this!

Page 112: two Bellini *Madonna and Child*s in museums in Milan show a distinctly "languid" baby, and the one at the Brera, at least, was familiar to Forster: "The child seems pushing with its feet against the picture frame, and leaning backward rather wearily into its mother's arms." (Diary, 20 October 1901.) Signorelli does not habitually "fling" his Infants "wriggling on pavements of marble"; Forster probably had in mind the *Nativity* in the National Gallery, London—likewise the same Gallery's *Adoration* by Lorenzo di Credi.

Page 117: "the Palazzo Pubblico, the Collegiate Church, and the Caffè Garibaldi". A corresponding photograph from San Gimignano is reproduced in Wilfred Stone, *The Cave and the Mountain: A Study of E. M. Forster* (Stanford and London, Stanford University Press and Oxford University Press, 1966), plate 17.

Page 118: the fictitious Giovanni da Empoli here stands for Domenico Ghirlandaio (1449–94); in "A Helping Hand" (see *The Life to Come, and Other Stories*) he appeared to stand for Antonio Pollaiuolo.

Page 119: the accuracy or otherwise of Forster's fictionalized account of Ghirlandaio's *Pope Gregory appearing to Santa Fina* can be gauged from the reproduction in Stone, *op. cit.* (note to p. 117), plate 16.

Page 121: Philip, in stipulating that "each lady retire to her bedroom with a book", appears to have forgotten that "we have no books" (p. 92).

Page 125: "Blessed be the Lord my God", etc., is a not quite accurate version of Psalms 144: 1. (For "God" read "strength".)

Page 128: Judith is the heroine of the eponymous book in the Apocrypha; for Deborah and Jael see Judges 4 and 5 *passim*. Two of these "prophetesses" are best known as slayers: Judith of Holofernes, Jael of Sisera.

Page 138: "Latte! Latte freschissimo! Bianco come neve!" Milk! Fresh, fresh milk! White as snow!

Page 146: Pasiphaë, legendary wife of Minos, king of Crete, had intercourse with a bull and gave birth to the Minotaur, half man and half bull.

Page 147: Endymion, an exceptionally beautiful young man, was loved by the Moon.